HEARTBEATS
OF A
KILLER

AGENT JAXSON LOCKE FBI MYSTERY THRILLER SERIES BOOK 1

MICHAEL MERSON

Edited by Novel Nurse Editing

G•S Cover Design Studio
https://www.gsstockphotography.com/

PROLOGUE

The ground under Tammy was hard. She couldn't move, and her hands and arms ached from the bindings that bound them together behind her back. She lay naked, looking through the tall pines at the Colorado moon glowing brightly overhead.

She was afraid and just wanted it all to end. She no longer tried to fight him or persuade him to stop. He was determined to finish what he had started, and he had already hurt her when she'd tried to reason with him earlier. Her left eye was now swollen shut, her nose was surely broken, and she could feel blood running down the back of her neck from a wound somewhere on her head.

She thought she knew him, and she felt she had always been nice to him, even when the other girls made fun of him behind his back.

Was this my fault? Did I ask for this? Tammy asked herself. She hoped and prayed that he would leave her there in the woods, but in her heart, she knew that wasn't part of his plan. Like most people, Tammy had heard about the killer who hunted victims in the Olympic City. Until now, she never imagined that she would be one of his victims.

Tammy replayed the events of the day in her mind. She remembered arriving at the mall for her shift at Landings

Department Store. She talked with Jennifer from the security office and later had dinner with her in the food court before Jennifer went on her trip to Las Vegas.

She remembered seeing him walking through the mall and how he had awkwardly waved at her when she passed by. She was in the parking lot next to her car when he approached her, and that was all she could recall. The next thing she remembered was waking up in the back seat of his car, tied up.

When he took her out of the back seat, she tried to protest. That was when he'd punched her in the eye and nose. He then picked her up, placed her over his shoulder, and brought her up the trail to this spot.

Jeramiah was proud of what he had done, and as he basked under the tall pines, he felt exhilarated, powerful, and full of life. For the moment, he was the one in control. He was the one who was seen and admired. Once again, he had the power to decide between life and death.

"Please let me go," Tammy pleaded from a few feet away.

Jeramiah turned around and looked at her for a few seconds. He then walked toward her and stood over her beaten and bloody body. "Do you love me?" he asked as he bent down and straddled himself over Tammy's stomach. He then placed his head on her chest and listened to the beating of her heart.

Tears rolled down the sides of her face. "I just want to go home!" she cried.

Jeramiah placed his finger over her mouth. "Shh," he whispered.

"Please let me go."

Jeramiah lifted his head and looked into her eyes. "I can't. You're mine now," he declared as he pulled his knife from behind his back. The blade was large, and he admired it in the light of the moon while dragging the tip softly over her bare chest.

"I won't tell anyone! Please, just let me go!" Tammy cried out.

"I can't let you go. Your heart belongs to me now," Jeramiah proudly proclaimed. He then quickly pressed her head hard onto the ground with his left hand while he ran the knife blade across her throat with his right.

Tammy tried to breathe, but she could not. The airflow into her lungs had stopped. The blood sprayed onto the killer and then began to pool under her as she squirmed on the ground. Jeramiah stood and backed away, watching intently as she fought for her life.

Tammy rolled onto her stomach, and to his surprise, she was able to stand. She continued to fight for air as her blood spouted outward with each beat of her heart. Jeramiah shook his head from side to side. He walked toward her and punched her in the face. The impact sent the young woman onto her back once more. Tammy did not attempt to stand again. She lay on the ground, desperately pulling at her restraints to no avail. Jeramiah walked around her body, excitedly watching as his victim fought for her life. After she stopped moving, he turned her head and body downhill so her blood would flow away from him. Once again, Jeramiah straddled her and watched as the last bits of life left her body.

"Now to get what's mine," Jeramiah said right before he got to work at retrieving his prize.

Jeramiah was about to remove Tammy's heart when he heard the voices of a man and woman walking up the trail. He quickly moved into the brush and ducked out of sight. A couple appeared and walked right up next to Tammy's body.

Jeramiah sat very quietly, not moving a muscle. The woman screamed loudly. Jeramiah panicked. He moved to his right, down the hill, and through the brush just as their flashlight skimmed past his hiding place. Unfortunately for Jeramiah, the only thing he left with was his precious tool in hand. Tammy's heart remained with her.

CHAPTER 1
PIKES PEAK

SUNDAY, JULY 1ST, 3:00 AM

I t was three o'clock in the morning, and from a distance during the day, Pikes Peak served as a beautiful backdrop for the city of Colorado Springs. The famous mountain was the subject of many photos and paintings and had been since its discovery. As Detective Frost left the bright lights of the city streets behind him, he quickly snaked his way through the many switchbacks of the mountainside that would eventually lead him to his destination.

Detective Axel Frost was all too familiar with the area known as North Cheyenne Cañon Park. The vast foothills with its many hiking trails surrounding Pikes Peak were an accessible playground for any outdoor enthusiast with a pair of hiking boots or a mountain bike. This section of the foothills was littered with large evergreens that seemed to stretch endlessly upward until they peeked into a sea of blue skies during the day.

North Cheyenne Cañon was populated with few residents whose homes were scattered throughout the mountainside. There were many hiking trails for residents and visitors to trek that crisscrossed through the trees and eventually disappeared into and around the rolling hills and valleys. The entire area was part of Axel's patrol sector when he had been a rookie officer fresh out of the police academy. When he patrolled North Cheyenne Cañon, he always felt more like a park ranger than a police officer.

Thoughts of those first unforgettable years on the department kept coming to mind as Axel traveled the familiar switchbacks one after another. As he continued his slow and steady climb up the gravel-packed road, he remembered the many nights when he had found sexually charged teenagers parked in the darkness at one of the many overlooks. He never arrested the kids. After all, he had been a teenager once.

He recalled helping the many lost newbie hikers find their way back to their parked cars after they got lost in the forest. They would get lost, then find their way back to some unknown location on the main road, where Axel would find them wandering around with no clue as to where they were. Axel thought those years were a much simpler time in his career. Back then, his only worries were the people who resided around North Cheyenne Cañon and those who visited it.

Eventually, the winding road passed through the first of two tunnels in the mountain. There had been three tunnels, but the third was closed off to traffic after it was determined to be unsafe. All the tunnels were rumored to be haunted. Some nights, usually around Halloween, high school kids would drive to each one and dare each other to walk all the way through the tunnel alone, in the dark, and without a flashlight. Some would make the trip through the tunnel and come back to their friends sharing their "ghost experience," while others never even made it halfway before they'd turn back around.

As he exited the tunnel, Axel saw the bright floodlights in the distance, near the visitor's center to Helen Hunt Falls. The sight of the busy police officers and news reporters brought him back to the situation at hand. He was no longer a rookie patrolling North Cheyenne Cañon for teenagers or lost hikers; he was a lead detective with the Colorado Springs Police Department who had a job to do. He slowed his car as he drove past the mixture of marked and unmarked police cruisers lining the parking lot. He pulled into an open space and parked between two cruisers numbered 1616 and 1620.

As Axel climbed out of his car, he had to grip the door tightly to prevent the strong winds from pulling it from his hand and hitting the cruiser next to him. He shut the door quickly, stood straight, stretched his arms to the sky, and swayed back and forth, mirroring the tall pines that surrounded him. Upon lowering his hands, Axel brought them to his face and wiped his eyes to wake himself a little more. He collected his flashlight, found his way past the parked cars to the entrance to the trail, and made his way up the mountainside. He was halfway up the trail when he found a large boulder to lean on to catch his breath.

"I need more cardio," he whispered.

He wiped away the sweat that had accumulated on his forehead. He decided he had made the right choice in wearing his hiking boots but the wrong choice in not keeping up with his New Year's resolution of more exercise. With each step, his hiking boots pressed into the loose gravel on the trail that took him deeper into the forest surrounding the mountain.

The trail was littered with large boulders, rocks, and wooden posts marking each mile on the trail. Axel's pants and windbreaker whipped loudly as the westerly wind found its way through the army of trees, across the rocky trail, and past him; then it continued down through the valley toward the city. Axel had grown up in Colorado, and he was all too familiar with the Colorado mountains and its unpredictable weather. The forecast for earlier in the day called for high temperatures followed by a warm evening that would eventually be cooled by winds from the west.

The floodlights along the trail were bright, and his route to the crime scene was clearly visible; his flashlight remained at his side as he continued the gradual climb upward. When he walked around one bend in the trail, two uniformed officers passed on his left, silhouetted only by the lights illuminating the darkness behind them. He heard the two officers before he saw them, and he was able to make room on the trail for them by stopping and pressing himself against a fence post marker. He deduced they were part of an earlier shift and the two had just been released from the crime scene by someone in Axel's office. Their conversation, the small portion that Axel heard, centered on the amount of overtime they were making tonight and how much they had made this summer so far. He tried to reason for a moment at the awkwardness of their conversation about money while an innocent girl lay lifeless a short distance away.

Eventually, he found his way into an area just off the trail where through the shadows of the trees, he saw a familiar figure carefully squatting next to the victim on the ground. Gary, his partner, was wearing his all-too-familiar, worn-out, brown leather coat, blue jeans, brown leather boots, and one of his signature cowboy hats. As Axel moved closer, his shadow crossed over Gary and the victim's naked body. Gary turned toward Axel and used his hand to block the floodlight shining behind the two of them.

"Her name was Tammy Johnson, and before this evening, she lived on Simmons Road in the 'rich' part of town. I think that's who she is, based on the identification we found," Gary said softly as he slowly turned away from the bright light back toward the victim. Axel knew the "rich" part of town was the Woodlake Estates Neighborhood Community.

Axel moved closer for a better look. "Do you stay up at night waiting for your cell phone to ring, or what?" He asked.

4

Gary nodded. "Yes, I do. Don't you?" He replied as he continued to look over the victim.

Gary had been Axel's partner for more than ten years, and he was a wise man. Axel had learned a great deal from him. Axel was close to Gary and his wife, Carol. He even spent some Christmas evenings and other family holidays at their home. They treated the lonely thirty-eight-year-old bachelor like a brother—or as Carol liked to put it, an adopted son—but truth be told, Gary and Carol weren't old enough to be his parents.

Gary had passed the recommended age of retirement years ago, but he continued to stay on the department and work one homicide right after another. Gary had worked for more chiefs than any one cop on the payroll, and he always let the new police chief know that he held "badge one" in the department. Personally, Axel believed Gary stayed on the job just to piss the brass off whenever he had the opportunity. He wasn't known for having a filter when it came to saying what he was thinking, no matter his audience.

Axel squatted, careful not to disturb anything behind Gary, and listened as his partner filled him in on the victim, who he had presumably already identified.

"I got the name from the purse I found over there," Gary explained as he pointed toward a pile of clothes and personal belongings lying near the victim while he held the victim's license in his other hand.

Axel looked at the picture on the license after Gary handed it to him and realized it wasn't going to be much help in identifying the victim. The girl in the picture he was looking at was a happy, smiling sixteen-year-old who had just passed her driver's test. The girl on the ground was beaten, bloodied, and covered in dirt.

While Gary spoke, Axel looked down at the lifeless form and tried to imagine her preparing herself for prom a few short months ago. For a moment, he imagined her at the mall with her girlfriends scouring the racks for the perfect dress—not just any dress, but the special one. The dress that would set her apart from the other girls at the dance. It would keep the attention of the young man who was lucky enough to have escorted her that night. For a few seconds, Axel imagined her dress and the color she had chosen, and for a brief moment, he allowed a slight smile to form across his face as he thought about the happier occasion. But, just as quickly as the smile appeared, it disappeared. Axel brought himself back to the current situation. It wasn't a joyous occasion. This was a cold, premeditated murder.

Tammy's torn and cut clothes were next to a Colorado blue spruce that swayed back and forth as the wind blew through its branches. It was evident that Tammy was a popular girl and was probably preparing to go away to college. The designer labels from her clothes and her manicured fingernails supported the idea that she was from a financially well-off family.

Tammy, like the other victims, had a deep cut in her throat and one down her chest. She lay flat on her back with her head pointing downhill. It was reminiscent of a method used by hunters to help expedite the flow of blood from a recent kill. The only difference between Tammy and the other victims was that her heart appeared to be where it should be, in her chest. Axel assumed the killer had been interrupted before he had the chance to retrieve his trophy.

Tammy's arms and wrists were tied behind her back, and Axel recognized the familiar brown rancher's rope used to subdue her. It was the same type used in all the other murders as well. The rope was a small detail discovered after the second body was found in the woods a few months ago. Unfortunately, the rope itself wasn't unique. It could be purchased at most any hardware store, but the lengths of rope collected previously from other victims were positively identified as being from the same roll.

One piece of rope remained a few feet away from Tammy. At one time, it had undoubtedly bound her long legs at the ankles; it was cut away after she was carried here. Axel didn't need the autopsy report to tell him what he already knew. Like some of the other victims, Tammy had been alive when she arrived here, and it was here where she was sexually assaulted and then killed. The rope that once bound her ankles was cut away only to facilitate the killer's twisted fantasy of sexual domination.

The crime scene was very much like the others. Axel continued to look over the entire scene, looking for anything unusual. He moved through the different aspects of the murder in his mind, trying to recreate the events that had taken place.

She was over there at first. Then somehow, she ended up here. There's blood around her neck, on her chest, and on her feet, Axel thought to himself.

"Wait, look at the area below her chest," Axel said to Gary.

Gary looked at the victim. "What am I supposed to be looking at?" He asked.

"There's a void," Axel answered confidently.

"A void?" Gary asked.

Axel stepped closer to the body. "Yeah. It's like a V, where blood should be," the detective explained as he pointed over the top of Tammy's torso.

Gary shook his head in agreement. "I see it. What do you make of it?"

Axel began circling the victim. "I think he sat on top of her and cut her throat. The blood spurted out onto her chest and his thighs, his knees, and maybe his chest, leaving the void around her abdomen."

"How do you explain the blood on her feet and ankles?" Gary asked.

"I think he raped her and cut her throat over here, closer to the clothes where this blood is pooled in one area on the ground." Axel walked Gary through it while Ken Beck, the crime scene supervisor, watched and listened from the side of the scene. "And then I think she somehow stood up, and blood spurted out and down onto her ankles and feet until she fell in this area." Axel continued while Gary followed him through the crime scene listening to his theory. "Then he positioned her this way with her head facing downhill," Axel concluded and then looked at Gary and Beck.

Beck nodded. "Makes sense to me."

"I know, and it makes sense to me. I just wanted to be the one to figure it out first," Gary admitted.

"Well, that's our working theory for now. I'll put all the evidence together and see if it fits," Beck replied.

Chapter 2
Voices In The Dark

The bedroom was almost completely dark. The only light came from the glow of a small candle that sat upon a dresser in one corner. The flame flickered in the darkness allowing the man to see his dark reflection in the mirror.

Jeramiah closed his eyes as he felt the familiar pain in his head slowly build bigger and bigger, more intensely with each breath he took.

"Are you crying up there, boy?" Jeramiah heard the voice echo through the house, but it was especially loud in his head.

He cleared his throat. "No, Father."

The sound of footsteps and the creaking of the staircase warned of his father's approach. Jeramiah listened intently as each step grew closer and then stopped just outside his door. There was a long silence, and Jeramiah took the time to wipe his tears away as he moved to the side of the bed to cower on the floor. Suddenly the door flung open, and once again, the boy's mountain of a father stood in the doorway with his large frame blocking the light in the hall.

"I told you about candles up here! This is my house, and you

will do as I say and abide by my wishes when you are staying under my roof!" His father's voice thundered somewhere in his mind.

The large man walked toward the scared boy who had placed himself into a fetal position for protection as his heart raced uncontrollably. His father unfastened his belt from around his waist and moved even closer to Jeramiah.

Jeramiah begged and pleaded with his father for forgiveness, and when that failed, the boy remembered the prayer his mother had taught him. He whispered, "Even though I walk through the darkest valley, I will fear no evil, for you are with me. Your rod and your staff, they comfort me."

His father heard his words, and it fueled his anger even more. *"You ask God for help? Well, your God has no more control over me than you do,"* he said coldly.

The voice torturing Jeramiah would not stop, and he burst from his fetal position and spun in circles. He crashed feverishly into the furniture that lay hidden in the shadows, and he held his head between his hands. He had his palms covering his ears, all while screaming for his father to stop. The candle danced in wild movements in the darkness as the boy moved about the room violently.

The madness quickly came to an end as Jeramiah stumbled over a chair and struck his head against the bedpost. As he fell to the floor, his father's voice grew silent in the darkness as the scared child faded into unconsciousness. Underneath his now-still body, the hardwood floor collected a small pool of blood from the cut on his head. The flickering flame that had danced a few moments ago faded as it burned to an end. The frightened boy's figure gradually disappeared into the blackness that slowly engulfed the room.

While the evidence techs completed their jobs of taking photos and gathering the last bits of evidence from the scene, the two detectives made their way back down the trail toward their cars. The sun had begun its crawl out of the east into the Colorado morning sky just as Beck caught up with the two of them.

"Based on Axel's theory and what I've seen so far, I believe she's PPK's latest victim. I took a quick look at the cut wounds in her throat and chest. They appear to be the same type of injuries the others had," Beck explained as he opened the rear door of the van and placed his crime scene bag inside.

Axel placed his hands on his hips. "What about the X mark that we found on the other victims, did you find it on this girl?"

"It'll probably be there too."

"When will you know for sure?" Axel asked.

Beck closed the van door and turned to Axel. "I can blow up the photos I just took of the injuries and then I can make a comparison to the other victims' photos. I should know sometime later today if they might be the same, but to be honest, I think they will be. Everything else matches. Dr. Ryan will complete the autopsy, and it'll help in making a final determination on whether it was the same weapon."

Beck then turned and walked back toward the floodlights off in the distance, carrying more plastic evidence bags. Gary explained to Axel the details he had gathered so far before Axel's arrival, which included how a man by the name of Richard Lambert had come to discover Tammy lying in the woods in the middle of the night.

"Lambert claims he was out here alone. Apparently, he had a few problems that were keeping him from sleeping, and he wanted to clear his head. He believed a walk up the trail in the middle of the night would do it," Gary explained in a sarcastic tone.

Axel huffed. "Do you think he has any idea how stupid his story really sounds?"

The corners of Gary's mouth turned upward. "He didn't at first, but he does now after speaking to me. But with his wedding ring on his finger, he knew he had to have a good story to tell his old lady if by some chance his name appeared in this morning's paper. I'll interview him later today and find out how long it took him to drop his girlfriend off after they stumbled across poor Tammy in the woods."

Axel opened his car door and was about to get in when he had a thought. "Do you think he took his girlfriend all the way home before calling us?"

Gary shrugged his large shoulders. "I don't know, Axel, but if he didn't, he probably dropped her off at the convenience store on Twenty-First Street and called her a ride from there," he answered.

"Well, call me later!" Axel yelled from his car window as he backed out onto the gravel road once more.

The early morning sun to the east blinded him for a moment when he pulled around a bend where the mountains no longer provided cover from the bright star bringing in a new day.

Instead of going home and climbing back into bed, where he wished he was now, Axel drove to the police operations center and parked in the four-story parking garage. At his desk, he once again reviewed the previous murders involving the Pikes Peak Killer, the name that had quickly been assigned by the media to the current monster running around the Pikes Peak region, killing young girls. The same local press were undoubtedly filming near Tammy's crime scene at this very moment. Axel guessed the name, Pikes Peak Killer or the PPK acronym some reporters used, could have been worse, but at the moment, he didn't know how.

He sat at his desk studying old crime scene photos for about an hour, hoping to see something new he may have missed the first few thousand times he had looked at them. He guessed he was really into what he was doing or was just tired. Either way, he didn't see or hear Lieutenant Wilson enter the office. Wilson had been in charge of the homicide division for two years now, and in all fairness, he had done an excellent job so far, at least in Axel's opinion.

"Good morning, Axel."

"Good morning, Lieutenant."

"Sorry I wasn't out there last night. I was on my way, but a gang shooting occurred, and the patrol sergeant needed me there. I figured that you guys could handle the scene and would have called me if you needed something."

Axel nodded in agreement. "We would have."

"Did you guys find anything helpful out there this morning?" Wilson asked as he stood there with his hands on his hips. He, like Axel, wasn't getting much sleep lately and was growing tired of PPK.

"No, but it was him. I'm hoping Beck and his lab guys will find something we can use."

"Axel, I need something soon. If you don't get something in the next few days, I'll be forced to call in the FBI. This son of a bitch is off the charts, and he's got to be stopped."

Axel nodded. He understood PPK was causing significant problems for everyone involved. He also knew that the FBI's involvement in this case was a possible scenario, no matter what he thought of them. Thus far, the FBI had only sent over a generic, at best, profile of the killer based on the crime scene photos. Now, just the thought of the feds coming into the investigation turned his stomach, and it only added to his building anxiety. He knew if they had a chance, they would come in and take over the investigation, probably hampering it more than helping it. Not to mention how bad it would make the department look and how he, the incompetent detective in charge of the investigation, would look.

With the FBI involved, and whether they solved the case

or not, Lt. Wilson and Detective Axel Frost would probably be reassigned to robbery or property crimes, and Gary, well… Gary would just tell everyone to fuck off and climb into his RV with Carol. He wouldn't give the department a second thought as he drove toward white beaches, tiny bikinis, and sunny skies.

Axel quickly dismissed the thought and brought Wilson up to speed on the newest victim. Wilson got up and walked toward the elevator with his notes in hand. With the latest details, he would make his way upstairs and pass the information on to the brass, who was just now getting to the office. Axel hoped Wilson's meeting upstairs would go well. Everyone knew Wilson was getting more than his share of pressure from the police chief, who in turn was pressured by the city council, and of course, all of them were pressured by the damned media.

Axel hated the press in town, as they taunted the department in their efforts to catch PPK. By their accounts, PPK lived in the community and, at his own discretion, moved about the city at night, killing the innocent while the police department slept.

He looked at the bookshelf in his cubicle that held fifteen three-ring binders, filled with every detail of the murders he had amassed since the first body was found. In one drawer of his desk sat stacks of high school yearbooks. The victims involved in all the killings had graduated or were getting ready to graduate from the surrounding high schools. Axel had been using the yearbooks to identify friends of the victims before their untimely deaths at the hands of this savage serial killer.

Axel made a note for himself to find a yearbook from Woodland Mountain High School, the school Tammy had graduated from about three weeks ago. Her student ID had been found in her purse with the rest of her belongings at the crime scene.

He made a second note reminding himself to contact the school resource officer at Tammy's high school. The SROs at the high schools had, in the past few years, proven their usefulness. They were valuable resources to the community and to other officers who were investigating crimes in which juveniles were thought to have participated. Axel was utilizing them to help build a victimology for each of the girls.

He thought for a moment back to a few weeks earlier when he had to contact an SRO about PPK. Axel needed a yearbook that would have a picture of one of the victims, named Christy Jared. She had been a senior at Mesa High School and was a month from graduation when her body was found on Rampart Range in an open area of the national forest.

Christy, like Tammy, had also been found beaten, with her throat cut, and she had been sexually assaulted. She also, like Tammy, was a popular girl and was making plans to start college somewhere out of state in the fall. But unlike Tammy, PPK had been able to cut Christy's heart out and take it with him. The killer had six hearts now.

Axel had been sitting at his desk looking at crime scene photos for more than a few hours when he received a phone call from Dr. Ryan, the pathologist completing the autopsies. He informed him that the parents of Tammy Johnson had come in a few hours ago and made a positive identification of their daughter.

As Axel reviewed the case file, he glanced at his inbox. It was overflowing with new memos, faxes, and department information that was circulated to all sections of the department. For the past few weeks, it all had gone unread, and for a second, he almost reached over to clear it out but decided it could wait one more day.

Not that I'm procrastinating or am busy with anything else, he thought.

"Who was at the door, Richard?" Elaine asked of her husband as he walked back into the living room from the foyer.

Elaine was wearing her customary Sunday white dress that extended below her ankles. Her shoulders were covered with a white sweater, tied along her chest, and she stood with the posture and elegance of a respected lady.

Richard Lambert walked toward the couch holding his cell phone in his hand. "It was a salesman. I told him we weren't interested." He scanned the local headlines and hoped there was nothing on the internet with his name on it.

Elaine followed closely behind her husband and waited for him to sit down. "What was he selling on a Sunday in the middle of the afternoon?"

Richard turned from his phone and looked at his wife. "Elaine, I didn't bother to discuss anything with him. I told him I wasn't interested, and he left!"

Elaine moved closer to her husband cautiously, as she knew she was treading on thin ice. "You were certainly outside with him for a long time, just to tell him you weren't interested. I mean, was he carrying a bag with merchandise or something in it?" Elaine remarked casually as she bent over and fluffed the pillows on the sofa next to her husband.

"Elaine, are you trying to piss me off?" Richard asked, raising his voice louder. It was an indication to Elaine that he was tired of her interrogation.

Richard knew he needed to end this discussion. After all, he couldn't very well tell her who the man at the door really was, and he knew that the louder he became, the quicker his wife would back off.

"Richard, I'm sorry I annoyed you. I just thought it was odd that a salesman would come calling on a Sunday," Elaine replied in a soft tone as she attempted to calm her husband. At the same time, she reached for his hand.

She had learned from her marriage counselor, whom she often saw without the company of Richard, that affection from one party in a relationship could sometimes put the guard down on the other and deescalate the situation.

Richard pulled away. "Elaine, I don't know why he came by on a Sunday!"

"Oh, all right. My father asked where you were this morning at church. I told him you got in late from the office last night and you were too tired to come with me," Elaine offered, trying to change the subject.

Richard rolled his eyes. "Great. Did you cry on *Daddy's* shoulder once again? Did you also tell him I was out on the town partying all night again?" He asked sarcastically as he stood.

"No, Richard, I did not. Why do you speak to me this way? I've done nothing to you. When you're out late, and I call your office and no one answers, I don't question where you are. I should, but I don't. I love you more than you'll ever know," Elaine declared as she turned toward the window and cried quietly.

Richard moved toward his wife, clenching his fist. "I've told you, Elaine. I turn the ringer on my phone off because I know you can't get through the day without pissing me off by calling and nagging me and asking me when I'm coming home."

"I know, Richard, and I'm sorry," Elaine answered abruptly. She put her head down while Richard hovered over her.

She agreed with him in the hope it would end the argument. Elaine always worried Richard would leave, as he had done in the past. That simply would not do for her family and their reputation in the community. She had come to accept the fact that having him home and not speaking to her was better than having him gone and not knowing where he was or who he was with.

Richard unclenched his fist, composed himself, and caressed her shoulder. Once again, he had won. He then walked into his office and closed the door behind him.

Chapter 3
Good Neighbors

Axel was still sitting at his desk. He asked himself a few questions in his head as he attempted to wrap his mind around PPK.

"Why did he cut his victims' hearts out?" He whispered. Axel then closed his eyes and thought about the case.

Okay, here's what I know:

He takes the heart as a souvenir or for some morbid trophy. He took it from each of the previous six victims, but with Tammy, he was likely interrupted by Lambert and his unknown friend.

I think he selects his victims after some careful consideration, based on the victims' profiles, which leads me to believe he's a patient man and an organized killer, like the FBI profile suggests.

Damn, who is this guy? Why's he doing this in my city? Why can't I figure out anything more about this guy? How does he always seem to be giant steps ahead of me?

Maybe the feds should come in and try to stop this guy before he kills another girl... Perhaps I'm not the detective I think I am... Maybe I should be working robbery or some bullshit property crimes, and well... just maybe I'm too tired to be working on this now.

It was after twelve thirty and Axel was about to leave the office when Gary called with information about their midnight hiker, Richard Lambert.

"Mr. Lambert refused to speak with me at his house. He insisted that I call him in the morning at his office so we can arrange a better time to go over what he saw," Gary explained in the voice he only used when he was agitated or pissed off.

Apparently, the first interview with a witness—maybe the only witness—to Tammy's murder didn't go over as well as Gary had planned.

Axel listened to Gary rant about how Lambert met him at the front door, closed it behind him, and refused to answer any questions about his or any other person's involvement in the case until tomorrow, when it was more convenient for him.

"I should've charged his arrogant, pompous ass with obstruction!" Gary proclaimed and unleashed an army of obscenities about people who were rich, self-centered, and too damn big for their own britches.

When he was finished venting, he told Axel how he had contacted the city's taxi services as well, and they had informed him that a driver by the name of Juan Garcia had picked up a fare at the convenience store on Twenty-First Street at around two in the morning.

Gary also told Axel that he would have to wait until tomorrow to speak with Juan Garcia. Axel was okay with that. Unfortunately, he really wasn't in the best physical or mental state of mind to take on a proper interview with a witness this afternoon. He was finding it harder to concentrate as the hours without sleep began to take their toll on him.

"Juan Garcia works nights, and he doesn't have a phone. His boss said you can get in touch with him at their office tomorrow," Gary said.

He thanked Gary for his help and told him he would see him sometime the next morning at the office.

Axel made his way down to the parking garage and pulled out of the police operations center a few minutes later. He soon headed west on Highway 24, toward the city of Woodland Park, where he called home. The trip to work and home was twenty-one miles one way. He enjoyed the daily commute, as it afforded him the opportunity to clear his mind from the things he longed to forget.

The morning drive was his favorite because of the view. The rising sun created an unforgettable image. It was a glorious sight to start one's day. During the spring, the mountains would come to life and sparkle from the rays of the morning sun as it melted the evening dew that had settled along the rolling mountain grass.

The top of Pikes Peak would on many occasions be covered with snow in the early spring. That was the local photographers' moneymaker, as the mountain itself seemed to awaken with the rising sun for the purpose of having its photo taken.

As Axel drove home, he tried to clear his mind of PPK, the victims, and the whole case in general. He turned the air conditioner on low, with the hope it would help keep him awake. Axel was tired, and after a few minutes on the road, he noticed he had begun to drive slower than the posted speed limit. Axel thought about the previous night and how he had attempted to go to bed early but had just lay there and thought about the case, wondering if or when his cell phone would ring. In the darkness of the bedroom, surrounded by the large pillows that adorned his bed, he had pondered when and where another innocent girl would fall prey to the elusive monster. Axel questioned if there was any way possible that he could be out there stopping him.

Before long, the drive was over. Axel pulled into his driveway sooner than he had expected. He quickly determined the lack of traffic on a Sunday afternoon was probably the reason the drive went by so fast, or maybe he was just so tired that he'd blanked for most of the way home.

By the time Axel pulled into his driveway he was beyond exhausted. He slowly got out of his car and stretched for a moment. The sound of children laughing in the distance made him stop and turn toward his neighbor's home.

Matt, his friend and neighbor, stood in front of the grill, burning what smelled like hamburgers. His wife, Jill, was spraying their two girls with a water hose as they ran around the yard. The girls cautiously moved closer to their mother, who pretended not to see them until they were really close. Their laughter and screams filled the air, and for a moment, Axel forgot about where he had been earlier.

He watched for a minute and then started toward the opened garage. He knew that in a few minutes, he would be in his bed, and hopefully, a few minutes later he would be in a deep sleep.

"Axel! I hope you're just going inside your house to put your stuff away, because I know you see us over here grilling some fine bison burgers!" Jill yelled, taking a break from spraying the girls.

The detective stopped and turned back to the happy family. "Hi, Jill," he called back. "I really would love to come over, but I had a long night, and right now, my bed is calling my name," he explained tiredly.

"Axel, you can't say no! I've tried, but she'll keep nagging you until you're sitting over here with a burger in one hand and a beer in the other. Now put your stuff away, get your ass over here, and have a burger and a wiener with the rest of us," Matt demanded. A flame shot up from the grill, startling him and forcing him to back away quickly or lose the hair on his arm.

Axel grinned. "Matt, somehow I don't think you mind losing to her that much."

Jill was an attractive, athletic woman in her mid-thirties. Axel often saw her on the trail behind their houses running or biking. She was also the type of woman who had met the man of her dreams, married him, and with him, created a fairytale family. Axel believed that when she and Matt had taken their wedding vows, it was in their minds, as it should be, that it really was until death that they would part.

He swore the two of them were the type of neighbors only found in movies and books. He smiled as he recalled the times when Matt, the master griller, was encouraged by Jill to walk across the yard in January with snow a foot deep, carrying a dinner plate to the lonely bachelor who lived next door.

They were the neighbors who knew what was going on in the neighborhood, and they also knew when Axel was called out at night, during the day, or over a holiday weekend. Axel believed Jill prepared extra food on those occasions to ensure he ate something other than a microwaved burrito from a convenience store.

Before walking across the lawn toward the burned wieners and burgers and cold beers, he had to put his gun away. It was an item that Jill was uncomfortable with having around the girls. He knew a cop was always a cop, but he was respectful of his neighbors' home and their wishes. If he wanted to eat a great meal, he'd have to leave the gun at home. After putting it in the drawer next to his bed, he took the opportunity to trade his hiking boots and pants for flip flops and shorts. He then walked next door.

"Axel, did you catch the game yesterday? The Rockies won eight to four," Matt happily announced.

"I saw the end of it. That grand slam sealed the game for them in the eighth," Axel replied.

Matt rolled a few hotdogs over the open flames. "How do you like your wiener?"

Axel quickly glanced at the grill, and he knew right away by the number of hotdogs and hamburgers that his neighbors had once again made extra.

"Not burnt," Axel answered with a sarcastic edge to his tone.

"I hope you aren't complaining," Matt replied.

Axel stepped back. "Nope, just making a statement based on my direct observation."

"Whatever! After dinner, if you don't mind, we'll go in and catch the game in my man cave where we can enjoy some cold beers."

Axel ran his hand across his forehead. "I wish you'd just call it the basement instead of the man cave. It sounds better."

Matt placed the food on a plate and turned and faced his neighbor. "It's a man cave. Don't be afraid to say it. Are you saying yes or no to the game in my man cave?"

Axel raised his eyebrows and smiled. "Yes, I'll go and enjoy the game in your manly man cave."

"Now see, when you say it like that, it sounds dirty," Matt explained while shrugging his shoulders.

Axel laughed. "My point exactly."

By the time the game started, Axel had eaten one hamburger and one hotdog, and he had washed it all down with a couple of cold Coors Light. Now it was time to sit back and watch the game in one of Matt's leather recliners. The coolness of the basement, a full stomach, the cold beers, and the recliner created a concoction too hard to resist. Axel closed his eyes for just a moment while the Diamondbacks started to warm up for game two of the series against the Rockies.

Chapter 4
PPK Strikes Again

H ours passed before light once again made its appearance into the room through a small circular window located on the east side of the house. The sun brought light and warmth into the cold, damp bedroom. The morning glow found its way to Jeramiah's eyes, awakening him from his slumber. Slowly and carefully, he sat up and propped himself against the footboard of the bed, where he sat for a moment. He placed his hand to the back of his head and felt the open cut he had sustained the previous evening. He rubbed around the wound for a few seconds and then turned and looked at the clock beside the bed. The flashing numbers read 7:30 a.m., he had been unconscious for over twenty-four hours.

"Damn!" he snapped as he pulled himself to his feet.

After a quick shower, Jeramiah grabbed a handheld mirror. He positioned his back to the sink mirror and used the smaller mirror to view the cut on the back of his head.

"I could probably use some stitches," he mumbled to himself, but then he thought it was better to just clean it and not go to the hospital.

After making himself presentable in the short amount of time he had, Jeramiah was soon walking outside. He locked his front door behind him, climbed into his SUV, and headed toward Denver. The traffic was light, and Jeramiah relaxed while listening to the radio. He thought about the evening's events and how he may have been seen by the two midnight hikers.

I need to try to find out who they were. Damn! he thought.

There were times after each kill when Jeramiah would tell himself he wasn't going to do it again, and there were periods of time when he would go without having the urge, but eventually, the urge always found its way back to him. Before long, his thoughts would drift back to his last kill, and he would find himself reliving the moment again and again. Before he knew it, he was fantasizing about someone new.

Now, as he drove into Denver, he wondered when the urge would return once more.

"Mr. Axel, Daddy says it's time for breakfast and you should come upstairs and eat."

Axel heard the little voice of Cindy, who was standing in front of him in a pink ankle-length nightgown. In her hand, she held a small plush brown puppy with rather large eyes. Her disarrayed hair circled her face, and when she tilted her head and smiled, it invited him to smile back. She quickly disappeared behind the corner of the wall, and Axel listened to every step as she ran back upstairs.

Looking around the basement, he slowly remembered the previous evening and determined that sometime during the game, he must have fallen asleep in the recliner. Later during the night, someone, most likely Jill, had covered him with a blanket. He walked up the same stairs Cindy had recently run up and entered the dining room, where he found Matt sitting in front of a rather large stack of homemade pancakes. A smile appeared on his face when he looked up from his mountain of flapjacks that had rivers of syrup running down the sides.

"You can stay at our house anytime you like," Matt declared and shoveled in a mouthful.

Cindy sat next to her sister, Sam, who was running her finger around the edge of her plate, catching the syrup leaking over the side. She apparently enjoyed the pancakes as much as her father. Jill was at the stove, placing a final layer onto another already-large stack.

"Sit. You need to eat before you go to work, and if you hurry, you'll even be on time," she insisted.

"Yes, ma'am," Axel replied.

Matt looked up from his breakfast at his houseguest. "You fell asleep before the game even started, but it wasn't until the third inning when I heard you snoring and saw the girls applying the makeup."

"Matt, stop it! Axel, you didn't snore, and the makeup will come off with some soap and water," Jill said jokingly.

Axel glanced at his reflection in the toaster oven sitting on the counter for peace of mind. Matt was the only one who saw Axel. He laughed and nearly choked on his last bite.

Jill placed a cup of coffee in front of Axel. "I came down with two beers, and you were sound asleep. Matt noticed your cell phone was on your side and we figured it'd be okay if you stayed here and slept. I mean, you did look pretty tired yesterday."

"Man, you look like crap in the morning," Matt managed to say between shovels.

Matt had apparently already showered, shaved, and dressed in his usual work attire: brown denim pants, a plaid shirt, and work boots. Matt owned his own landscaping company and had a few employees working for him, which allowed him to manage rather than set stone walls. Axel admired Matt for being so successful, knowing he had grown up in a poor family in Florida. That was something Matt had shared with Axel after a six-pack some time back.

"Daddy had too much beer last night. Mommy said he was sitting on the toilet until the wee hours of the morning," Cindy innocently shared, adding to the conversation as she giggled and hid behind the big-eyed puppy.

"Eat your breakfast, young lady," Matt growled jokingly.

Axel finished some of his pancakes, thanked his generous friends, and walked to his lonely house next door. He figured there was still time to get cleaned up. Axel waved from his front door as Matt backed his truck and trailer out of his driveway.

Jaxson Locke sat at his kitchen table, eating cold cereal while reading over the national news on his cell phone when he came upon the story.

PPK Strikes Again!

Jaxson had been following the PPK case in the news and at work. He wondered when the Colorado Springs Police Department was going to officially ask for help from the FBI. Jaxson knew the police department had sent crime scene photos into the Behavior Analysis Unit (BAU) and that they had sent back a profile of the UNSUB, or Unknown Subject, based on the crime scene photos.

Through a friend, Jaxson had been able to get his hands on the profile, but based on what he was able to get, he thought there was more that could have been added. He wanted the opportunity to review the photos for himself, but he didn't currently have the authority or the clearance. After all, Jaxson Locke had only been with the FBI for three years. He held a doctorate in forensic psychology but had not been accepted into the BAU yet. Instead, Agent Jaxson Locke spent his days as an FBI agent reviewing cold cases concerning the ever-growing internet ring of child pornography. He currently completed psychological profiles on those offenders from the confines of his desk.

When he contacted the BAU a short time ago for the chance to share his own profile and to see if he could participate in the UNSUB profile of PPK, he was informed that he wasn't adequately trained in the study of serial murder. He felt he had been blown off, and he felt humiliated by those he had reached out to in the unit.

He sat thinking about how he could get involved without anyone knowing.

They won't let me be part of it in the BAU. But what if I just went to the lead detective? I do have some vacation time I could take, Jaxson thought.

Axel arrived at the department a little late. He doubted anyone would say anything. After all, he had been called out over the weekend and deserved a little comp time. Besides, he was usually the first into the office before eight most days.

Linda, the major crime unit's receptionist, was sitting at her desk near the entrance to "Cubicle City." She served as the buffer between detectives and visitors. She was in the perfect spot to stop and ask people who they were and who they needed to see. She was great at delaying someone whom someone else was trying to avoid, which earned her wonderful gifts on Secretary's Day.

"Good morning, Detective Frost," Linda greeted in an upbeat manner. She always enjoyed greeting and looking at Detective Frost. Although he was younger than she was, she still found his perfectly groomed dark hair, his bright white smile, and olive skin attractive. Not to mention his blue eyes and the way he smelled.

Wow, Linda thought to herself when he'd walked in. Linda always dressed professionally, and today was no different as she had decided to wear a blue dress suit with a red flower pinned to her chest. She had a larger than usual smile that accompanied her greeting.

Axel grinned. "Good morning, Linda. Did you have a good weekend?"

"Yes. Larry and I drove up to Cripple Creek Friday night, and I won a thousand dollars on a slot machine," Linda replied excitedly.

"Well, I guess that means you're buying lunch today."

"Oh yes, you can count on that, Blue Eyes," Linda responded flirtatiously.

Everyone in the office knew that Linda and her husband, Larry, were always in the gambling town of Cripple Creek, Colorado, on the weekends, and they had probably spent fifteen hundred dollars to win that thousand. They then would have continued to play the thousand dollars they won back into the slot machine. When it was all gone, the two of them were probably actually down a few hundred.

"Good morning, Axman!"

Axel was about to sit inside his cubicle when he heard Gary's familiar morning greeting.

"Good morning to you, Bernard," Axel said as he sat and spun around toward his desk, patiently waiting for Gary to come unglued.

Gary, wasting no time, ran around the cubicle wall that separated them and stood dangerously close to Axel. He cautiously looked around the office for witnesses. "We talked about the Bernard thing, Axel. You agreed not to tell anyone my middle name," Gary whispered in a serious tone, while once again looking around the office.

Axel gave his partner a lopsided grin. "I didn't tell anyone your middle name, Bernard. I just spoke it a little loud."

Gary's lips pursed. "You keep being a little loud, and you may find yourself alone on Christmas this year," he said smugly as he stood and crossed his arms, smiling as if he had his young partner over a barrel.

Axel shook his head. "Carol wouldn't allow that to happen," he replied just as smugly and then crossed his own arms and leaned back in his chair. "Remember, I bought her that nice coat last year, and you got her what, a vacuum cleaner and treadmill? Right?"

"Yes, I do remember, and this year, we shop together, Santa Claus. Do you know that every time we go out during the winter, I have to listen to how sweet and nice you are as she rubs that leather coat?"

"I'm sorry. Carol doesn't say things like that about you when she's vacuuming?" Axel asked in a pathetic voice, followed by a smile.

A smile formed on Gary's face as well, and the two of them laughed aloud.

"If you two are finished joking, I'm sure there's some police work needing to be done somewhere in this city," Wilson barked from the door to his office.

Gary looked up. "Oh yes, I was just about to tell Detective Frost that we have interviews to conduct with our two witnesses from the latest homicide," he quickly replied.

Lieutenant Wilson walked back into his office, shaking his head, and shut the door.

"I was just about to tell Detective Frost that we have interviews to do," Axel mimicked.

Gary shrugged.

"You are such a kiss-ass," Axel declared.

"We do have interviews to do, and I'm not a kiss-ass," Gary said in protest. "Now come on and get your keys. I'll tell you where we're going on the way to the parking garage."

As they exited the building, Gary explained that Richard Lambert had called early this morning and agreed to see Gary at 9:45 a.m. at Mountain Air Deli on Tejon Street. Gary also informed Axel that he was scheduled to interview Mr. Garcia, the driver of the taxi, at 9:45 a.m. as well at the taxi company's office on West Colorado Boulevard.

"I'll meet or call you later, and we can discuss what we learned from our interviews," Gary offered as the two walked into the parking garage.

"Sounds good."

Chapter 5
Schizophrenia

Dr. Trevor's office was decorated modestly. There were no family photos, no trophies, nor anything else that would lead one of his patients to believe he had any interest outside of psychiatry.

Jeramiah had driven to Denver and made it to the appointment with the doctor on time, the same as he had done for the past year on every other Monday. He found the leather chair comfortable. The room always seemed to be the right temperature, had the right amount of lighting, and smelled of mahogany.

Jeramiah looked at his watch impatiently. He needed his appointment with Dr. Trevor to be done on time today because he had an afternoon appointment back in Colorado Springs.

"How are things at home?" Dr. Trevor asked after seeing his patient fidgeting in the chair.

"Fine," Jeramiah answered quickly. He thought Dr. Trevor was nosey, especially when it came to asking questions about his home life. He also thought Dr. Trevor was overweight and a slob, but he allowed Jeramiah to pay in cash. Dr. Trevor at the request of his mother, had provided him with a prescription that kept the voice and hallucinations out of his head.

It was about a year ago when he first started hearing his father's voice, and it was about six months ago when he stopped taking the meds because he missed the urges. The urges came with a price. That price was his father's voice in his head. He had decided it was an acceptable nuisance if he could indulge in his urges and fantasies.

"How are your parents?" Dr. Trevor asked, attempting to get his patient to converse on some topic.

"They're fine."

"And the voices, do you still hear them?" Dr. Trevor asked as he wrote in his notepad.

"No. I take my medication as directed." *Not really, but that's what you want to hear. My father still talks to me,* Jeramiah thought.

"How are things at the mall? Are you still working nights?"

Jeramiah pressed his lips together into a thin line, he was annoyed. "Yes. Someone has to clean the toilets," he answered sarcastically. *As if anyone would believe that I would actually clean up someone else's shit,* he thought again.

Dr. Trevor titled his head to the side. "You sound a little bitter today. Is there something troubling you?"

Yeah. I kidnapped, raped, and killed a girl the other night, and I think someone may have seen me... Oh, and my father is driving me crazy! "No, nothing at all," Jeramiah replied after a moment.

Dr. Trevor lifted his chin and looked down the bridge of his nose. "Jeramiah, Paranoid Schizophrenia is not a condition that you should take lightly. How's the chlorpromazine working for you? Are you having any side effects from the medication?"

Yes, actually. I don't feel the urge to hurt people as much. So I stopped taking it six months ago. The only reason I come here is so you don't alert anyone that I may be a danger to myself or others. "No. No side effects."

Jeramiah hated these appointments, but they were

necessary. His mother had found Dr. Trevor in Denver and set up his first appointment. If Jeramiah stopped coming to the appointments, he knew Dr. Trevor would try to contact his mother, or even come by the house for a home visit. That simply wouldn't do! He'd have to kill him. He still planned on killing the doctor but not right now.

"Do you have plans for the Fourth of July?" Dr. Trevor asked.

"No. Not yet, but I'm keeping my options open."

Axel entered the taxicab office right on time. The walls were painted white with a red-and-white checkerboard-track border that was midway up the wall. It ran around the office with cabs racing past each other on both sides. The receptionist was polite, and she escorted Axel into the break area where he found a Hispanic man sitting alone at a table, drinking from a coffee cup.

"Hello. You are Detective Frost, yes? I am Juan Garcia. Your friend say you come and talk with me," Mr. Garcia said as he stood.

The detective reached out and shook hands with Juan. He was in his forties, and he spoke with a thick accent, accompanied by broken English. Axel also noticed that Mr. Garcia appeared to be very nervous.

"Yes, I'm Detective Frost. I'm glad you could meet with me this morning, Mr. Garcia," Axel said.

"Ah. No problem. My boss say I should speak to you and tell what I know," Mr. Garcia said as he twisted his ball cap in his hands anxiously.

"That's wonderful, Mr. Garcia."

His uneasiness was visually apparent, and the other people

coming in and out of the breakroom seemed to make him even more uncomfortable. A breakroom wasn't what Axel had in mind, but it was better than the hallway. In the middle of the room was a large table, and in the corner sat a small silver garbage can that desperately needed to be emptied. Mr. Garcia motioned for the detective to sit down. Mr. Garcia sat directly across from him while he continued twisting his hat in his lap.

Axel took out a pen and placed it along with a notebook on the table. "Mr. Garcia, I want to ask you about a fare you picked up early Sunday morning near the convenience store on Twenty-First Street and Highway Twenty-Four," the detective explained in a friendly voice.

The taxi driver nodded. "Sí. I pick up pretty lady. She very nice to me," he explained.

"Did you happen to get a name from her?"

"No, I do not."

"Do you remember what she looked like?" Axel asked as he scribbled in the notepad.

"Sí. Long hair, tall, and thin, and very pretty," he answered as he looked up at the ceiling and to the left. It was an indication to the trained detective that Mr. Garcia was telling the truth as he tried to recall what the woman looked like from memory.

"Was her hair blonde, brown, or do you remember?"

"Yes. She blonde."

"Do you remember where you took her?"

"Sí. I take to house in Woodlake Estates. It was very nice big home."

"Do you remember the address?"

Juan pulled his notepad from his shirt pocket. "Sí, I write it down. It stucco house on mountain side of street of Valley View. One, four, four, four, five is house number."

"Did she say anything to you during your drive?" Axel asked as he continued to take notes.

"No. She just says street and point, but she pay me real good tip," Juan said with a smile.

Axel decided that Mr. Garcia was friendly, and he appeared to be telling the truth about his time with the unknown female passenger. By the time the two were finished, Mr. Garcia had relaxed. As Axel stood to leave, Mr. Garcia had one request of the detective.

"You tell boss I help you, please?" he asked as he reached out to shake Axel's hand.

"Yes, I will. Thanks again for the help," he replied. Axel then walked out of the building and back to his car.

Mountain Air Deli wasn't overly crowded, but the small dining area for customers placed the wealthy patrons of the establishment quite close to one another. The closeness of "these people" made Gary uncomfortable. "These people" were, as Gary called them, yuppies, and while he impatiently waited for Richard Lambert, he made the determination that the entire establishment was a yuppie zone. He avoided those places like the plague on most days.

Lambert was late for the appointment, and Gary was becoming agitated by the lack of cooperation and consideration. He took his frustration out on the young waitress who had walked to his table to get his order. Gary, since birth most likely, had started his day with a cup of coffee, black of course, and one sugar, which he ordered from the waitress. The whipped cream running over the top and down the sides of the cups on the tables around him, being slowly sipped by the yuppies he disliked, only added to his annoyance.

Richard Lambert entered the deli, and immediately, he wished he had chosen a more private location to meet the police detective. Richard had suggested the deli without a thought about how crowded it would be at this time of day.

"Detective Portland?" Lambert whispered softly as he approached the detective.

Gary looked Lambert over disapprovingly, as the man stood there in his expensive suit and two-hundred-dollar shoes. Lambert was extending his hand for the customary gentleman's greeting while at the same time looking the detective up and down in his off-the-rack suit and leather cowboy boots. For a moment, Gary thought about not shaking hands but quickly decided it was probably a good idea to start things off politely.

"Hello again. Thanks for meeting with me, Mr. Lambert. Please sit down," Gary said with a friendly smile. He had hoped this approach to the interview would facilitate a positive atmosphere between them. His experience over the years taught him to allow the interviewee to be comfortable in the hopes he or she would talk and not put up defenses.

Richard Lambert sat down and brushed off something he saw on the table. "I want to thank you for agreeing to meet me here instead of my home or my office. You see, Detective, I'm a very private man, and I prefer that neither my neighbors nor my employees know anything about my private life, especially when it comes to matters involving the police," he explained as he straightened his suit coat.

The words and body language Lambert used were indications to the experienced detective that Lambert was self-centered, pompous, and an extrovert. Someone with an extrovert personality like Lambert's thought they were going to run the interview and control the outcome. Maybe it was nothing, and maybe Gary really didn't see anything. Perhaps he just did not like the man, but either way, he quickly decided to use another approach for the interview.

"Well, that's fine, Mr. Lambert. Privacy can be very important to someone like you, who's involved in a situation like this," Gary said, acknowledging Lambert's comment while leaving the word "this" lingering on his lips a little longer than usual.

Lambert surveyed the room and then glared at the detective. "Yes, you are quite right, Detective," he said as he now put himself on the defensive by sitting back in his chair away from the police detective and crossing his arms.

Gary gave a half smile. "Well, with that in mind, let me begin by asking: What were you doing in North Cheyenne Cañon early Sunday morning?" The experienced detective asked with confidence as he slid his folded arms and torso forward across the small circular table as he moved closer to Lambert.

Lambert blew out his cheeks and shook his head. "I was simply walking alone, thinking about a personal problem I'm struggling with right now. Sometimes I go up to the trails where it's quiet and peaceful to be alone with my thoughts," Lambert answered. He repositioned his legs to the other side of the table, away from the detective.

"Really? Well, that's interesting because a lot of men take their girlfriends up to the trails to fuck. Not many people go up there just to be alone to think about personal problems in the middle of the night. I—"

Lambert placed his hand flat on the table and leaned in. "Detective, my wife wasn't with me that night," he protested and then uncomfortably looked around the deli.

Gary smirked. "I know. I said people take their girlfriends up to the trails to fuck… not their wives," he explained in a louder tone, momentarily drawing the attention of some of the other customers.

Lambert gritted his teeth. "First of all, it's insulting to accuse me of having an affair. Second of all, I have half a mind to call your supervisor and inform him about how you are treating a personal friend and advisor to the mayor of the city," he replied quieter and then paused as he looked around the deli once more before speaking again.

"Well, third of all," Gary interjected quickly, not allowing Lambert to start again. "I've got half the mind to call your wife and ask her if she was the woman who was picked up at the convenience store early yesterday morning. I might even call the store clerk and maybe get a video of the people coming in and out of the store early yesterday morning. Perhaps that same video will make its way to the nightly news where everyone in Colorado Springs can call in and help identify the mystery woman who most likely isn't your wife," Gary explained in an irritated tone and then quietly waited for a response from Lambert.

"Okay, Detective. I was up there with a woman, whom I'd like to keep anonymous and who would like to remain anonymous, I'm sure," Lambert said uncomfortably while he repositioned himself in the chair once more. "My wife and I are in an open relationship. So, on occasion I will keep company with different women. Sometimes I go to private places with these women to be alone. The other night, I went up the trail with one particular woman."

"In the middle of the night to…" Gary said, waiting for Lambert to finish his statement.

"To fuck, as you like to say. I'm trying to hold on to a bit of my dignity and be civilized right now, like someone who has a reputation to uphold," Lambert said in defense.

"That's fine, and I'll be sure to tell this poor dead girl's family about how your dignity and being a gentleman is so important to their daughter's case," Gary sneered as he leaned closer. "Now, I'm going to start asking questions, and I expect answers to those questions from you. If you don't believe you can answer my questions, then I can always arrange a trip to one of our interview rooms downtown. Furthermore, at any time if you think you're someone special and don't need to talk to me, maybe an anonymous call can be made to the media, informing them how a friend to the mayor is a prime suspect in a murder investigation." Gary allowed his last statement to set in before speaking again. "I mean, how would you explain to the media about being in the North Cheyenne Cañon in the wee hours of the morning, walking alone, pondering your personal problems?" Gary asked.

Lambert dropped his head and thought about it a moment. He then looked back up at the detective. "Okay, like I said, I was up there with a woman. She and I wanted to be alone. We walked up the trail, looking for a private place to throw a blanket, and as we came around the bend toward the clearing, we saw a figure on the ground. At first, I couldn't tell what it was, so I used my flashlight to get a better look at what I thought was an animal. When we moved closer, it became clear that it was a girl's body," Lambert explained and then paused for a moment as he looked down at the table in front of him.

"Go on, Lambert," Gary ordered.

"Sharon screamed, and I started shining my light into the trees around us. I half-expected an animal to come charging at us from out of the trees or something. After a few seconds, I quickly grabbed Sharon's hand, and we ran back down the trail toward the road where we'd parked."

Gary took notes as Lambert told his story, and once again Lambert paused. This time, he placed his face in his hands and rubbed his eyes.

"What happened when the two of you made it back down the trail?"

"Well, when we were in the car driving down the road, Sharon said she thought she saw someone in the woods. I thought I heard something behind us, but now I just think it may have been my imagination."

"And then?"

"I dropped Sharon off at the convenience store, and she

called a cab. I then drove back up the hill and called the police. I stayed in my car near the trail and waited. Honestly, I was afraid to get out of my car and go back up the trail alone."

"Who's Sharon?"

"She's Councilman Douglas's wife. Now do you understand why I'm so reluctant to speak about her? If our affair got out, it'd be very damaging to a lot of people and their families," Lambert explained quietly, looking around the deli for a third time.

Gary wrote everything down and then looked at Lambert. "Yes, I do. Now did you see anyone when you started flashing your light into the woods?"

"No."

"Did you see any cars parked along the road or near the trail before walking up the path with Sharon?"

Lambert closed his eyes for a second. "I don't remember. I know cars have been parked there before when Sharon and I went up the trail. I just thought they were other people trying to be alone like us."

"Have you spoken to Sharon Douglas since the other night?"

"Yes, but only once. I told her I'd try not to mention her name to the police. If this got out to the public, it'd really damage her in the community. I mean, she really does a lot for people who need help, and she should not be defined as a woman who has an affair in the woods."

"Are you going to leave your wife for her?" Gary asked without hesitation. It was a question that most people wouldn't have asked someone they'd just met, but Gary wanted to know, not for the case but for his own curiosity.

"Now, Detective, that's private, and I don't believe you need to know that information for your investigation. However, to satisfy your curiosity, I don't believe I'll ever leave my wife. For now, Sharon and I have a good time with each other, and we will continue to have a good time until we get tired of each other's company and decide to move on."

"Interesting. That's all I've got for you right now, Dick, but I may call on you again if something needs to be answered or if I think you can help," Gary said with a bit of sarcasm, to which Lambert simply laughed and rolled his eyes without comment.

"Please make any further contacts with me through my office," Lambert ordered. He stood, buttoned his coat, and walked away without shaking hands with the police detective.

"Okay, I'll do my best, Dick," Gary shouted from the table after waiting for Lambert to get close to the door and far enough away so that he would have to shout.

CHAPTER 6
OLD FRIENDS

A xel was walking up to the elevator when his cell phone rang. He quickly recognized Gary's number and was eager to learn what Lambert had told him.

During a lengthy phone call, the two detectives exchanged information concerning their interviews with the two witnesses. Gary told him what was said during his meeting with Richard Lambert, and what he thought of him, and in turn, Axel shared what he had learned from Juan Garcia. At the end of their conversation, they decided they needed to speak to Sharon Douglas, especially if there was a chance that she may have seen something or someone in the woods.

They also decided that Richard Lambert should be the one to call her and arrange the meeting. It was Gary's suggestion to have Lambert call her. He knew she would give Lambert hell for bringing her name up during the interview after he'd told her he wouldn't mention her by name.

Gary made a quick call and spoke to Lambert once more, who, just as Gary had thought, was reluctant to call Sharon Douglas. He finally agreed to the detectives' request after a few more comments about how the media was thirsty for a suspect.

Axel was walking to his cubicle, carrying a new three-ring binder, and looking it over, when he came across DJ Thompson sitting in Lt. Wilson's office.

"Hey, buddy," Axel greeted as he walked in.

"Hey yourself," a familiar voice replied from behind DJ. Axel recognized the voice, and he tilted his head and peered behind DJ at his old friend and sector partner, Jake Mean.

Axel was happy to see him. "Well, what brings the two of you up to the fourth floor?"

Jake stood and walked out from behind DJ. "I wanted to come by to say good-bye to you and Gary. DJ here told Commander Williams on Friday he'd escort me up here and then also promised he'd make sure that I wouldn't misbehave or touch anything."

The word "escort" lingered a second. Axel knew that active-duty police officers did not need an escort, but civilians did. So did police officers who were no longer police officers.

"So this is it? You're done?" Axel asked, even though he already knew the answer.

Jake took a deep breath and then slowly let it out. "Yes. After everything that's happened over the past few months, there's just too much to deal with in my own personal life. Honestly, the department isn't pleased with me. Don't get me wrong. I don't think they had any other choice after everything that's happened," Jake explained.

"Are you leaving town?"

Jake darted his eyes toward the ceiling and then back at Axel. "Yeah, but not immediately."

Axel could tell that Jake was having a hard time. "Can we get together and have a few beers or something?"

Jake nodded his head. "Of course we can. You still have my number. Just call me and let me know when."

"Sounds good. Where are you off to now?" Axel asked, already knowing the answer.

Jake pointed downward with his index finger. "I'm going downstairs to clean my locker out, which is why I brought DJ here with me. I need some help with the heavy lifting," he joked as he reached up and patted DJ on the shoulder.

"You know I really enjoyed the time we spent getting into it on the streets together. I wish I could've done more to help you," Axel confessed as he reached out to shake Jake's hand.

"I enjoyed it too, and I always knew, and I still know that you have my back," Jake replied.

Axel stood there for a moment, wishing he could have done more for Jake after his pregnant wife was killed about a year ago. Jake was a great cop, but when River was killed by a group of bikers, he couldn't handle it and he may have taken matters in his own hands.

The brief distraction from an old friend was a welcomed one, but Axel was soon back at his desk, looking over the case files again. He dictated his continuation report to Tammy's case concerning the interview with Juan Garcia and left the office early. The overworked detective decided he wanted and desperately needed to get plenty of rest for his early morning appointment with Dr. Ryan, the pathologist at the medical examiner's office.

Tuesday, July 3rd

After Axel got home the previous day, he made his way to his bedroom and lay down for a few minutes to relax. Before he knew it, he had fallen asleep to the sound of an old Western movie playing on the television. He awoke to the sound of the alarm, got up, showered, and drove to Derby's Diner for a quick breakfast before driving to the medical examiner's office.

Axel always gave himself ample time for his breakfast to digest before attending an autopsy. Over the past few years, he had observed many autopsies as a homicide detective, but for reasons unknown to him, he still felt uncomfortable, and he usually couldn't eat after attending one.

He arrived at the medical examiner's office, and once again, he felt it was cold in both temperature and atmosphere. He was permitted access to the examination room by the front desk receptionist. He found Dr. Ryan standing over the body of Tammy Johnson, speaking into a microphone that hung from the ceiling. His hands were gloved, and he wore a green surgical scrub that was covered in the front with a white surgical apron.

Dr. Ryan was a large man in both shape and height. He had been a pathologist for over thirty years, and he was recognized by many as a leading expert in the field of forensic pathology.

The doctor looked up from the body when he heard the detective walk in. "Nice to see you again, Detective Frost."

"Nice to see you as well," Axel replied.

"Wally, will you please get a new bag for the stomach contents?"

"Yes, Doctor," Wally, Dr. Ryan's assistant, answered and walked to a counter to retrieve another plastic bag.

"I think you already know, but I'll say it out loud for your report. Based on my medical examination of the body and on my experience as a medical pathologist, I've determined that the victim's manner of death is a homicide," Dr. Ryan stated as he removed the contents of Tammy's stomach and placed them into the plastic bag Wally had opened and held out toward the doctor.

"Wally, please place this in the scale and turn it so I can see the weight," Dr. Ryan instructed.

Axel was always amazed at how Dr. Ryan never seemed affected by the sheer violence he saw daily. He watched and listened as the doctor looked at the scale and spoke his findings into the microphone.

"Based on my postmortem examination, I've determined the cause of death was a deep laceration across the victim's throat that started approximately two inches below the right ear of the victim and moved horizontally across the throat to the left side, stopping approximately two and a half inches below the left ear. Both the left and right carotid arteries were severed. The right carotid artery was completely severed, and the left was partially severed. The cut started deep on the right side and finished shallower, which resulted in the left carotid artery only being partially severed."

Axel listened and took the notes he needed as Dr. Ryan continued with his examination. When he finished, he reached up and turned the microphone off and looked at Wally.

"Wally, will you please go into the cooler and prep the next autopsy?" Dr. Ryan asked his assistant and then turned and looked at Axel.

"I know that look. What else do you have?" Axel asked.

"Nothing. What do you have?" Dr. Ryan asked and turned back toward the body of Tammy Johnson.

The detective moved closer to the doctor, took a breath, and began. "I think the deep cut is from him sitting on top of her pushing her head back into the ground below. When we found her, we noticed a void where there should have been blood. There wasn't any around her midsection or just under her chest. We think he straddled her, held her head down, and cut her throat from right to left. The blood from her carotid artery spurted onto her chest, shoulders, and onto him, which left the void under her chest and around her abdominal area," Axel explained as he held a stack of photos from the crime scene of Tammy's body toward Dr. Ryan for him to examine.

"I agree with your theory. The blood from her right carotid artery would have been shooting out with each heartbeat. The left would have spurted too but not as much as the right. But how do you explain the blood on her lower legs and feet?" Dr. Ryan asked as he looked at another photo from the scene.

"We think she somehow stood after he cut her throat and moved around. The ground was disturbed in a few places at the crime scene. We also think we found the spot where he sexually assaulted her, cut her throat, and then stood up to watch her die. In this photo, you can see where we found her, and in this next photo, you can see the different areas that Beck identified. Where she was sexually assaulted, where she stood, and where she fell to die," Axel explained as he moved through the different photos with Dr. Ryan.

"I'll call a friend of mine who's an expert in blood spatter analysis and send him everything we have thus far. It'll be helpful, when you finally catch this guy," Dr. Ryan said while emphasizing the last six words.

"I'm working on it," Axel replied.

"I know you are. Call me if you need anything," Dr. Ryan offered as he walked to the next body that Wally had brought in.

"I will," Axel said and left the building.

Jaxson made it to the airport early and grabbed a bite of breakfast in the terminal before heading to the boarding gate. He arrived just as the plane was boarding, and he handed the airline gate attendant his boarding pass and stepped onto the boarding ramp. Once inside, he stopped and looked around and discovered the plane was nearly empty of passengers. The attractive flight attendant standing at the cabin door smiled at the six-foot-one, blue-eyed, and slightly dark-skinned passenger as he approached her.

"Sit in any seat you'd like," she instructed with a friendly smile.

Jaxson unconsciously looked her over before speaking. He liked her long blonde hair and green eyes. "Does that include first class?"

"I think that'll be all right too," she answered and smiled flirtatiously.

"Great," Jaxson said as he walked down the aisle and found an empty row in first class.

Jaxson was tall, and he always hoped for either aisle seats or emergency exit rows when traveling by plane so that he fit more comfortably. He placed his carry-on in the overhead bin and made himself comfortable in the aisle seat. He took his cell phone out, switched it to airplane mode, selected the right music, and placed his earphones into his ears. He then rested his head on the headrest and closed his eyes.

Jaxson was sound asleep when he felt someone tapping him on the shoulder. He opened his eyes and found the attractive blonde flight attendant standing over him. He quickly removed his earphones and sat up straighter in the seat. "Yes?"

"Would you like a beverage or a snack?" she asked.

"No, thank you."

She tilted her head to the side and smiled flirtatiously once more. "Are you sure? About ninety percent of passengers want something. Trust me, I know. Now, are you positive you don't want anything?"

"How about some company?" Jaxson heard himself say. He was embarrassed. "What I meant was…"

"Sure. Let me put my cart away, and I'll come back and sit with you. There are only eight people on the flight, and Sara, the other flight attendant, can take care of them," she answered before he could finish his comment.

Jaxson watched her walk toward the front of the plane, and he, like most men, was focused on one specific asset of hers.

Nice! Stop being an idiot, he thought. *You should move over and let her have the aisle seat.*

Jaxson took his own advice and moved into the window seat. He waited for what he thought was an eternity. He tried to look himself over without the advantage of a mirror. He wiped his eyes and mouth and then he covered his mouth and blew into his hand to check his breath.

"Can I sit next to you?" she asked.

"Of course."

She sat down and leaned toward Jaxson. "I'm Brandi," she said with another smile as she extended her hand toward Jaxson.

"I'm Jaxson. It's nice to meet you," Jaxson replied nervously as he shook her hand.

"Business or pleasure?" she asked.

"Business," Jaxson answered.

"Me too, but every flight is business for me," she joked and laughed. Jaxson liked the sound.

He laughed too. "I imagine it is," he said in agreement.

"What kind of business are you in?" she asked.

Jaxson cleared his throat. "I work for the department of treasury." Jaxson, like other agents, had been told to tell strangers who asked about his profession to lie to them and say he was a treasury employee and not an FBI agent.

Brandi's forehead furrowed. "Are we really going to start our friendship off with a lie?" She asked.

"What do you mean?" Jaxson questioned. He was surprised by her comment.

"I work for the airline. I know about every passenger who comes on this plane with a gun. They tell the pilots and me. So, Agent Locke, can we try once more?"

Jaxson embarrassingly darted his eyes downward and then back at Brandi. "Yes. I'm sorry. It's just that we're instructed not to identify ourselves as agents of the FBI unless it's in an official capacity. I forgot that I had to declare my firearm when I checked my luggage," he explained.

Brandi's mouth curved into a smile. "Now see, that's better. How long are you going to be in Colorado Springs?"

"I don't know for sure. How about you? Are you laying over or continuing on to someplace exotic?"

"I'm actually visiting my sister and her husband for two weeks. I'm celebrating the Fourth of July with them. And then I'm off to the Bahamas for a week," Brandi said enthusiastically.

"That sounds like fun," Jaxson replied.

"What about you?"

"Mostly work, unfortunately," Jaxson answered.

Chapter 7
Uncle Wilber

Sharon drove her Lexus north on Nevada Avenue, being cautious of the many families crossing the street in front of her as they made their way toward Acacia Park. There they were preparing their children to march in the annual parade on Tejon Street. After seeing all the families, Sharon was slightly annoyed with herself for choosing this location to speak to the police department.

The park is too crowded, she thought to herself.

She had known very well it would be overflowing this time of year. The parade itself was an annual event for the city. The many underprivileged families with whom she worked and volunteered for had children, and there was a good chance one or some of them would be here today.

Turning right onto Bijou, she spotted a blue van pulling out of a parking space close to the park. The driver of the van slowly made her way out of the space, being careful of the many kids running around unsupervised. Sharon waited patiently and guessed that the van belonged to a soccer mom who was making good use of it, carrying multiple kids back and forth to games and other activities.

After what seemed an eternity, Sharon pulled her car in between two other vans. She was ten minutes early, according to her watch, and decided to wait in the comfort of her car with the air conditioner on to keep her cool.

Sharon turned the radio up and watched as a group of boys in one corner of the park lit firecrackers and kept busy by throwing them at one another. A local band was playing in another corner of the park. She turned and watched as children ran through the water of the Uncle Wilber Fountain. Sharon smiled as it sporadically shot streams of water into the sky and then fell upon the children. She thought the children's behavior was somewhat comical as they stood impatiently waiting for the burst of water and then scrambled for cover when it finally flew from Wilber's mouth. Sharon contemplated for a moment the decision she and her husband had made many years ago about not having children. For her, there would be no games, no minivans, and most of all, no children calling her Mommy.

A tapping on her window surprised her. She turned and smiled at the friendly face staring back. She reached over and pressed the automatic window button. With the window down, the aroma of hot dogs, hamburgers, and firecrackers filtered inside the car.

"Hello," Sharon said, just as her attention was drawn back to the boys lighting firecrackers in the corner. They were louder now that her window was down. She watched as one boy used a lighter to ignite a fuse. At the same time, she caught a flash of light from the corner of her left eye. She heard no bang but felt her head growing heavy as her body slumped forward. As her head rested on the steering wheel, she noticed the lights around her slowly growing darker.

Sharon's killer put the gun away, walked toward the sidewalk, and quickly blended into the crowd. The band continued, and children still screamed and ran away from the water. No one realized what had just happened until a few minutes later, when a mother walking her son to the park passed the idling car.

The mother covered her mouth and her child's eyes. She gasped and tried to speak but could not. As she backed away, she pointed at the car, and it drew the attention of others. The news spread quickly, and people started gathering around the car, hoping to catch a glimpse of what was inside. Officers ran over and promptly set up a perimeter protecting the crime scene.

Axel drove from the medical examiner's office to Acacia Park, located in the center of downtown Colorado Springs, and waited for Gary. He had called him earlier and informed him Richard Lambert had gotten in touch with Sharon Douglas and that Sharon had agreed to meet them in the park, away from the police station.

Children were running around the park like a swarm of bees around a hive. Tejon was closed off at both intersections with bright yellow police tape to stop traffic from entering the parade route. Police officers, on their day off, collected overtime pay to guard the barricades and intersections. Axel found an empty picnic table and sat.

"Hey, Satchel Ass."

Axel heard Gary's familiar voice and turned and saw him moving toward him through the crowd, carrying two hotdogs.

"I got you a hotdog. I hope you're hungry," Gary announced as he reached out toward his partner with one of them.

Axel took the hotdog. "What do I owe you?" He asked.

"Eight bucks."

Axel gave his partner a bug-eyed expression. "Eight bucks! For one hotdog?" Somehow, he knew he was being taken advantage of once again. He was also surprised he felt hungry and that he wanted the hotdog after viewing Tammy Johnson's autopsy earlier in the day. *Maybe I'm just getting used to them,* he thought.

"No. Two hotdogs cost eight dollars. It was your turn to buy."

"Well, I don't have any money on me," Axel replied.

"I'll add it to your tab."

"I imagine you will. Do you know what this lady looks like?" Axel asked and then took a bite of his eight-dollar lunch.

"She's supposed to be in a white summer dress with red flowers. She has blonde hair and long legs," Gary said with a smile and a wink.

"That's quite the description. Did Lambert tell you all that? I mean about the legs and all?"

Gary shook his head. "Nope! He just mentioned the dress and blonde hair. I imagined the rest."

Axel shook his head and continued to eat his food, while Gary talked about the Colorado Rockies and their season. The band and other participants started to march down the street, and people clapped and cheered from every corner of the park as the firecrackers ignited. The parade did not interest the smaller children who were running through the Uncle Wilber Fountain.

"What time did she say she'd be here?" Axel asked as he finished his food.

"Eleven thirty," Gary said and ate his last bite.

"Well, it's eleven forty now. Call Lambert and ask him what kind of car she drives. She could be stuck in that traffic on Nevada Avenue."

"Okay, Mr. Impatient. Come on. My phone with his number in it is in my car," Gary explained.

As the two started across the park, Axel noticed a large crowd of people standing on the sidewalk with a few police officers nearby. Another officer was standing next to a Lexus parked on Bijou, facing the park.

He was wondering what the gathering was about as his phone started to vibrate. He looked down at it. He then looked at Gary. Axel answered his phone and listened to Lt. Wilson on the other end.

"We got a homicide over there," Axel said and pointed toward the Lexus after getting off the phone.

The two detectives walked toward the other officers and surveyed the scene. They observed a female victim inside the car, sitting in the driver seat with her head slumped over the steering wheel. She had an apparent gunshot wound to the left side of her temple and an exit wound on the right side.

The passenger seat and window were covered in blood and brain matter, indicating the bullet's direction of travel. There was a small hole in the passenger door where Axel determined the round had finally come to rest.

"It looks like the shooter was standing next to the driver's door and shot downward. The bullet struck her high on the left side, exited low on the right, and finally came to rest in the passenger door," Gary explained.

Axel pulled his notebook out and took notes on what he observed. The victim was blonde and wearing a white summer dress with red flowers. He didn't need the victim's driver's license or a family member for identification purposes. The victim was Sharon Douglas.

Maybe she did see something the other night. What she may have seen will now remain a mystery, along with the identity of PPK, Axel thought to himself.

Axel noticed the driver's side window was down. This minor detail seemed strange. It was scorching outside, and when the detectives arrived, the car was still running, and the air conditioner was on.

"That's odd," he said quietly. *Why's her window down with*

the AC on? Was she talking to someone? Did someone she knew come up to her? He asked himself.

The only thing Axel could conclude was that she knew who shot her or she saw who it was, and she wasn't afraid to speak to the shooter. *Hence the window being down.*

The scene took a few hours to process, and as Gary was completing his interviews, the coroner arrived and collected the body from the car. Gary walked toward Axel just as he was reaching into the vehicle to turn the engine off.

"Damn. She was our witness. The car is registered to David and Sharon Douglas," Gary explained.

"Did anyone see anything?" Axel asked.

Gary shook his head. "No, everyone was watching the parade," he answered.

Axel placed his hands on his hips and slowly turned in a circle surveying the area. *There were so many people around,* he thought.

"The woman who found her had parked across the street and was walking by with her son when she saw the body slumped over the steering wheel," Gary explained as he looked down at his notes.

His so-called notes consisted of a few napkins that had come with his hotdog lunch.

"Who do you think could be a suspect?" Axel asked.

Gary glanced up in the direction of a tall tree and thought about the question for a second. "Well the way I figure it, we got PPK… and Mr. Douglas if he knew about the affair with Lambert. Who are you thinking of, Axel?"

"Same as you, but I'd like to know where Lambert was during lunch as well. Do you want to go and speak to Lambert again while I go see Mr. Douglas and tell him that his wife is dead? After that, I'll go over and speak to Tammy's parents."

"You haven't talked to the victim's family yet? Are you waiting for an invitation? I thought you would've spoken to them earlier this morning."

"No. I was giving them time to collect themselves. Lt. Wilson and the chaplain already did the notification. I still need to get statements from them, which I'll do later. Besides, I had to meet Dr. Ryan for the autopsy this morning."

That was a lie. Axel was putting off visiting Tammy's family because he didn't want to see another family in mourning. Axel figured that if he had captured PPK by now, their daughter would still be alive.

Gary could tell that his partner was agitated. "Okay, I'll finish things up here and then I'll speak to the cheater again and find out where he was today. I'll also find out if he owns a gun," he said as he walked back toward his car.

As the coroner's van pulled away from the curb, Axel stood and stared at it as it turned south on Nevada, carrying away his only possible lead.

CHAPTER 8
FORENSIC PSYCHOLOGIST

"What exactly does a forensic psychologist do for the FBI?" Brandi asked.

That was the one question everyone asked, but it still put a smile on the agent's face. "I put profiles together to help identify a perpetrator of a specific crime," he answered.

"How do you do that?"

"Well, I look at observable behaviors and try to determine what type of person exhibits those types of behaviors."

Brandi's curiosity was piqued. "I think I need a little more of an explanation than just that," she replied.

Jaxson thought for a moment. "Okay. For example, this plane has three seats on both sides of the plane for passengers to sit in."

Brandi nodded. "Right."

"I have an idea about what type of passenger sits in each seat."

"Really! Do tell," Brandi encouraged.

Jaxson leaned into her. "The aisle seat is for the passenger who is an extrovert. The aisle-seat passenger is comfortable around other people and likes to converse with strangers and learn more about them, while at the same time being in control."

"Control?" Brandi asked.

"Sure. The aisle-seat passenger controls the other two passengers' movements in and out of the row. He or she may not necessarily understand that they have that control, but psychologically speaking, they do."

"I can actually see that. What about the window-seat passenger?" Brandi asked with interest.

"That passenger is more likely an introvert. They sit there, closing themselves off from the rest of the passengers except the middle seat, which they have no control over. They'll most likely put their earphones on and pretend to sleep or look out the window. As long as they don't have to converse with anyone, they're content."

Brandi's eyes lit up. "Wow! You're absolutely right. I've seen it. Many window-seat passengers will get on the plane and immediately put their earphones in and ignore everyone else."

"Now this isn't exact, and sometimes a behavior analysis profile like in this scenario can be incorrect for any number of reasons. Sometimes, new information that comes to light changes the profile. I made this passenger seat assignment analysis off the belief that the passenger selected their seat. If the airline assigned the seat, then the profile is useless," Jaxson explained.

"I get it. But what about the center seat?" Brandi asked.

"That's just poor travel planning by the passenger who usually gets stuck with the seat that they waited until the last minute to book. Nobody wants the center seat," Jaxson said and then laughed.

"But you've moved to the center seat," Brandi keenly pointed out.

"Like I said, the profile can change. In this scenario, I want to be in the center seat next to you," Jaxson happily admitted.

He was happy with the relaxed and easygoing companionship of Brandi.

Axel maneuvered his car down Lake Avenue through a roundabout, one of many that could be found in the Woodlake Estates community, on his way to the Douglas home. The homes that lined either side of the street were expensive, most of which belonged to prominent families and wealthy business owners in and around Colorado Springs. At one time, the community had its own police department patrolling the quiet neighborhood.

He pondered how the city of Colorado Springs could justify the construction of the many roundabouts in the expensive neighborhood while ignoring the potholes and cracks in the less affluent communities. These streets were well lit at night, and the flower arrangements along the road were comparable to that of the White House in Washington, DC. The expense to keep this neighborhood looking the way it did had to be high.

As he pulled into the Douglas driveway, he noticed it was surrounded by a wall of river rock. The lawn was immaculate with its perfectly manicured green grass. There were beautiful spruce trees sporadically placed around the property. The home, like many others in the area, screamed to those passing by that people with money lived here.

Axel pulled under a covered driveway near the front door. He stepped out of the car onto a cobblestone patio and then walked toward the large pine double doors that were held in place with black cast-iron hinges. He shook his head as he thought about the people who lived in this area away from reality, the reality where people knew their neighbors, said hello, and watched out for each other.

From the front porch, Axel saw a red sports car parked under a tree near the garage, out of view from the street. As he reached for the doorbell, he paused and listened to what he believed were the voices of two men arguing inside the home. At first, it was verbal, but then he heard furniture being pushed around the floor. Axel rang the doorbell, then knocked on the door loudly. The argument inside stopped, and Axel positioned himself to the side in preparation for the unknown. One of the large doors opened and standing in front of him was a medium-sized man with dark hair, wearing a yellow dress shirt, a loose tie, and blue slacks—all of which seemed to be slightly disordered.

"Can I help you?" he asked.

"I'm Detective Frost with the Colorado Springs Police Department, and I need to speak with Mr. Douglas concerning his wife," Axel answered directly as he tried to look past the man into the home.

"I'm David Douglas. Please come in, Detective," he said with some hesitation.

The inside of the home had its own personality. It was decorated with expensive wall paintings, lavish furniture, and hardwood covering the floors from wall to wall. He believed an expensive interior decorator deserved credit for the grandeur displayed. Axel continued to look around at the home as he followed Mr. Douglas from one room to the next. He made polite comments about the beauty of the house as he walked. It was nothing more than small talk, as Axel was still concerned about the second man he had heard from the outside.

Mr. Douglas quickly moved in front of him near the kitchen and asked that they continue their meeting in the living room, where they could sit and talk. As he took a seat, he noticed Mr. Douglas had a red mark on the side of his face, as if he had just been hit by someone. His eyes were also bloodshot and swollen.

"Would you care for something to drink?" Douglas asked.

Before Axel could answer, his host yelled for someone named Abigail. A woman, apparently Abigail, had been hiding around the corner. Upon hearing Douglas call for her, she made her appearance. She, too, was visibly upset, but she wasn't the other voice Axel had heard from the door.

"What would you like, Detective?"

"Do you have a diet soda?" Axel asked Abigail.

"Certainly," she replied and quickly left the room.

She disappeared behind the corner, and Mr. Douglas took a seat across from Axel.

"Is everything okay here?" Axel asked.

"Yes, Detective." Douglas lied.

Axel decided to dig a little deeper. "It's just that I heard some people arguing when I came to the door, and I thought it was another man's voice I had heard."

"Oh. I was watching the game and yelling at the players," Douglas explained quickly.

Douglas wasn't going to break and Axel knew it. It was time to move on. "Mr. Douglas, I'm sorry, but I come here as the bearer of bad news. You see, I'm here to inform you that your wife was killed this afternoon," Axel explained softly.

Douglas took a deep breath. "Yes, Detective, I know."

"You already know? How did you find out so soon? I mean, I just left the scene," Axel said in shock.

"I have many friends in this town, and when someone dies or is killed, especially someone who was as special as my wife, the news gets out pretty fast."

"I mean, I just left the park and came straight to your home. Maybe I'm out of line, but hell, for lack of better words, her body wasn't even cold yet."

"Detective, let's just say that, well… Someone I know saw my wife's car and everything else that was going on near the park and called me. In turn, I made some phone calls myself."

"I understand. So, do you think I could ask you a few questions?" Usually, the detective tried to be more compassionate when interviewing the family of victims, but if this guy was going to be secretive, then he saw no reason to delay the inevitable.

Outside, he heard a car start, and seconds later, he saw a flash of red pass by the window. When he looked back into the room, he met the hypnotic eyes of Abigail, who had returned with the drinks. He smiled and thanked her as she placed the soda on a coaster in front of him. He then watched as she walked to David Douglas, where she bent over and handed him his drink. He couldn't help but notice that Abigail appeared to be remorseful or sympathetic to David. She passionately, or with compassion, rubbed his hands with hers after she placed the drink in his hand. She then stood back upright, smiled, and slowly caressed his shoulder.

Axel noticed that she was an attractive Hispanic woman in her mid-thirties, and she had a body that would rival twenty-year-old models. She was tall, dark-skinned, beautiful, and walked through the room with confidence. Axel suspected that Abigail was something more than just hired help. Abigail was someone he may have to investigate later, but for now, he turned his attention to the man whom he believed had answers. David stared at him from across the coffee table. Axel sat there for a moment, thinking.

Why would anyone want Sharon Douglas dead? Well, besides PPK. Was there a possible reason David would want to kill his own wife? If so, what was his motive? Maybe David's motivation just brought me a soda. Axel thought.

"Abigail is a friend of the family. She's here visiting my wife and me for the summer. She lives in Spain, and she and Sharon met in college," David explained without being asked.

"Mr. Douglas, where were you today between eleven and twelve o'clock?" Axel asked, as he figured it was time to start the interview.

David took a drink and sat the glass back down. "I didn't kill my wife, Detective, if that's what you want to know," he answered.

"I didn't say you did. I'm simply trying to eliminate the possibility. You know. I'm just looking at all the angles and eliminating the obvious," the detective explained.

"I was here, with Abigail, watching the game. You can ask her yourself if you would like."

Abigail is his alibi, Interesting. Axel said to himself as he wrote in his notes.

"Do you know of anyone who may have wanted to kill your wife?"

"No. Sharon was a wonderful woman. She volunteered at soup kitchens, the church, and anywhere someone needed her. Everyone loved Sharon."

"Do you know why she was at the park today?" Axel asked, not knowing how to react to a yes or no response from Douglas.

"Yes. To see you, Detective," David answered without hesitating.

Axel was taken aback. *Why would a woman who was cheating on her husband tell him she was meeting with a detective to discuss her involvement in a murder case that happened when she was in the mountains with her lover?*

The look on Axel's face said it all. Suddenly, without another question from the detective, David spoke again.

"I know my wife was in North Cheyenne Cañon, and I know who she was with and what she was doing. Sharon and I had an open relationship. It was a type of understanding, if you like. At home or at a special event, it was the two of us in the loving relationship that religious and morally strict members of the community expected from people in our position. Away from the house and in secret, and away from public scrutiny, whatever happened just happened," David explained plainly.

"Well, with that in mind, did your wife share with you the

events that took place in North Cheyenne Cañon the other night?"

"Just some of it. I understand the two of them were walking on a trail and came across the young girl on the ground. They got scared and ran away. Sharon's companion, if you will, called the police, and Sharon got a ride home in a taxi."

"Do you think Richard Lambert would want your wife dead in the hopes of concealing his affair with her? As you probably already know, he, too, is married."

David huffed. "No. I know Richard, and even though he's a cheating son of a bitch, he wouldn't kill anyone."

"Do you know his wife? What I mean to say… is do you know if he and his wife had an open relationship too? Maybe Lambert and his wife had the same type of relationship you and your wife had." Axel already knew the answer, from speaking to Gary, but he wanted to hear what Douglas knew about it.

"I've seen Elaine at parties. She's not the type. Richard only married her, in my opinion, to help his own political career, and no, I've never had a relationship with her. That's why her husband is a cheater. Sharon and I were open about our relationship and respected each other's privacy. Richard hid his and Sharon's affair."

"I don't understand. I thought Lambert was wealthy."

David sat forward. "Okay, here's the story. Richard was poor when he met Elaine. He went to college on some academic scholarship. When Richard met Elaine, he was in law school, and he was flat broke. Once when he was drunk, he told me that in college, Elaine came on to him all the time. She wasn't his type until he learned who her father was and how wealthy he was. Elaine was a very homely girl—still is too—but she's the daughter of Johnathon Willard Davis, a rich bastard from the South who moved here when his wife, Elaine's mother, died giving birth. He's a mean old crab who bought his way into Colorado politics. He raised Elaine on his own, within their church, and spoiled her rotten. Anyway, after they were married, her father bought his new son-in-law a place in our own local government," David explained.

Axel listened and watched Mr. Douglas's body language. The trained interviewer deduced that David was telling the truth. He was open, direct, and didn't appear to be searching for answers.

"If he has it so good with his wealthy father-in-law, why would he cheat on his wife and risk the chance of losing it all?"

David slightly chuckled. "Have you seen Elaine?"

"No."

"Don't get me wrong, Detective Frost. Elaine isn't ugly per se. She's homely, and I mean very homely: no makeup, long dresses, hair in a bun, and right with God. Sharon, on the other hand, was, as you can see, gorgeous," David explained as he pointed at the numerous pictures of his wife that were displayed around the room.

"Have you spoken to Lambert today?"

For the first time David paused before answering. "No. Richard and I still have to work together, and right now, I'm angry with him over this whole mess. I don't want to say or do anything that could be harmful to either of our careers. Don't get me wrong, Detective, I'm not angry about their relationship. I'm upset because they were sloppy with their relationship."

Axel couldn't believe what he was hearing. The guy had just lost his wife, and all he was concerned about was his career. Axel ended the interview at about the same time he finished the soda. He thanked David Douglas for his time and was escorted out the same way he had come in.

After leaving the Douglas home, Axel looked at the map on his phone and found Simmons Road. The house where Tammy Johnson had once lived was also in the Woodlake Estates area.

Chapter 9
Dick

The home was easy to find. It was the one with all the cars on the street in front of it. Tammy's home was blue with white trim and had four garages. Above the last garage, a sign read "Tammy's Parking, All Others Will Be Crushed." Once again, the lawn was well maintained, and the trees were in full bloom and trimmed. The other homes along the street were evenly spaced apart, and all the yards were like the Johnsons'.

After parking four houses down, Axel walked up to the front porch and rang the doorbell. After a few moments, he was greeted by a woman in her mid-forties. She was dressed in black, her hair was pulled back, and she wore no makeup. The area around her eyes was red from wiping many tears away.

"May I help you?" she asked softly.

"Yes. I'm sorry to intrude like this, but I'm Detective Axel Frost, and I hoped to speak with the parents of Tammy Johnson." He knew before he said it that the woman was Tammy's mother.

The sound of Tammy's name brought the woman to tears once more. She covered her face just as a man walked up behind her.

"Clare, are you okay?" he asked. He placed his hands on her shoulders while he looked Axel up and down.

Axel looked back at the man. "I'm Detective Frost, and I think I've upset her. I'm truly sorry."

"That's all right, Detective. Please come in."

The man opened the door wider and escorted the woman back into the living room where an older woman took her by the arm and led her into the other room. The house was just as nice inside as it was outside. The home décor reflected a country setting with handmade quilts on the furniture. The paintings were religious in nature, with brilliant colors that changed with the amount of light shining on the canvas.

"Detective, we can talk in here."

Axel followed the man into a study, where he shut the door and offered Axel a seat.

"Are you Tammy's father?"

"Yes. I thought someone from your office would be coming by. My name is Boyd Johnson. My wife, Clare, is the one who greeted you at the door. She still can't believe Tammy is gone. Every time the doorbell rings, I think she goes to it hoping to see Tammy standing there. I don't know what to do. Family from all over have come in for the funeral that isn't even scheduled yet. I just hope that we've called everyone. We still have so many things to do. Have I ordered the flowers yet?" Boyd asked himself, temporarily forgetting about the detective sitting across from him.

Axel listened as the grieving father rambled over the funeral preparations for his daughter. He had visited families just like the Johnsons in the past few months, and unfortunately, he was getting used to the behavior of grieving parents.

"Mr. Johnson, where was Tammy last seen?" Axel asked.

Mr. Johnson was looking down at the carpet, focusing on something other than his daughter.

"Landing's Department Store. She worked there. I

wanted her to have a summer job where she could learn some responsibility before going to college. Clare was against it. She wanted Tammy to just play around this summer, but I insisted Tammy find a part-time job. I guess this is my fault. You know, college can be tough. You must get your priorities straight and prepare your kids for the real world. You got kids?" Johnson asked.

"No, I don't," Axel replied as he watched Boyd wipe his eyes to stop tears from streaming down his cheeks.

Mr. Johnson took a moment to collect himself. "Even though everyone was against her working at first, Tammy got the job and seemed to enjoy it. She was so happy when she received her first paycheck. Tammy ran in the door, waving it in the air. Her mother and I sat down with her in here, and she asked us who FICA was and why they got some of her money. Clare and I laughed at her, but Tammy still took us out for pizza. I think she made about a hundred dollars in that check," Boyd said as he recalled the happier moment.

Axel just listened. He felt that a good listener was what others needed the most, especially in times like this.

"You know, I could have given her a hundred dollars every day. She didn't need the job," Boyd whispered. He looked down when his eyes started to fill with water once more.

"Mr. Johnson, it's okay to want your kids to understand responsibility, and this isn't your fault in any way," Axel reassured.

"Thank you for that, but it's hard to imagine what could have been if I—"

"Now, did you talk to Tammy that day?" Axel asked, stopping him mid-sentence.

The grieving father cleared his throat. "Yes. She was closing that night and called to tell us she'd be home in about an hour. When she was two hours late, I drove over the route she takes to get home, looking for her car. When I got to the mall, I found it in the parking lot and called the police. They were sure she went out with some friends after work and would probably come home later." Boyd shook his head and breathed deeply. "Clare and I were home Sunday when the police chaplain and Lieutenant Wilson came by and gave us the news. They then went to the coroner's office with us, where I identified my daughter's body. 'The body,' our Tammy, 'the body.' It sounds so horrible, and cold, and final."

"Did she ever mention anyone new in her life whom she may have hung out with?" Axel asked.

"No. Well, she did like this other girl who worked there in the security office. I think her name is Jennifer. She's a bit older than Tammy, maybe twenty-nine. Tammy thought it was exciting how Jennifer took down shoplifters."

"Tammy worked in the security office at the store?" Axel asked.

"No, she worked in apparel. One day, Tammy saw this boy stealing some pants, and she called security. Jennifer showed up and arrested him. From that day, they started a friendship. They went to the movies and walked around the mall during their lunch breaks, talking about their futures." Boyd, for the first time, smiled at the image of his daughter spending her last days without a care in the world.

"Thank you, Mr. Johnson. Here's my card. If you need anything, call me."

Axel reached a hand toward Boyd, who grabbed it tightly and pulled the detective closer.

"If you find this man and can't kill him, you call me." Boyd was angry, and Axel believed he meant what he said.

Axel did not acknowledge Mr. Johnson's comment. Instead, he nodded, gave his condolences, and walked out the front door past the family and friends who were still arriving. They all stopped their idle conversations and watched as the detective stepped out of the house.

Do they blame me for what happened to Tammy? Maybe if I caught this guy sooner, she'd still be alive. What am I overlooking? Perhaps I should turn this over to the FBI, Axel thought to himself as he drove out of the neighborhood.

Gary parked in front of Lambert's office next to a red Porsche, hoping to surprise him by arriving unannounced. Upon walking in, he saw the receptionist, a short and portly woman sitting behind an oak desk, looking down at some papers. Gary stood there, waiting for her to address him. After a moment, the detective cleared his throat and announced himself.

"I'm Detective Portland, and I need to see Mr. Lambert regarding a matter," Gary snapped.

The woman looked up from her papers and peered at the badge in front of her. She then looked up between her glasses and eyebrows and relaxed her shoulders and let out a breath of air. Her body language indicated she wasn't impressed with the badge and that the interruption was unwanted. "May I tell him what this is about?"

"Nope," Gary replied smugly as he smiled and placed his badge back in his pocket.

"Well then, he's probably busy," she replied with an equal attitude.

"Well, why don't you wipe away that peanut butter on your finger and pick up your phone to ask him if he can see me?" Gary's patience with the overweight receptionist was growing thin.

He watched with a smile as she picked up the phone and announced that Detective Portland was there. The receptionist nodded and said "yes" and "no" a few times and then hung up the phone.

"You can go in," she mumbled almost inaudibly as she pointed at a door to her right.

Gary smiled once more and walked toward the door. He let himself in, but not before turning around to see the rude woman looking at her finger with the peanut butter on it, which she quickly stuck into her mouth.

"I told you not to come here and that I'd deal with you people outside of my home and office," Lambert protested from behind his expensive desk.

Gary was unaffected by Lambert's attempt to intimidate him. The detective walked forward without saying a word. When he reached the edge of the desk, he placed his hand over his mouth and rubbed at his five-o'clock shadow, still not saying a word. Lambert appeared uneasy as he watched the detective.

"Get out, or I'll—"

Before Lambert could finish what he was about to say, Gary reached across the table and grabbed him by the tie. He wrapped it around his hand in one motion and pulled him across the desk, pushing the papers and pens to the floor.

"All right, *Dick*, let's get something understood," Gary said as he looked into Lambert's eyes while holding him in place and off balance.

"I'll ask a question, and you'll answer it. Is that clear, Dick? I think we've done this before. And another thing, Dick. You might believe you're untouchable behind this desk, but you should think about how easily you can be taken out from behind it. Have we reached an understanding, Dick?" Gary released his hold on Lambert, who fell back into his leather chair. "I hope we don't have to do something like that again," Gary said with a smile as he unfastened his coat and sat down. He gave Lambert a few minutes to collect himself. "Now, where were you today around lunchtime?"

"I was here," Lambert said quickly.

"Are you sure you weren't at the park earlier?"

"Yes."

"Dick, what if I told you someone saw that red Porsche at the park?" Gary asked, bluffing his suspect.

Lambert straightened his tie. "Okay, I was there, I went to see Sharon. I wanted to know how her interview went with you guys. I wanted to know what she said to you."

"Why would that be important for you?"

"Because of who I am and who I work for. The mayor can't be blindsided by a police investigation. Do you know how that would look to the public, if my affair got out?" Lambert asked pathetically.

"Pretty damn bad, for you, but I don't think you care about the mayor. You only care about yourself. You're worried that your own little world will come crashing down around you if your boss hears you are having an affair and that you are under police suspicion for murder."

Lambert sat forward and pounded his fist on his desk. "You don't know shit about my life. I could call and tell your boss about the police brutality that just took place," he said, feeling confident once more.

Gary sat there for a moment. Then he got up and rushed around the desk. He grabbed Lambert by his ear and forced his head down onto the table.

Lambert tried to push him away, but the detective was too strong. He squealed in pain when his arm was forced behind his back.

"You and I both know a complaint won't be made. You're afraid to call anyone and tell them what happened here. They may ask why I was here. Then you'd have to explain everything, especially the affair and the dead body you found. Now, don't piss me off again," Gary ordered and released Lambert.

He walked back to his chair and sat down once more. Lambert sat back in his own chair and straightened his shirt and tie again. He was angry and shook his head in disbelief. He wasn't accustomed to being treated this way. He simply wasn't used to not getting his way.

"Get over it, Dick! I got a few more questions," Gary asserted. "What did you do at the park today?"

"If you're asking me if I killed Sharon, then the answer is no. I went there, and I saw all you cops standing around her car and then I saw blood on the window. When I saw the coroner's van arrive, I knew she was dead. I drove past without stopping. Then I went to her house and told her husband."

Gary's eyes widened. "You told her husband?"

"Yes."

"Did you also tell him why you knew she was at the park?"

"He and Sharon had an understanding that benefited me, if you know what I mean."

"So, David Douglas knew you and his wife were doing the deed?"

"Probably, but when I saw him today, I told him everything."

Gary listened and wrote everything in his notepad. *I can't believe the lives these people live. They are supposed to be admired people in the community,* Gary thought to himself as he listened to Lambert.

"If that covers it, I'll say good-bye. You know nothing about me, Detective, but I suggest you back off if you know what's good for your career," Lambert said.

"Dick, you can expect me to be in your business daily if I need to be. By the way, do you own a gun?" Gary asked while holding the door open.

"No, I don't."

"All right. I've been doing this job since you were in diapers. Having me as an enemy could be very bad for you," Gary explained confidently before walking out the door.

Jaxson's flight arrived in Colorado Springs at four thirty in the afternoon, and a short time later, he was in a rental car driving west on Highway 24 toward North Cheyenne Cañon. Jaxson had made a call to his friend in the bureau. His friend was able to get the location of all the known crime scenes where PPK had killed his victims. He was also able to get a few more photos of those scenes as well. As Jaxson drove, he thought about how he had requested two weeks' vacation and how surprised he was when it was approved on such short notice.

At first, the young agent questioned why Special Agent in Charge Joe Wright had approved his request for a vacation so quickly, but right before he left for his flight, he received a call telling him to enjoy his time off because he deserved it. Agent Wright said Jaxson had been working hard, and he had been very successful with his assigned cases. On the flight, Jaxson felt guilty for not sharing his plans and not telling his boss what his real intentions were.

How do you tell your boss that you plan on inserting yourself into the PPK case without permission from the bureau or an invitation from the Colorado Springs Police Department? Jaxson asked himself.

Chapter 10
Commando

J axson made his way up the winding dirt road, looking for the parking lot for Helen Hunt Falls. The information Jaxson had received from his contact in the bureau indicated that PPK's latest victim had been discovered just off the hiking trail toward the west, about a quarter of a mile up in the dark timber. After about ten minutes of driving up the dirt road, he soon found the sign for the falls and pulled into the parking lot. When he got out of the rental car, he couldn't help but admire the tall pines that reached upward into the clear blue Colorado sky.

Jaxson was athletic and a strong man, but the trail was a little steep in some places, and after a short climb up one section, he got his first taste of how the high mountain altitude affected those who lived at sea level. He was slightly dizzy and felt uneasy on his feet.

He stopped and placed his right hand on the split-rail fence that lined one side of the trail to rest and catch his breath. After a few minutes, he began once again, and before long, he found the crime scene. Yellow police tape still blocked it off from the trail. Jaxson bent down and ducked under the tape, and after he took about twenty steps into the dense brush, he found the murder site.

An eerie feeling swept past him that seemed to be carried by the westerly winds. The ground was still disturbed, and dark dried blood stained the pine needles that littered the ground. Jaxson opened the file and read Detective Axel's report concerning his theory on what had taken place, and when he was finished, he turned to the accompanying photos.

He tied you up to control you. It wasn't part of his fantasy. But how did he first approach you? How did he get close to you? A ruse? Did he trick you into allowing him to get near you? No, you weren't afraid of him, were you? You trusted him, didn't you? Who would you trust? Someone you knew or someone else? What is this X imprint from the knife? Jaxson thought to himself.

It was later in the afternoon by the time Gary and Axel reached the office at about the same time. The two found Lt. Wilson standing at the entrance to Axel's cubicle. The look on his face hinted to the two seasoned detectives that something was up.

"Axel, I need you to do something for me," Wilson said as the detective walked by him to sit down.

Axel couldn't imagine what he was about to be asked to do, but he knew it wasn't going to be good. "What's up?"

"The press needs a statement, and it came down from the chief's office that you're going to give it. I told them I'd do it, but they said the press needs a fresh new face to discuss the PPK killings. Personally, I think the higher-ups believe by putting you out to the public, it will get the media and others off the chief's back," Wilson said as he watched Axel turn his chair around while shaking his head no.

They're throwing me under the bus! Axel thought.

"Don't shake your head no, because you gotta do it, like it or not," Wilson ordered.

"Okay… When?" Axel asked as he threw his pen across the desk in frustration.

"I think they're already downstairs waiting for you."

Axel's eyes narrowed and his brows turned downward. "What?! I thought I'd at least have some time to think of something to say."

"Damn! That's not right," Gary protested.

"Move!" Axel said as he pushed past Gary toward the bathroom.

Gary caught himself on the cubicle wall. "Hey, don't get pissed at me. The lieutenant is the one throwing you to the wolves, not me," Gary said in his defense and looked over at Lt. Wilson.

The lieutenant glared over his glasses. "You're lucky I didn't have you do it," he said to Gary as he turned back toward his office.

"You and I both know you knew better than that. I'd just embarrass the department... By the way, a Mr. Lambert may call with a complaint." Gary allowed the last sentence to slip out quietly as Wilson was shutting his office door.

Axel stood in front of the mirror in the men's bathroom, looking at his hair and teeth. He knew he needed to make sure he looked presentable in front of the camera. A few minutes later, he walked out of the bathroom and toward the elevator, with Gary right behind him.

Axel glanced over his shoulder. "Why are you coming?" He asked.

"Well, the way I see it is when you fall on your face, someone needs to be there to pick you up," Gary answered with a smile.

"I won't fall on my face," Axel huffed as he straightened his suit.

"Who do you think will be here to interview you?" Gary asked.

"I don't know, and I don't really care who it is."

Gary tapped Axel's shoulder. "Hey, maybe it's that fox from Channel Twelve News."

"I doubt it, and who uses the word 'fox' anymore?"

"I do, and Amanda Crosse has been the reporter covering the killings since they began. It'll probably be her. Wow, are you lucky or what? Carol thinks Ms. Crosse goes commando," Gary said excitedly.

"Commando? What does that mean?" Axel asked.

Gary smirked. "It means she doesn't wear any underwear. You really should read a men's magazine occasionally. I don't believe you sometimes, Axel. It's like you live in a bubble. No contact with the outside world and no women in your life," Gary said as the elevator doors opened.

The news team was setting up their equipment in front of a large Colorado Springs Police Department badge painted on the wall. It was a familiar spot where other members of the department had addressed the city via the local news. An attractive woman standing alone looking into a compact mirror caught the detective's eye. She wore a flattering pantsuit that fit tightly over her body. She stood about five foot four and couldn't have weighed more than one hundred and twenty pounds. Axel recognized her as Amanda Crosse.

Gary was right, Axel thought to himself, just as Gary nudged his arm and winked at him.

The two detectives walked in and stood next to the wall. They notified a cameraman that they were ready to begin the press conference. Ms. Crosse, after being informed of the detectives' arrival, made her way past the news crew and walked up to the two of them.

"Hi, my name is Amanda Crosse, and you must be Detective Axel Frost."

"Hello, my name is Detective Gary Portland," Gary stated, interjecting. He moved around and in front of Axel as he smiled at the reporter. Axel thought Gary looked like a ten-year-old on Christmas morning.

Amanda turned her attention from Axel and reached out to shake Gary's hand. Axel did not stop his partner. He just smiled at Amanda from behind Gary's shoulder.

"Hello, and yes, I'm Detective Frost. Gary here is my partner. Are you going to be conducting the interview?" Axel asked as he stepped in front of Gary.

"Yes, I am. I hope I'm not keeping you from something more important," Amanda answered as she looked at the detective.

Axel escorted the reporter to a bench, where the two of them discussed the questions that Amanda was going to be asking. As they talked, Axel had trouble concentrating on what she was saying because he was drawn toward her beautiful face and friendly smile. He noticed the woman's blouse was unbuttoned near the top, and her cleavage was partially exposed. Axel tried not to look but found it a bit difficult. He wondered if she had left a few buttons undone on purpose to distract the person she was interviewing.

Axel politely listened to her as she went over each question. Some of the questions she had prepared for him, he told her he couldn't answer, and although she disagreed, she accepted his request and removed those questions from the interview. The reporter then reached up with both hands and placed a microphone on Axel's shirt collar, straightened it, and ran her hands down the front of his coat. He thanked her and smiled, and she smiled back, which brought about an awkward silence between the two.

"Amanda, can you come over here for a minute?" one of the crew members asked from across the room.

When Amanda walked away, Gary stepped forward and

stood next to Axel. He was about to say something when she suddenly dropped her papers and bent over to pick them up.

Gary's eyes widened. "See that? She definitely goes commando," he said quietly.

Axel shook his head and grinned sheepishly.

"Seriously, there were no panty lines on that ass. I know you noticed," Gary insisted.

Before Axel could respond, he was motioned over by Amanda. The two stood in front of the camera as the spotlight came on, and the interview began.

Axel was in front of the camera for less than five minutes, and Amanda stayed right on script with the questions she and Axel had discussed. When they were finished, Axel returned to where Gary was sitting on the bench leaning against the wall behind him with his arms folded.

"Man, why didn't you look at me? I was trying to get your attention. You had a huge piece of something between your teeth," Gary said.

Axel was about to respond when Amanda Crosse walked over. She smiled at Axel and asked him if he thought the interview went well. Gary, in his usual fashion, made a few comments about how he felt the interview went and what he would have liked to have seen and heard.

"Well, thank you for your thoughts, Detective Portland, but I was really interested in how Detective Frost thought the interview went," Amanda said as she removed the microphone from Axel's shirt.

"Amanda, we got to go," a crew member said.

The reporter shook her head at her coworker and then turned back to Axel. "Maybe we could get together for coffee or something and talk about the interview," she suggested.

"Like a date? Where exactly would you be taking my partner, Ms. Crosse?" Gary asked in a parental tone.

"W-Well, wherever he'd like to go," she answered.

Axel, seeing how uncomfortable Amanda was becoming, gently took her by the arm and led her away from Gary, who stood there smiling.

"I'm sorry, Ms. Crosse. My partner has an odd sense of humor, but he means well."

"Amanda, call me Amanda," she offered.

Axel smiled at her. "Okay. Amanda it is, but only if you call me Axel."

"It's a deal, Axel."

"Where shall we go?" he asked.

"I asked you out for coffee, so where would you like to go?" Amanda asked.

"You know, if it's later in the evening, why don't we make it dinner? And I like steak," Axel answered.

Amanda nodded. "Well, so do I. How about we go to Mike's Steakhouse?"

"I'll see you there at say, eight o'clock?" Axel suggested.

"Eight it is," she replied.

The two exchanged numbers and Axel watched as she walked out of the building and to her van, where the rest of her crew had assembled. Watching from the window, he noticed the entire group turn around and look back toward him and then start laughing. Amanda shook her head and quickly hurried the rest of them into the van.

"Nice ass. I bet you could bounce a quarter off it."

Axel rolled his eyes and turned toward Gary, who had quietly walked up behind him. "I wasn't staring at her ass."

"Neither was I. I was talking about yours," Gary declared, which made both of them laugh.

"I can't believe what happened. So many people. I couldn't

have planned it any better. She was just sitting there, and wham, her brains are on the other side of the car. No one saw anything!" Jeramiah said excitedly as he drove away from the park. He had stayed there for hours watching it all.

Jeramiah had made sure to arrive at the park early with the hope of getting to her first. He knew he had to eliminate any possible witnesses, but today, the whole set of circumstances had worked out perfectly. The chances of getting caught were high, but if that woman had seen him the other night, she could have identified him.

She needed to die, Jeramiah thought to himself.

Jeramiah had long ago decided that prison wasn't an option. He would never go. He slammed his hand against the steering wheel at the mere thought of going to prison for the rest of his life. After the witness was killed, Jeramiah had been able to stay in the large crowd near the sidewalk, and after the officers started to gather, he walked away without anyone trying to stop him.

"It was so invigorating," he said out loud.

Jeramiah smiled as he thought about his victims and how he felt when the murder was complete. After killing his first victim so easily, he had transformed into a man on a mission. He believed there were many others like him in the world. They were the ones who were constantly ridiculed and made fun of by the popular, pretty ones in society. If they weren't pointing or laughing in his face, then they were doing it behind his back.

The constant shaming and the lies they spread hurt people. Making fun of him and putting him down made them feel better about themselves. Jeramiah had created a way of stopping them, those women and their looks and lies.

Bitches, he thought.

He may never win their hearts through the power of love, but he would have them by any means necessary.

He hated women. Jeramiah killed them because he believed

they humiliated him and others like him, first as a boy and later as a man. Now, it was time to return the hurt.

Jeramiah drove through the mountain pass, thinking about the day's events. The large rocks on both sides of the road tightened the closer he got to his house. After twenty minutes, he pulled off from the highway onto the gravel road that led to his hidden driveway. For Jeramiah, there were no neighbors to wave to, no pets running out to greet him, and no wife standing at the door wearing an apron, asking how his day went.

After parking his SUV, he walked into the large foyer of his home and removed his shoes. He proceeded into the living room, sat in the recliner, and turned on the television. He was tired. It had been a stressful day, although it had ended nicely. He closed his eyes, and before long, he fell asleep.

It was about six o'clock when the music that seemed to blare from the television speakers woke the sleeping giant. On the screen, he saw the all-too-familiar image of the hunter. The hunter had been tracking Jeramiah for the past few months. Jeramiah smiled as he listened to the hunter answer pointless questions about him.

The smile soon faded, and Jeramiah became angry when the woman reporter referred to him as being insane or psychotic. She was humiliating the killer in front of thousands of viewers. Her accusations made Jeramiah furious, and he sat forward in his recliner, watching and listening to every word she said.

As the interview closed, Jeramiah looked at the reporter and thought about what it would be like to have her in the woods or in his room. His mind squirmed over the different possibilities, and he smiled at the fantasy playing out in his mind. Suddenly, from across the room, Jeramiah heard his father.

"Why do you watch this shit, boy?"

"I don't know," Jeramiah answered quickly.

"You like to look at that girl on television, don't you, boy? Get it out of your head!"

"Yes, Father," Jeramiah said as he stood and excused himself from the room. He tired quickly of his father's conversations, all of which eventually led to arguments. Jeramiah decided to end this one before it started by removing himself from the room.

As he left the living room, he listened to his father turn his attention and frustrations to Jeramiah's mother.

"Don't tell me how to speak to my son. I'll say whatever I want!" he yelled as Jeramiah reached the top of the stairs.

In his room, Jeramiah closed his door softly and sat at the edge of his bed. He reached over and slid the drawer to his nightstand open. He then turned and looked around the room to ensure he was alone. He slowly removed the knife from its resting spot. The sun was going down, but a few rays of light from his west window peeked through and danced across the blade. He turned it back and forth, so the glare passed over his eyes.

He felt unstoppable. The power to end a life with his knife was personal, powerful, and exhilarating. Even his own father was useless against him when Jeramiah held it. He had bought the knife at a sporting goods store and made some slight changes to it to make it his.

Jeramiah had been lying on his bed for an hour with his knife in hand, fantasizing about the reporter, when he heard his father's voice calling to him from downstairs. He quickly sat up and put the knife back in the drawer. *Maybe I'll go for a drive into the city. Maybe I'll pay Amanda Crosse a visit,* he thought to himself.

Chapter 11
Mike's Steakhouse

Axel and Gary worked in their cubicles after most people went home. For them, the day had been an eventful one. Both the detectives had completed their continuation reports concerning the investigations involving Tammy Johnson and Sharon Douglas. Axel took longer than usual dictating his report. Gary kept sending emails with pictures of Amanda Crosse in them that he had retrieved from the station's website, one of which Gary spent considerable time on by cutting her head out and placing it over the head of a soldier standing in the familiar camouflage uniform with the word 'commando' written underneath it.

As they rode the elevator to the main lobby, the friends talked about what they would be doing the next day. When the doors opened, the two stepped out, walked down the hallway, and then outside toward their cars in the parking garage. Axel was unlocking his door when he heard Gary yell from across the lot.

"Is there a chance you'll find out if she's a true American hero?"

Axel smiled, shrugged Gary's comment off, and climbed into his car.

"Really, brother, I hope you have a good time tonight," Gary yelled again from his car as he drove past his friend. Axel turned, smiled, and waved at his partner.

On the way home, he worried about his dinner plans with Amanda. He had been too busy during the day to think about it. She was a beautiful woman, and when was the last time he had been on a date? His hands started to sweat as he drove. Butterflies took to flight in the bowels of his stomach as he thought about her face, her eyes, her hair, and her body, of course.

"Hey, you've dated pretty women in the past. She's no different than the rest of them. Now calm down." Axel said, reassuring himself.

When he pulled into the driveway, he saw Matt in his front yard, adjusting a sprinkler that was attached to a green hose.

"Are you ever going to install that underground sprinkler system for your lawn? I mean, moving that hose around all day must get tiring after a while," Axel yelled from his front door.

Matt looked up and shook his head. "Jill asks me that same thing every summer. Have you ever installed one?" He yelled back.

"No. Mine came with the house. That's one of the few things I negotiated into the price before closing the deal. Maybe you should've thought about that when you bought your house," Axel said with a slight laugh.

Matt looked back at the house and around the yard before extending his middle finger into the air toward his neighbor. Axel continued to laugh and walked inside.

He looked around the living room and thought, *I have four bedrooms, three bathrooms, a living room, a sitting room, a dining room, and a breakfast nook. This house is huge. Why did I ever buy such a big place? I'm single. Oh yeah… wishful thinking!*

Upstairs, he showered and then debated several times over, *Casual jeans or slacks, buttoned shirt or a pullover, tennis shoes or leather shoes, white socks or black socks?*

At seven thirty, the debate was finally over, and Axel left the house wearing a blue V-neck shirt, blue jeans, and a brown leather belt with shoes to match. The drive back into town wasn't nearly as congested as it had been during his commute home. The sun was still setting in the west, and the evening shine that lit up Pikes Peak was now growing dark as the light slowly descended behind the mountain.

While he listened to the music pouring out of the radio, he thought about the case, and one thing continued to bother him.

Who killed Sharon Douglas? Was it Richard Lambert? Did her own husband kill her, or was it PPK? Who benefited from Sharon's death?

Axel pulled into the parking lot of Mike's Steakhouse right at eight o'clock, with all the same questions and more running through his mind. He found a parking space in the back of the restaurant, and as he climbed out of his car, he once again felt the butterflies in his stomach preparing for an all-out attack. He straightened his clothes and looked around the parking lot for his date.

"What am I doing? I don't even know what she drives," he said out loud and then took a deep breath. As Axel entered the restaurant, he wondered if he should really call it a date. He had a brief inclination it could be nothing more than a business dinner for her, where she would try to get more information from the detective to use in her story.

No, she seemed sincere when she made plans with me. She never mentioned the killer or murders again after the interview was over, Axel thought.

The aroma of steak grilling permeated the air around him. He walked to the hostess and stepped on a peanut shell that had been discarded to the floor by another customer. The peanuts were a part of the restaurant's laid-back atmosphere. The steak house allowed customers to momentarily stave off their appetites with peanuts until they could be seated to devour a steak of their choice. Country music played in the background, while the servers crossed the room carrying large trays to different tables. They wore boots and cowboy hats and occasionally danced a two-step with an intoxicated guest.

Axel didn't figure himself a cowboy, but he did respect the all-too-familiar Colorado lifestyle that many people lived. After a few minutes of waiting, he was greeted by the young hostess, a petite girl with brown hair and brown eyes. From her demeanor, Axel determined she disliked her summer job.

"How many are in your party?" she asked unenthusiastically.

Axel held up two fingers. "Two. I'm expecting someone else, and I'd rather wait for her before I sit down, if that's all right."

The hostess huffed slightly but agreed to his request. She added his name to the list, and Axel took a seat next to a sizable barrel overfilled with peanuts. He sat on a wooden bench, where he watched others walk in and grab a handful of peanuts before being seated.

Amanda made her way across town toward the date she had with Axel Frost. She was excited but nervous at the same time. She contemplated canceling the date more than once, but in the end, she decided to go for it. She hadn't been on a date in a long time, and deep down, she wanted to go on one. She had decided to dress casually and chose the clothes she felt she looked good in.

Does he think I'm just going out with him for a story? Am I just going out with him for a story? Oh shit, what if he doesn't consider this a date? Wait… Is this a date? Amanda asked herself as she pulled into the parking lot and looked for a parking space.

She saw a truck backing out of a spot close to the entrance and was waiting for it to back out when a honk came from the driver in the black SUV behind her.

Impatient and rude! she thought to herself.

Axel was distracted and failed to see Amanda enter the restaurant. When she came up and tapped him on the shoulder, he was surprised, and he began to choke on a peanut he had just shelled and tossed into his mouth. Clearing his throat, he dropped the shell and reached his hand out to Amanda.

"Hello," she said.

He looked at the beautiful woman and was amazed by how put together she looked. She wore a pair of jeans and a simple T-shirt, and he noticed her skin was bronzed brown. Her shirt was white with a blue stripe across the center. She wore tennis shoes with white ankle socks. Her blonde hair was pulled back into a ponytail. She looked comfortable, he thought, and he was glad he had chosen jeans for the evening.

"Hello. I'm so glad you made it," Axel said as he released her soft hand and cleared his throat once more.

"You didn't think I was going to stand you up, did you?" she asked.

"No! Not at all," Axel answered.

"Sir, your table is ready, if you and your date are ready to be seated," the hostess announced from her podium.

Amanda smiled at Axel as she walked past him, following the hostess who led them to a corner booth. The hostess placed menus in front of the couple and walked away.

"I didn't tell her I was waiting for a date," Axel said, red-faced and embarrassed by the hostess's assumption.

"Oh. So… are we here on business?" Amanda inquired as she smiled and then raised her menu in front of her face to cover her expression and pretend to read it.

"Well, no. I just—"

"Then I guess it's a date," Amanda said as she lowered the menu and winked at him.

Amanda browsed the entrees. She continued to smile and peek over the top of her large menu, occasionally checking out her dinner date. When she was at the news station earlier, she found herself pausing the recorded interview with him on her computer screen just to look at his blue eyes.

"What are you going to have, Axel?" she asked.

"I don't know."

"Howdy, can I take your order?" the waitress asked as she stood there with her hand on her hip.

Amanda ordered the special, which consisted of a garden salad followed by a twelve-ounce steak with mashed potatoes. Axel was surprised by her order but ordered the same.

"Who do you think killed the woman in the park today?" Amanda asked before thinking about what she had asked and to whom she had asked it.

Axel's forehead wrinkled and his nostrils flared a bit. "I'm sorry, but I thought you said we were here on a date. It sounds like we're now on the record. I can't say anything about an ongoing investigation," he replied in a sharp tone, suddenly feeling ambushed.

Amanda shook her head. "We're not on the record. I was just trying to make conversation. If you like, we can talk about something else," she said, embarrassed. Amanda pretended to wipe something that wasn't there from her mouth with her napkin.

"Well, it's just that I can't say anything else about the PPK investigation that I haven't already told you during the interview earlier today," Axel explained, now embarrassed by his overreaction.

"I should've asked something else. Besides, I didn't know today's homicide was related to PPK," Amanda remarked.

Damn! I let that out all on my own, Axel thought.

"How about we start over and pretend you haven't said anything, and I didn't hear anything." Amanda kindly suggested.

"I think that's a good idea," Axel agreed.

"Okay, are you married, or do you have a girlfriend?" she asked with a flirty smile.

The question made him grin. "No," he answered.

"That's good to know. A girl has to know who she's eating with."

"Do you have one?" Axel asked.

"Well, I've never been married, and I don't have a girlfriend. Although, there was that time in college…" Amanda answered and then looked away.

Axel sat there, unable to speak, waiting for some thought other than the X-rated image that went into his mind. Amanda turned back around and laughed out loud when she saw the expression on Axel's face.

"I was just kidding. I don't have a husband, boyfriend, or girlfriend. I wish you could have seen the look on your face though."

Axel laughed along with his date. "You caught me off guard. For a moment, I was speechless."

"What about the whole experimental thing?" he asked jokingly.

"A girl has to have secrets," she replied.

Axel, once again, could not help but notice how beautiful Amanda was. When she laughed, her head tilted slightly to the left, and her long slender neck became more visible. Her eyes were moist from laughing, and they now sparkled in the light of the restaurant.

The two exchanged small talk that consisted of their personal histories, from where they were born to the colleges they went to and, of course, how they ended up in Colorado Springs. Underneath the table, the two rested their legs against one another's and never moved them through the entire dinner.

Time flew by as the two exchanged stories and smiles. Their dinner came, and their conversation continued through dessert. When the check arrived, the waitress put it in front of

Axel, and as he reached for it, Amanda pulled it out from under his hand.

"I invited you to dinner. This one's on me," Amanda said as she handed the girl the check back with her credit card.

"You know the man is supposed to pay," Axel retorted.

"Oh, and I bet you think women should be at home barefoot and pregnant in the kitchen."

"I didn't mean anything like that. I was trying to be polite," Axel said, defending himself.

"I'm just teasing you, honey."

A warm feeling came over Axel when he thought about her choice of words. After Axel demanded he be allowed to leave a tip, the two walked out of the restaurant and strolled toward Amanda's car. Both seemed to take their time, unconsciously extending the date.

"I had a nice time," Amanda said after unlocking her car door. She then turned to face her date.

"I did too. Maybe we could have dinner again sometime… I mean, if you wanted to." Axel was uncomfortable, and words seemed to fumble out of his mouth. He ran his fingers through his hair and shyly looked away.

"Are you asking me out on another date, Detective?" Amanda took advantage of the situation. She'd read Axel's body language and decided to have some fun with it.

"Well, I mean…" Axel didn't know how to reply and once again looked away, this time out toward the street at the passing cars.

"Because if you are, I'd probably say yes. I mean, if you were to ask me."

"Yeah, I'm actually asking you out, and I'm beginning to think you're playing with me. So, would you like to go out with me again?" Axel asked with more confidence this time.

"When?"

"How about this week sometime?"

"I'm free tomorrow. Is that good for you?" Amanda asked as she scrolled through the calendar on her phone.

"Yes, it is. Where would you like to go?" He asked.

"I don't know. What's good? Wait! Tomorrow night the Rockies play," she replied.

"You're right! I've been so busy, I haven't seen a game in a while. Lately, every time they play, something happens, and I miss the game," Axel explained.

"Well, I wouldn't want you to miss another game. How about we meet at a sports bar that serves a great dinner?" Amanda requested.

"I dislike sports bars, but I do like pizza in front of the TV as I watch the game at my house," Axel said, hoping she would agree to his suggestion.

"Okay, Axel. Maybe we can have dinner some other night then," Amanda replied, slightly embarrassed he preferred to watch a game instead of meeting her for dinner. She had not caught on to Axel's suggestion for her to join him at his place, and she started to turn toward her car.

"No, you misunderstood me. I want you to come over and eat pizza and watch the game with me at my house," he said quickly when Amanda climbed into her car.

"Do you think I'm the type of girl who would go over to some man's house on the second date?" Amanda asked, taking advantage of the situation.

"I didn't mean to insinuate that you and I would… umm…"

"Axel, it's fine! Give me the directions," Amanda said, quickly saving him from another embarrassing moment. She enjoyed the taunting but knew when enough was enough.

Axel quickly texted his address and directions to Amanda's phone.

"The game starts at seven. I'll try to be there at six, if that's okay."

"Six is good with me, and I'll start making the pizza at about six too."

Amanda's eyebrows raised. "You make your own pizza? You're just a man full of surprises now, aren't you, Detective?"

"Yep. It's my grandmother's recipe."

"You know, it's supposed to rain in Denver tomorrow."

"No. I didn't, but if the game gets called, maybe we can watch a movie or something."

"Sounds great. We can see if my favorite movie of all time is on Netflix."

Axel smiled. "Really? What kind of movies do beautiful reporters like to watch?" He asked, hoping it would not be something that required a box of tissues for her and a lot of caffeine for him.

"Commando," she replied.

Axel's mouth dropped. He was leaning in through the window, and her answer had caught him off guard.

"I watched it with my brothers when I was a little girl," Amanda said as she leaned over, kissed Axel on the lips, waved good-bye, and backed out of the space before he could say anything.

Axel was still in awe as he stood upright and watched as she drove away. He wondered if she had heard Gary's comment earlier. He walked back to his car, shaking his head and smiling. She was mysterious, and she excited him. For the first time in many years, he felt good, and he enjoyed the many thoughts he had of Amanda Crosse.

When he reached his car, he started to put the key into the door when he noticed a large scratch along the side of the door panel. He stepped back and bent down to look at the marks in the paint, then read the words out loud. "I'm watching."

CHAPTER 12
COWARD

Seventies music blasted from the speakers of Jeramiah's radio as he drove home. He hoped the loud music would block out his father's voice, who had been screaming at him a few moments ago. His plans were a bust. He had set out earlier in the evening, arriving at Ms. Crosse's home with the hope of spending time with the beautiful reporter.

His thoughts wandered back to the moment he had arrived, where he had parked on the street a few houses down. The neighborhood residents were out walking along the sidewalk, which forced him to park under a large spruce tree that obstructed the light shining from the streetlight positioned over it. He had watched from the dark confines of his SUV. It didn't take long after his arrival for Jeramiah to observe his newfound fantasy walk out of her garage and get into her car.

She backed out of the driveway and drove past him while he ducked out of view. He waited for her to pass and then quickly put his car in drive, turned around, and sped after her.

After a few blocks, he had caught up with her and followed her for a short time until she came into the downtown area of Colorado Springs. He was careful not to get too close, keeping at least two cars in between them. He watched and followed her into the parking lot of Mike's Steakhouse. He sat behind her while she waited for someone to back out of a parking spot.

He grew anxious at having to sit there, so he honked his horn at her. He wanted and needed her to park somewhere darker and more private. When she finally pulled into the empty spot, he drove past her car and found an empty space across the way, where he sat and watched.

Jeramiah decided to wait for her to go inside before he got out of his car. When he felt it was safe, he got out and walked across the parking lot. He then entered the front door of the restaurant. He passed the hostess podium and sat at the bar, where he was partially concealed in the dimly lit room. From there, he watched as she sat with Detective Axel Frost.

Jeramiah became jealous, and after one drink, he ordered another and then another until he heard the voice in his head once more.

"Look at her! She's cheating on you! You are such a fool. If we'd left earlier, we could be with her now and not him. Go on over and let them know you see them together... Or don't. They're probably talking about you right now. You should feel like an idiot," his father's voice said, tormenting him once again.

"Shut up! Shut up! Damn you!" Jeramiah shouted, disturbing the other patrons around him.

"I think you've had enough," the bartender said.

Jeramiah looked at the bartender but did not say anything. He just watched as the bartender took away the half-empty bottle of beer in front of him.

"This one's on me, but you need to leave now."

Jeramiah was angry. He got up, walked from the bar, and into the parking lot. Once outside, he walked to the back of the restaurant, where he started to feel sick. He vomited next to the building, and as he wiped away the residue from around his mouth, he looked up and saw the detective's vehicle.

How nice! He thought.

As he walked toward Detective Frost's car, he pulled his knife out from under his shirt and looked at the blade in the light. He was fascinated by its allure once more. Standing next to the car, he looked inside. He then bent down out of sight and scrawled his message along the door. When he finished, he walked to his car, where his father spoke to him again.

"Coward! You are such a little boy, afraid to confront them. I really don't know how I put up with you."

Jeramiah did not reply to his father this time. He climbed into his SUV and drove out of the parking lot. Once he reached the road, his father started again, but Jeramiah turned on the radio and listened to the music as it echoed through the speakers.

WEDNESDAY, JULY 4ᵀᴴ

Axel came into the office and sat at his desk. On top of his computer was a female doll dressed in a commando outfit holding a microphone. He looked at the doll and laughed.

"Well, it's nice to see that on some mornings, you get here early," Axel said when he heard Gary's laughter coming from the next cubicle.

"Are you talking to me, Detective Frost?"

"No. I'm talking to myself," Axel announced as he looked up and saw Gary peering over the wall.

"Hey, nice doll. Who gave you that?" Gary asked as if he didn't know.

"Axel, are you here yet?"

Axel looked out of his cubicle while still holding the doll in his hand. He saw Lt. Wilson, who was walking toward him.

"Yeah, he's here, but he's busy playing with his doll," Gary said from the confines of his cubicle.

Axel, realizing he was still holding the doll, quickly opened his desk drawer and put it inside, out of sight.

"What happened to your car last night?" Wilson asked.

"Did something happen to your car last night?" Gary asked as he stood from his desk and looked at Axel.

Axel took a deep breath and blew it out. "Outside the restaurant last night, someone damaged the door. The words 'I'm Watching' were scratched into the paint. They sent Officer Thomas out, and he took photos of it and completed the report," the detective explained.

"No one saw anyone around it?" Gary asked curiously.

"Nope."

"It was on the blotter this morning, and that's where I read about it," Wilson explained.

"Do you think it had anything to do with this case?" Gary asked.

"I don't know right now. It could've just been some dumb-ass kid walking through the parking lot. I mean, the car was parked in the back, away from the street and the entrance."

"Well, until we know what's going on, watch your six when you're at home, and you watch each other's six at work. From now on, I want the two of you going on all interviews and tracking down all witnesses and suspects together. If something is going to happen, I want you there watching out for one another," Wilson ordered and walked back to his office.

Gary waited until the lieutenant was out of earshot. "Axel, what do you really think?" He asked.

Axel shrugged his shoulders. "I think it's a good possibility that someone wants me to know they are watching me. Maybe it's someone involved in this case, or maybe it's someone who knows Amanda, and they're just jealous."

Gary looked at Axel with a raised eyebrow. "Are you thinking it's an old boyfriend?"

"I don't know, but maybe I should ask her if there are any ex-boyfriends still in her life."

Gary grinned. "Well, wouldn't that suggest you're in her life? Wow! Did the two of you have that good of a time last night?" He asked with a smirk, quickly changing the subject.

"Hey, are you guys busy over here?" DJ asked as he walked up to the two detectives with a yearbook in his hand.

"No, we're not," Axel answered.

"Here's the yearbook you requested, and here are some of the people who knew Tammy Johnson and went to school with her. I also checked with the principal, who told me that while Tammy was there at school, she never got into any trouble. She was a star athlete and had good grades," DJ explained.

Axel reached out and took the yearbook and list of people. "Thanks for the information," he said.

"Have you guys gotten anything new on the case, or is there anything I can track down for you?" DJ asked.

Axel placed the yearbook on his desk and glanced over the names on the list.

"Well, DJ, if you could talk to some of the people on the list and see if any of them hung out with Tammy the week of the murder, that would help."

DJ took the list of names back from the detective. "Yeah, I could do that for you."

"Not many people want to track down possible witnesses. When we solve this case, I'll have to buy you a steak dinner," Axel offered.

"Axel, look at me. A steak dinner could be costly for you. I have a ferocious appetite," DJ said jokingly.

"It'll be worth it if you can get any leads that would help solve this case."

DJ nodded his head in understanding and walked out of

the office. Axel looked at Gary, who was shaking his head as he held the doll he had retrieved from inside Axel's desk.

"We haven't finished our conversation about Miss Commando and you. Mostly, I just want the details about last night. Was it her place or yours where the deed was done?"

"Neither. We had dinner and conversation, and I walked her to her car."

"That's it?"

"Yes." Axel walked to his desk and picked up the phone.

Gary shook his head and walked back to his cubicle. "You're a loser. She goes commando, and I'm thinking you'll never find out," Gary said quietly but loud enough for Axel to hear.

Jaxson sat in his hotel room comparing his profile to the one the bureau had sent over. For the most part, he agreed with it, but things were missing that he felt should have been mentioned. He knew his theory would stun the community and the police department.

He was concerned about being there without permission from the bureau, without an invitation from the police department, and he knew his profile could change the entire investigation. If he was right, he would be congratulated, but if he was wrong, his career was over.

But what does the X represent? Did you put that on yourself?

Jaxson was deep in thought when he finally heard the phone ringing, and he answered it.

"Hello?" Jaxson said, greeting the unknown caller.

"Hello to you. How's work going?" Brandi asked.

"So far, nothing exciting. How's it going with your sister?" Jaxson answered and smiled at hearing his new friend's voice.

"Good. I was calling to see if…"

"If what?" he asked.

"If you're going to be getting any time off while you're here."

"Maybe. Why?" Jaxson asked.

"I don't know. I thought maybe we could take the train up to the top of Pikes Peak together this weekend, and you could tell me more about those passenger seats," Brandi suggested.

"You know, I would love to, but let me see how things work out here first. I can let you know. Is that okay?"

"Absolutely."

"Great. I'll call you later," Jaxson said.

Time in the office was spent with both detectives reading over forensic reports and dictating continuation reports that would be typed later by division secretaries. They looked over field reports conducted by beat cops who had stopped suspicious cars or people leaving or coming into or out of the areas of the murders.

Axel was placing one of the old case binders back on the shelf when something slipped out of the binder onto the floor. It was a five by seven photo of Emily Long, a nineteen year old girl. She was one of PPK's victims. She had gone shopping in the afternoon on Thursday, March eighteenth and was missing for over a week. Her beaten and battered body was found by hikers just off a trail in the national forest. Axel stood there, looking down at the photo of the beautiful eighteen year old, as he recalled the case.

CHAPTER 13
EMILY LONG

Emily walked through the mall quickly and without hesitation. She was on a mission to find one more bikini for her family's trip to Florida over spring break. Emily had spent every day for the last few weeks searching online and browsing stores from Colorado Springs to Denver, looking for the bikinis she felt she needed for the trip. She had made all the right choices thus far, and she knew each one would bring Austin to his knees, but at the same time, she had to make sure she wouldn't cause her father to have a heart attack. After all, it had taken all of February to get her father to say yes to Austin coming along on their family vacation in the first place.

Emily had liked Austin from the first day of high school when she saw him in homeroom. He was tall, athletic, and charming, which were all the right qualities that a high school girl like Emily looked for in a guy. But, unfortunately for Emily, Austin always seemed to be busy with football or baseball. He never seemed to have time for her, or any other girl for that matter, until the start of their senior year in August of last year.

As usual, Emily and Austin had homeroom together, but this year was different. Emily had caught Austin staring at her from across the room almost every morning. A short time later, he was following her on her social media accounts. Every so often, Austin made comments about an outfit she was wearing that she posted online. Sometimes he even commented or liked a funny video she posted. But still, Austin never approached her to ask her out until October when he surprised her at cheerleading practice. He, along with some of his friends, showed up wearing tuxedos from the seventies and serenaded her to "Kiss You All Over" by the group Exile. The boys sang, danced, and ended their routine with a banner that read: Emily Please Go With Me To The Homecoming Dance. Austin held a bouquet of white roses and waited nervously until she said yes.

Emily smiled when the memory crossed her mind while she held a skimpy red bikini she had found. It was something her father would never approve of her wearing. She started to put it back on the rack but then remembered her parents were going to spend time with some old friends on one day of the trip. That was when she and Austin were going to be alone at the beach house.

Maybe Dad won't approve, but Austin will! Emily thought to herself as she made her way to the register with her final bathing suit selection in hand.

He saw Emily from the time she entered the mall. He followed her from a safe distance as she walked from store to store. He had always been drawn to her. When he was working, he would go out of his way to follow her when she came to the mall. He'd even seen her at the football games cheering for her high school team on Friday nights. Emily was the prize above all others. She was the type who ignored him, made fun of him, and talked about him behind his back when he was in high school. Girls like her never understood a guy like him. Suddenly, it all came back.

"Jeramiah, why do you wear hunting clothes to school? Jeramiah, why do you smell like an animal? Jeramiah, do you live in a cave? Jeramiah, why do you have bruises on your body all the time?"

Jeramiah became angry as he recalled memories from his past.

"Jeramiah. Don't be a pussy and let this one get away. Follow her. Then take her. You deserve her, just like the others."

Jeramiah listened to his father's voice repeat it over and over again in his head. "I know I deserve her. I deserve her and so much more than what I was given," Jeramiah said to himself.

"That's right! Now stop acting like a pussy and get your shit together. Think of how you're going to get her."

"Yes, Father," Jeramiah answered and then quickly came up with a plan.

Emily made her way to the parking lot, found her car, and got inside. A heavy spring snow was falling across the Front Range. She turned the car on, activated the windshield wipers, and turned the heat up. She waited for the car to warm up and the windows to clear before heading onto the road. She took the time to look through her many shopping bags at her new clothes. She held her red bikini in hand, smiling as she thought about how she would surprise Austin. After a few minutes, she checked the mirrors and her makeup before backing out. She wanted to make sure she looked perfect, as she had dinner plans with Austin at his house and she was expected to be there by five thirty.

Maybe I'll give him a peek of this new bikini as a little hint of what's to come next week in Florida, she thought to herself as she left the parking lot and made her way to the interstate. She drove down the interstate for about five minutes and turned off onto the Fillmore Street exit. As she waited at the light, she saw a man pull up next to her. She looked over and realized he was motioning for her to roll her window down.

"You have a flat tire!" the man yelled and pointed at the rear of her car.

"Oh," she replied.

"Pull into that parking lot up ahead and let's see if we can fix it!" the man yelled and smiled.

"Okay," Emily replied. She recognized the man, and although she had always thought he was odd, she wasn't afraid of him. She drove the car forward when the light changed and then turned right into the parking lot of a convenience store that was no longer in business. As she maneuvered the car under the old gas station canopy, she didn't feel her car lean to one side, nor did it drive as if there was a flat. She finally came to a stop out of the snow behind the gas pumps still in place.

Emily got out and walked to the back of her car and looked at her driver's side rear tire. She didn't see anything that would lead her to believe it was flat. She then walked up and looked at her front tire as he got out of his car and walked to the passenger side of hers.

"It's this one over here," he said as he looked over the roof of her car while pointing down at the passenger's side rear tire.

"Oh. I was wondering because I didn't see anything over here on this side," Emily replied and casually walked to the passenger side of her car. When she got to the rear tire, she bent down to look at it.

Jeramiah was ready, so he quickly looked around for any witnesses. When Emily bent down, he pulled out his blackjack from behind his back and swung it at the back of Emily's head. She fell to the ground and did not move. The blow from the lead-filled leather weapon had done its job.

Jeramiah looked around the area once more before going over and opening the passenger-rear door of his car. He walked back and tied Emily's hands and arms behind her back. Her ankles were then bound and drawn up toward her hands at the small of her back. He then took a rag and tied it over her mouth. Finally, he carried her to his car and shoved her into the floorboard of the back seat. When he was satisfied that she wasn't going anywhere, he shut the car door and looked around the area once more. He casually walked back to her car, opened the passenger door, and pulled out the red bikini.

"Nice!" Jeramiah said as he held the tiny bikini up in the air. "I think we'll go back to my place and enjoy this together," Jeramiah said and walked back to his car.

Axel was still looking at the photo of Emily when he heard Gary walking toward him. Axel took the photo and placed it back into the binder from where it had dropped.

"You want to come over and watch the game at my house tonight?" Gary asked as he walked around the corner of the cubicle.

Axel shook his head from side to side. "No. I think I'll watch the game at my house, but thanks for the invitation, Mr. Portland."

"It'll do you good. Carol can make some nachos, and we can have a few beers and maybe forget about this place and this case for a little while."

"Gary, thanks for the offer, and I normally would accept the invitation, but I really can't make it tonight."

Gary rubbed the stubble on his chin. Axel was hiding something, and he knew it. "Look, I know I don't have a big screen like you, but my thirty-two inch will do fine."

Axel smiled, he knew that he couldn't hide anything from his partner but it wouldn't stop him from having a little fun. "It's nothing like that. I just want to watch the game at my house and eat my homemade pizza."

Gary's eyes lit up. "Are you making *the pizza*?" he asked,

knowing his partner never made his homemade "world-famous" pizza to eat alone.

Axel looked away with a smile and shook his head.

"You son of a... You got a date, don't you? I bet it's with Commando, and you weren't even going to tell me," Gary said as he bent down close to Axel's face.

"Yes, I've got a date," Axel replied as he put his pens back into his drawer. He then stood and walked past Gary toward the elevator.

Gary was speechless as his friend passed him smugly. "Why wouldn't you tell me, your best friend?" Gary asked as he moved toward the elevator behind Axel.

Axel didn't respond. He stood and waited for the elevator doors to open with a smile on his face. He enjoyed keeping Gary in suspense. Gary moved close to him and waited for an answer. When the doors opened, Axel looked at Gary but still did not say anything. The two walked inside, and Axel pressed the button for the first floor.

"If a man plays with dolls at work, I don't see the point of having an adult conversation with him," Axel teased with a wide grin.

"You're not calling me a child, now are you?"

The doors opened again, and they exited into the hallway and walked toward the doors leading to the parking garage. The two men casually made their way to their cars. Gary kept looking over at Axel, waiting for an answer.

"I know you're screwing with me, Axel, and payback is a bitch!" Gary threatened as he closed his car door and drove away.

Axel laughed as he watched Gary leave the parking garage. He knew the two of them would have a good time tomorrow when they met up again. Axel also knew Gary would not allow him to get away with anything. He wondered what Gary would have planned for him in the morning.

Axel made his way through the downtown traffic quickly and turned onto the highway heading west. His speed was only about five miles more than the posted speed limit, but still, other commuters passed him when the left lane was clear. He turned into the parking lot of the grocery store and quickly went inside as the rain fell from the threatening purple clouds above him. When he entered the store, he stopped and wondered if Denver was getting any of the downpour.

They may very well cancel the game if it doesn't clear up, he thought.

For a moment, he thought Amanda might not come over if she knew it was raining in Denver. His attention was redirected from the weather and the game when he rounded the corner of the aisle. There, he saw an item sitting on the shelf, an item he had not even thought about. Condoms were displayed there in the personal hygiene area. He stood in front of it, looking around to see if anyone was watching him. He wondered if he would need it tonight.

If he bought it, he would undoubtedly have to look at the store clerk, and of course, there would be a line filled with women and children watching him.

The clerk would also be a girl, probably sixteen, and she would look at me too, Axel thought.

Axel pushed the cart farther and decided if he needed something like that tonight, he would simply go to a gas station and use fifty cents to buy it from a machine.

How romantic. Just be an adult… buy them now, he told himself.

The rain was falling harder when Axel ran into his garage, carrying the supplies he needed to bake pizza. He went to the kitchen and prepared the dough. Eventually, Axel placed the dough with all the toppings into the preheated oven. He set the timer and decided he had just enough time for a shower. Before he headed for the bathroom, he looked out the garage door to ensure his garage was open so that if Amanda did arrive, she could come inside.

Axel quickly undressed and jumped into the shower. He ran the soap over his body and the shampoo through his hair, and he was out in less than five minutes. He then stood in front of his mirror, brushed his teeth, flossed, and rinsed his mouth out. When Axel walked out of his bedroom, he looked out his living room window and saw Amanda's car in his driveway.

"Damn," he mumbled.

Axel hurriedly opened the door to his garage and saw Jill, his neighbor, standing there wet, talking to Amanda. He could find no words to say, looking at the two of them laughing as they looked back at him. Amanda was wearing a white T-shirt and blue jeans. She was slightly wet from the rain.

"Amanda, this is my neighbor Jill. She and her husband, Matt, live next door," Axel managed to say as he moved toward them. His eyes met hers, and he leaned forward and kissed her cheek awkwardly. "Sorry. I was in the shower, and I thought I'd be done before you got here."

"That's all right, Axel. Jill here kept me company while I waited."

Axel looked at Jill suspiciously. "I noticed, and now I'm worried," he admitted.

"I saw your garage open and thought maybe you were gone. I was going to be a good neighbor and shut it for you," Jill explained.

"Amanda works for the local news here in town," Axel said.

"Yes, I know. She's on our television almost every night," Jill commented with a cheeky grin.

"Yes, I guess she is." Axel embarrassingly said after quickly realizing that anyone who watched the local news probably knew who Amanda Crosse was.

"Well, I'll go for now, but you'll hear from Matt and me later. Bye for now. It was nice meeting you, Amanda."

"It was nice meeting you as well," Amanda said.

Jill walked out of the garage and back to her house.

"Let's go inside and see if the game is going to be played," Axel said as he motioned his hand and arm toward the inside of his home.

Amanda walked in and started moving about the kitchen. "So does the single detective buy his pizza in a box and call it his own, or does he really bake it from scratch?" she asked.

Axel was amused by the suggestion. "I bake it from scratch. Living alone gives a guy a lot of time to experiment in the kitchen. Why don't you have a seat there in the living room, and I'll see to the pizza and grab you something to drink," Axel offered as he walked toward the refrigerator.

"Okay," Amanda said. She then walked into the living room and sat on the sofa in front of the television. "Wow! This is a big television."

"Yeah, it is. I got a terrific deal on it about a year ago. I had a smaller television in there, but with that large wall, it looked weird—tiny, you know? So I saw that one on sale and bought it," Axel explained right before he reached into the oven to take the pizza out.

Amanda looked around at the décor of the home. She quickly decided she liked it. She noticed a few paintings on the walls, along with some family photos. On the coffee table, there was a photo of an older couple smiling and sitting in a swing on a front porch surrounded by azalea bushes.

Somewhere in the South, I think, she thought to herself.

She presumed the couple were Axel's parents. The couch she was sitting on, surprisingly, didn't have one single stain on it. It was brown and made of leather, as were the loveseat and recliner. The home was big, much too big for a single man. For a moment, Amanda had the idea that Axel may have bought the house for someone he intended to settle down with—or maybe had.

"Did you do all the decorating yourself?" Amanda asked.

"Yes, I did," Axel answered as he walked into the living room, carrying two beers. "The house is too big for one person, but I like the openness of it. I decided to buy it when I was driving through the neighborhood, looking for a stolen car. I was in the motor vehicle theft unit at the time, and I was told by an informant that a car I was looking for was dumped in this neighborhood. When I got here, I saw the sign out front and knew I had to have it."

"Spontaneous…" Amanda called.

"Yeah, maybe a little. It was kind of funny. Jill was out front getting onto Matt about something, and their girls were running around the yard, chasing each other. I pulled up and asked them some questions about the previous owner and how long it had been on the market. They were both really friendly, and I decided to call this retired cop who's in the real-estate business, and before I knew it , Gary and I were unloading my furniture into the house," Axel explained.

"Well, it's very nice, but from the outside, I would have expected to see a Suburban parked out front that got a lot of use out of it from the large family living here." Amanda confessed. She then reached for her beer and looked around the room some more.

"Maybe one day there'll be a family living here," Axel said with a grin.

"Maybe," she replied.

The two talked about anything and everything and flirted in between as the rain continued to fall. Eventually, Axel served the pizza to his guest. The game was delayed, but the two found many things to talk about while they waited. The exchange of flirtatious smiles eventually escalated to slight touching of the hands and knees. The butterflies in Axel's stomach took flight once more. Axel thought about what the two were leading toward.

Amanda put her drink on the table and placed her right hand onto his. She began to stroke it as she looked into his blue eyes and friendly smile. Axel was feeling comfortable but excited as he stared into her green eyes. He leaned in toward her face, hoping she would do the same, and she did. Before he knew it, his lips were touching hers. He smelled her perfume and her hair as he held the back of her head in his hand. The butterflies continued to circle faster and faster in his stomach. He moved his arm under hers and pulled her closer. She reciprocated by reaching around him and pulling him closer to her.

The two sat on the couch in each other's arms, making out like two teenage kids. Axel reached back under her arm with his hand, slowly moving toward her breast.

Would she allow me to or am I moving too fast? he asked himself. Axel stopped his hand short of his target. *Too fast. Slow down,* he thought.

Suddenly, Amanda moved over on top of him, straddling him with her legs as she held his face in her hands. The two looked at each other. Axel slid his hands under her shirt and followed her waist upward. Amanda moaned out loud and kissed him deeply.

Chapter 14
Black Forest

The rain continued to fall as Jeramiah pulled his SUV to the side of the road. He only waited a few minutes before he got out and walked into the woods next to the roadway. There were no neighbors around. The house was a light-brown stucco rancher that was set back on a dirt road in the woods of an area called Black Forest.

The homes in the area were built on five-acre lots with many tall pines between them providing privacy and concealment. The sun was setting, and the dark thunder clouds concealed what would typically be a bright moon. Jeramiah knew he needed to move under the cover of darkness.

Patiently he waited and watched from the cover of the tree line until the car pulled out from the driveway, carrying two passengers. He saw on social media that the people in the car had to be at a Fourth of July fundraiser later in the evening, which was when she would be alone.

The evening grew darker, and the rain fell heavier. Jeramiah carefully made his way through the dark timber and across the lawn toward the house. The outside lights cast shadows out toward the front of the home, allowing the occupants full view of visitors approaching from the front or back.

Jeramiah used the shadows of the trees to cover his movements toward the side of the house. When he reached the window to the garage, he paused, squatted, and surveyed the inside with the use of a mirror he had brought with him.

Once he was satisfied no one was inside the garage, he stood in front of the window and tried to open it, hoping it was unlocked. The window moved slightly, and a smile appeared on Jeramiah's face. He lifted the window without any resistance and without making a sound.

He looked left and right to ensure he wasn't being watched, then placed one leg inside and pulled himself through. The three-car garage was occupied with one expensive car parked in the end bay, which was next to the window he was climbing into. The other two spaces were empty. Jeramiah walked to the door leading into the house. He placed his hand on the knob while he put his ear to the door. Standing quietly, he listened for any possible sound or movement coming from the other side.

Slowly, he began to turn the knob and open the door, but the garage light came on. Jeramiah ran across the concrete floor and hid between the car and the wall under the window. He ducked out of sight and sat quietly, listening to the garage door opening. A moment later, he heard a car pull up to the house. When the engine turned off, he listened to a girl's voice call from the door he had been standing in front of a few seconds ago.

"I thought you'd never get here," Shannon yelled to Tony, her boyfriend, as he parked his car in the driveway.

The car door opened, and Jeramiah heard a male voice. He sat quietly beside the car, listening to the two of them talk.

"I saw your parents drive away and gave them a few minutes to get out of the area. You never know. They may have forgotten something and had to come back. That wouldn't have been good," Tony said as he entered the house and reached for Shannon to pull her close to him.

"I missed you!" Shannon said as she leaned in and kissed his lips. She then shut the garage door and pulled her boyfriend inside.

After the door shut, Jeramiah waited a few minutes to ensure no one would come out again.

"Play some music, and I'll fix us a sandwich, Tony," Shannon said as she walked into the kitchen.

"You don't mind that we are staying in and not going to watch the fireworks show tonight, do you?" Tony asked.

"No. We'll make our own fireworks," Shannon teased.

"That sounds good. Hey, I downloaded that song last night onto my phone. Shit! I left my phone in the car. I was listening to it on the way over. I'll go out and get it." Tony moved toward the garage door, while Shannon continued to make the sandwiches.

Jeramiah finally decided to get up and leave. He stood and opened the window to make an early exit. He was upset and angry that, once again, his plans had been ruined. He bit his lip as he looked out the window through the rain, toward the tall pines in the distance. He shook his head and reached up to pull himself out of the window when he heard the door open. Suddenly, the overhead light illuminated the garage.

Jeramiah quickly turned around.

"What the hell are you doing here?!" Tony yelled from the door.

Jeramiah moved quickly as he pulled the gun from his waist and faced his target. Tony never saw the gun, nor did he hear the shots, so before he knew it, he was on the ground. He reached for the wall and tried to stand but couldn't. He looked up from the cold concrete at the intruder who was now standing over him.

"Why?" Tony asked.

Jeramiah didn't answer. He raised the gun from his side and pointed it at Tony's head.

Tony closed his eyes and waited for the impact.

The concrete under Tony turned bright red as parts of his brain exited the back of his skull. The gun recoiled in Jeramiah's hand. He looked down at his victim and watched, fascinated, as blood pooled around Tony's head. Jeramiah was momentarily hypnotized by the ordeal. It was the screams from Shannon that redirected Jeramiah's attention toward the direction of the door and toward her.

"No, no, not me, please don't!" Shannon begged as she moved back toward the kitchen.

Jeramiah placed the gun under his shirt, smiled, and walked toward her. He slowly pulled his knife from behind his back. Shannon continued to scream, but Jeramiah couldn't hear her. His attention was on the reflection of light from his blade as he turned it back and forth. Jeramiah continued toward her, he reached out, grabbed her by the hair, forced her against the wall, and pulled her head upward violently. He then placed the knife against her throat just as Shannon screamed louder.

"Why are you doing this to me?" she asked and cried out loud.

Jeramiah slowly pulled the knife across her throat. Blood ran from under the knife, down her neck, and onto her chest. She tried to stop the knife with her right hand, but Jeramiah pulled her up off the floor, forcing her to lose her balance. She coughed and gagged. Without warning, he released her. Shannon dropped to the floor and lay on the cold white porcelain tile, fighting to stay alive. She tried to stop the blood shooting from her neck. Jeramiah watched as she violently twisted from side to side, knocking over a stool that was next to her as she struggled to breathe.

Jeramiah squatted next to her and reached under her shirt

to run his hand along her body. He then placed his ear to her chest to listen to the last beats of her heart. When there were no more beats left, he kissed her lips while he continued to fondle the other parts of her body over and under her clothes. As his excitement built, he quickly removed her shirt and bra, looked into her eyes, and slowly pushed his knife into her stomach. He twisted it back and forth before pulling it out to change the knife blade.

With the hook blade securely attached to the handle, he inserted it just under the skin and pulled it upward toward her neck. Her eyes were still open, and Jeramiah felt she was looking at him… judging him. Shannon was one of his tormentors who he had wanted to kill for over two years now. When he saw that the twenty year old had come home for the summer, he couldn't resist tracking her down.

"Stop it!" he screamed at her lifeless body.

He changed blades once more and cut through her breastbone with the short bone saw.

I'll have your heart! We will be together forever now! Jeramiah thought as he reached into her chest and pulled her heart from her body.

"I am sorry though. This wasn't supposed to happen like this. I had planned for us to be alone. I wanted to drive you up to the mountains where we could've had some privacy. The mountain air is wonderful this time of year, and it's so much cooler there," Jeramiah confessed as he stood over her.

He waited a few minutes, taking it all in, before he collected himself. He found a bag on the kitchen table and placed his trophy in it before exiting the home through the door leading back to the garage.

As he stepped into the garage, the garage door opened, and the headlights of a car shined onto the lifeless body of Tony. Jeramiah quickly covered his face with his hand and ran out the open door, directly in front of the oncoming car.

By covering his face, Jeramiah blinded himself, and he did not see the car coming at him so fast. His right leg was knocked out from under him, and he soon found himself flying into the air. Jeramiah landed hard on his shoulder. His knife flew just past his head and stuck into the ground next to his bag. Without hesitation, Jeramiah pulled his gun from his pants and fired at the now-parked car. The bullets struck the roof and windshield, causing the two occupants inside to duck.

Jeramiah stood on his injured leg and ran for the concealment of darkness that the woods afforded him. Once he entered the foliage, he sprinted as best as he could for his SUV, parked a short distance away. The pain in his leg intensified. It felt as if a nail was being driven farther into his thigh muscle with each step he took.

The rain was falling much harder, lightning flashed in the sky, and cracks of thunder boomed above him as he ran. He stopped to catch his breath, and for a moment, he found himself disoriented. A brief flash of light across the night sky allowed the road to appear a few yards away, and just beyond the tree line, he saw the silhouette of his SUV. He felt slightly rejuvenated and began to run once more.

When he reached his SUV, he dug into his pocket and pulled out his keys. He leaned against the door for balance, wincing in pain. He sat in the driver seat and wiped the water from his forehead. He took a moment to catch his breath. The pain in his leg and shoulder was getting worse with each breath. He closed his eyes and turned the ignition to the start position and flipped on the windshield wipers. He then opened his eyes and surveyed the area around him.

I wasn't followed, he thought reassuring himself.

Jeramiah placed the vehicle into drive and slowly pulled onto the dirt road with his lights off. Once he was on the main road, he turned on the lights; he was careful not to speed and ensured he used his turn signals appropriately as he watched police cars speed past him, going in the other direction.

Jeramiah felt safe for the time being, and he thought about the situation he was in. Like a soldier returning from a mission, he started to take inventory.

My gun. I have it here on my waist. Gloves are still on. I'm not cut or bleeding anywhere… My knife, where is my knife?

Jeramiah forgot about the pain in his leg and shoulder as he became acutely aware he no longer possessed his knife. He thought for a second about returning to where he had parked, in the hope he had dropped it on the road when he leaned against his door. He slowed his SUV and started to pull over when he saw the red-and-blue lights approaching through the darkness in front of him once more.

They're setting up a roadblock! Jeramiah thought to himself.

He sped up again, turned right down the first available road, and shut his lights off. In the darkness of the sideroad, he sat there looking behind him through his rearview mirror. He reached into his waistline and pulled his pistol out once more, then waited with it in his lap.

Another police cruiser flew by in a flash of red-and-blue lights. Jeramiah held his gun and closed his eyes for a moment.

CHAPTER 15
'ROD'

"**A**xel, this feels really good," Amanda said as she took a deep breath. She really enjoyed his touch and thought about letting him go further.

If I sleep with him, will he think I'm easy? If I stop him, will he think I'm a tease?

Those two thoughts kept running through her mind, but she was feeling too good, and deep down, she knew what she wanted. She was with a man who was holding her and clearly wanting her as much as she wanted him.

The vibrating sensations on her thigh from Axel's pants startled Amanda.

"Damn… Work's calling," Axel said as he reached into his front pocket to collect his phone.

Amanda stood and pulled her shirt down. Axel lifted himself from the sofa and squinted at the phone before answering it. She sat in the recliner and drank from her bottle. Outside, rain continued to fall, and water could be heard running through the gutter near the window. The television indicated with a message across the bottom of the screen that the game was officially canceled.

"Give me the address again please," Axel said to the person on the other end of the phone.

Amanda shifted her eyes from the television to Axel.

"Yes, I know how to get there. Has everyone else been notified to respond to the scene? Good. No, I'm not close. Tell Lieutenant Wilson I'm on my way," Axel ordered. He then stood and looked at his guest, not knowing what to say.

"I guess I should go now," Amanda said as she stood.

Axel anxiously glanced around the room. "Wait! Uh... Can we get together tomorrow night for another dinner?" he asked as he walked toward the garage door to put on his shoes.

Amanda stood over him and smiled as she rubbed the top of his head. "Yes, we can. Where would you like to go?"

"Where would *you* like to go?"

"How about if I fix you dinner at my place? I make a mean casserole."

"Casserole, huh?" Axel asked as the two walked toward the door leading to the garage.

"Yes, casserole. My mother taught me how to make it, along with other things an adult should know before leaving home," she explained.

You know something, Amanda, you just don't look like a casserole eater," Axel admitted as he opened the garage door.

The rain outside appeared to fall sideways as the wind blew it into the open garage. Amanda looked at her car and saw that her left front tire was flat.

"I need to change that before I go," she huffed.

"No, I have a better idea. You should stay here tonight, and we can fix it in the morning," Axel suggested.

"Where would I sleep?"

"In my bed," Axel blurted.

Her eyes widened. "Your bed?"

"Well... I... um... What I mean is that I can sleep in the spare room when I get back from this call. Besides, I'll be gone most of the night, and I might not return until the early morning. You can stay here, eat the rest of the pizza, and we'll get you on the road after breakfast," Axel offered.

"Are you sure you don't mind?"

"No, not at all."

"Okay then. I'll see you in the morning."

Axel smiled at her and ran out to his car and quickly got in. He sat there a moment before running back inside. Amanda was still standing in the doorway when Axel reached her. For a moment, he just looked at her with a smile. She smiled back, and suddenly they both leaned forward for a kiss.

"I'll see you later."

"Yes, you will, Detective."

Streams of water flowed down both sides of Woodmen Road as Axel drove toward the scene. His thoughts should have been on what was waiting for him down the road, but his mind was on Amanda. He knew they had just met, but he felt so close to her already. She was beautiful, intelligent, and funny. Axel chuckled out loud as he thought of her incredible sense of humor. *There's just something irresistible about her.*

The rain was worsening as Axel approached a four-way stop, as another vehicle approached from his right. Axel allowed the other driver to go first. The rain made it difficult for Axel to see, but he could tell it was a dark SUV. He watched as the vehicle turned right onto Woodmen Road. He thought for a moment that it appeared as if the driver had covered his face when he turned, but he wasn't positive.

Axel turned right toward Black Forest and drove for about six miles before he started to slow down so he could locate the right street. He was unfamiliar with the area, and the rain made it hard to see street signs. The crime scene itself was in El Paso County, and he had been requested to assist with the investigation by the sheriff's office.

This wasn't the first time Axel was called by an outside agency to assist or to lead an investigation that fell outside the city's jurisdiction. The El Paso County Sheriff's Office and the Colorado Springs Police Department had an agreement in place, and the two agencies assisted each other in some investigations, all of which depended on the circumstances of the crime. Some of the other victims of PPK had been found in other counties as well.

Since PPK's first murders were in the city of Colorado Springs, Axel had been given all of the cases that followed, even if they took place in other counties. The other agencies helped in every way possible but were generous enough to allow Axel to carry the full weight of the investigation and all its responsibilities.

Through the rain and darkness, Axel eventually found Rolling Hills Drive, where he made a right turn and drove down the dirt road toward the flashing lights. The road was filled with water that had collected in puddles. Axel came to a stop in the road and was greeted by a uniformed officer with a flashlight.

Jeramiah opened his eyes and was careful not to move too fast. He allowed his eyes to adjust to the darkness, and he surveyed his surroundings. After he saw he was still alone on the road, he glanced at his watch and was surprised to see he had slept for so long.

He turned his lights back on and quickly placed the SUV into drive and then he turned around on the road. His weight shifted as the vehicle spun around, and his leg moved slightly. The shooting pain in his leg returned. He reached down and rubbed his now stiff and swollen thigh. He drove toward Woodmen Road, approached the intersection, and stopped as another vehicle came to a stop to the left of him. He turned right and used his left hand to conceal his face from the other motorist.

He made it back home without incident and pulled into his driveway about forty-five minutes later. After shutting the engine off, Jeramiah opened the door and stepped out slowly. He attempted to stand on his right leg, but it refused to bend entirely like it should have.

Limping to the rear of his vehicle, Jeramiah opened the trunk and took out a screwdriver and a set of Colorado license plates. He slowly bent down and removed the rear plate and replaced it with the other one he had in the back of his vehicle. He did the same to the front. When he finished changing the plates, he walked inside his house and lay on the couch, then lightly massaged his sore leg and shoulder.

"Well, I guess you screwed up again, didn't you? What the hell are you going to do now? Am I supposed to fix your leg for you?"

Jeramiah listened to his father carry on until he fell asleep. He was too tired, too angry, and too hurt to argue with him.

"The road is closed, sir. You'll have to drive up to Lange Avenue and come in that way," explained the deputy as he shined his light into Axel's car with one hand and covered his weapon with the other.

Axel held his badge out the window with one hand and shielding his eyes from the flashlight with the other. "I'm Detective Frost with CSPD," he replied.

"Oh. Then you'll need to park over there and walk into the house from the other side. The crime scene goes from the house out into the woods and then out to the road somewhere. The others are waiting for you inside," the deputy explained before retreating to the dry interior of his cruiser.

Axel pulled to the side of the road and used a paper towel from an old lunch bag on the floorboard to wipe the rain away from his door. He looked at the mass of cars in front of him, took a deep breath, closed his eyes, and sat quietly for a minute.

He let the air out from his lungs, opened his eyes, and pulled the door latch as he shut the motor off. The rain fell onto his head as he stepped out into the night air. He used a flashlight to help him dodge the mud puddles as he walked closer to the house.

"Are you Detective Frost with the city?" a voice asked from the dark doorway leading into the house.

"Yes, I am," Axel replied.

"I'm Detective Harris with the El Paso County Sheriff's Office." Harris was a tall man in his sixties. He extended his hand toward Axel as he entered the house.

"I was just about to fall asleep when I got called!" Gary shouted as he approached the house.

Axel turned to see Gary walking in out of the rain, holding an umbrella over his head.

"I should be on the beach somewhere with a beer in one hand and a fishing pole in the other," Gary said as he shook out his umbrella and looked at the two detectives.

"This is my partner, Detective Gary Portland," Axel said, introducing his partner to Harris.

Harris reached out and shook Gary's hand. He looked him over for a minute and noticed Gary was wearing blue jeans, boots, and a shirt that had images of sailboats on it. Gary quickly looked at Axel, who was also casually dressed but slightly better, as usual. He noticed Harris was also dressed better.

"I'm sorry for my appearance, but my wife took my clothes to the cleaners and forgot to pick up the other ones that were ready," Gary explained.

Axel and Harris looked at each other and grinned.

"Oh, forget it! Screw you guys for judging me!"

Axel and Harris chuckled.

"Call me Bill," Harris said. "What we got here is a double homicide. The two victims are boyfriend and girlfriend. The girl was stabbed in the kitchen. The boyfriend was shot in the garage," Bill explained as he walked Axel and Gary through the crime scene.

Axel looked around the room and got angry. There was a mass of people he observed standing around, possibly contaminating the scene and any evidence that may have been left behind by the suspect. He decided to put his frustration aside for now.

Until I'm asked to take over the investigation, I'm not in charge, he thought.

He stopped at Shannon's body, and he knew from his previous investigations that PPK was the monster responsible for this gruesome murder as well. This scene wasn't like the others though. Something had gone wrong here. PPK had never used a gun in any of the other murders.

This time he was surprised by the boyfriend who now lay in the garage dead, Axel surmised to himself. He turned and asked Harris, "Are you guys giving this to me?"

"Yeah, if you think it's tied to your guy. We want to be kept in the loop though. If you guys get anything on a suspect, we want to know about it. I'll be your contact at the sheriff's office. If there's anything I can help you with, just call me. Here's my card," Harris said as he handed Axel his business card. "I got everything I need for my report. I'll type it up and send it to you concerning my actions upon arrival here tonight, which isn't much," Harris explained.

"Thanks, Bill," Axel said as Detective Harris walked out.

Axel looked at Gary and whispered, "ROD."

"Yeah. Retired on Duty. I don't think Harris is going to be much help," Gary said quietly.

Axel looked around the home and estimated there were probably twenty people inside, doing nothing important except staying out of the rain.

"Everyone, stop what you are doing!" Axel yelled to the uniformed officers standing around him.

"I'm Detective Frost, and I'm in charge of this scene. Everyone needs to exit the home now. Whatever you brought inside here, you take back out with you. Before anyone speaks and tries to explain that there's a good reason for them being here, I'll tell you now, I don't care what you are going to say! I'm going to start writing names down that will go in my report. I don't care if you are a supervisor or the chief or sheriff himself. This is my case, and I will not allow anyone to screw it up with a cup of coffee from the local diner," Axel announced to the room.

The officers whispered their frustrations to each other and slowly started to gather their things.

"Detective Portland, will you please stand at the front door and write down the names of the people who are inside here right now as they leave?" Axel then yelled into the garage, "Deputy! Please make a list of everyone in there. I want a written report from you with all of their names and their assignments listed. I want to know who they work for and how they came to be here, what they touched, why they touched it, and why they were here. If anyone has a problem with the way I'm doing things, don't speak up. You can contact my lieutenant in the morning. But you will provide the information I've asked for before leaving this crime scene."

"No need to contact me in the morning. I'm here right now if anyone has a problem with Detective Frost's instructions," Lt. Wilson called from the front door.

The crowd whispered once more. They slowly moved around as if they weren't included in the group who was asked to leave.

"Everyone, the only people I want to see in that house alive are Detective Frost and his team. That means you need to start moving toward the door. If you don't think it includes you, please come and ask me. Also, if I find fingerprints or footprints belonging to any of you, I'll have your ass. Clear this house now!" Wilson yelled, and this time, it was in his command voice.

The whispers stopped as the crowd of uniforms finally made their way out of the house. Axel stood alone while it got quieter around him. He ran scenarios through his mind of what could have happened. There was no sign of forced entry at the front door. The sliding glass door leading to the deck out back was latched shut. The air conditioner was on, so the windows around the house should have been closed. The detective pulled a notebook out from his pocket and started writing his observations down.

"Detective!"

Axel turned toward the garage and saw Beck, who was standing there in a raincoat.

"Axel, I got something out here you need to see," Beck said as he walked out toward the driveway. Beck walked with a limp most days, but it seemed to be worse when the air was wet and cool like it was tonight.

"Yeah, what you got?" Axel asked as he followed Beck outside where the rain had eased to a slight sprinkle.

"When the uniforms got here, they were told the suspect may be injured. And that he ran into the woods."

"So did they catch him?" Axel asked hopefully.

"No, but they did find a knife near the driveway," Beck smirked as he held a plastic evidence bag in the damp air. Inside the bag was a black knife with a long blade.

Axels' eyes bulged. "Does it have any unusual marks on it?" he asked quickly.

Beck used his other hand to hold up another bag. It had a piece of putty pressed into it and an -"X" mark carved into that. Axel smiled upon seeing the first good piece of evidence that had finally been found.

"Finally, the X. That's great, Beck."

"It's not an X. It's a skull and crossbones. Look at the knife again," Beck instructed.

Axel grabbed the bag and looked at the base near the blade. Sure enough, there sat a skull and crossbones.

"Wow! You got anything else?"

"I give you a murder weapon, and you ask for more?"

"Well, I...-"

"Hold that thought. I do have more. I got some of my guys pulling a plaster from a footprint found outside the garage window. We'll also have some bullets from a gun shortly. And he dropped his bag with the trophy he took from the victim."

"We're getting closer, Beck. He's slipping. We're so close!"

"I know, finally," Beck said in agreement.

"Let's finish this one!" Axel shouted as he walked back into the house where Shannon lay on the floor.

He squatted down, staying on his feet, and looked over her body for anything else that could help. He was pleased PPK hadn't been afforded the opportunity to do anything else to her. She was dead, but she hadn't been raped and left lying in the woods.

Chapter 16
Flats

Axel turned into his driveway and smiled when he saw Amanda's car was still there. He noticed the flat tire had been replaced with a smaller spare. He parked beside her car and went inside the garage. It had been a long night, and he was exhausted. As he took his shoes off at the door, he wondered what she was doing.

Should I go into my bedroom, or should I go to one of the other bedrooms?

Axel entered the house and walked toward the guest bedrooms, trying not to make a sound while his heart pounded. As he moved through the home, he stepped on a squeaky board. He paused and waited.

"Axel, is that you?"

"Yes, it is," he answered in a surprised voice. "Where are you?"

"I'm in the kitchen."

Axel turned and walked back toward the living room. He surveyed the kitchen from where he stood. Amanda wore a T-shirt from one of his dresser drawers with her long legs on display. The shirt just covered the bottom of her buttocks, and he could see more than he should when she leaned over. She looked up from her coffee cup and smiled at him as he walked toward her.

"I made coffee and then breakfast from some things I found in the refrigerator. I replaced my flat tire with the spare," Amanda said as Axel stopped in front of her and took the cup she was holding.

"Is there any sugar in the coffee?" Axel asked and drank from her cup.

"Well, I did put my lips to the rim before you came in," she replied as she traced her finger down the front of his shirt toward his pants.

"It tastes sweet." Axel leaned forward into her inviting lips.

He placed his left arm around her waist and brought her close to him. Amanda closed her eyes, ran her arms around his back, and held on to him. Their lips met, and he placed the coffee cup on the counter. He used his free hand and ran it around and behind her. The T-shirt started to rise higher, but her cell phone rang.

Amanda regrettably pushed herself away from him and reached for her purse to retrieve her phone.

"Hello? This is Amanda. Yes… I'm on my way… I know… I'll be there as quickly as I can… Okay, good-bye."

Axel figured his work was done at the crime scene, so now it was time for Amanda to go to work and report it to the public.

"Axel, I'm sorry, but I need to go."

"I thought you might've left last night when I got called out."

"I didn't know you were going to a possible PPK murder scene when you left last night. Although, I thought it could be. I really wanted you to know I wasn't here with you for a story. So last night I gave you your space to work without me being a reporter."

Axel nodded. "Thank you, but now I feel like shit. I didn't want to give you the impression I thought that. I don't think for a minute you are that type of person."

She smiled. "I'm not that type of person."

"I know you're not, and I'm glad you're not," Axel said as he looked into her eyes.

Amanda started to walk away. "I need to get dressed and go out to Black Forest," she replied.

Axel leaned on the counter. "I know, but I still wish you could stay."

"Me too." Amanda crossed the floor back to him and kissed him once more.

"I got to go," she whispered and pulled away once more.

"By the way, don't wear high heels. It's really muddy out there!"

"I won't, and thanks for the tip," Amanda said as she started up the stairs toward the bathroom.

Axel moved toward the living room from the kitchen, carrying the coffee cup. When he looked up toward the balcony from below, he saw Amanda go by and caught a glimpse of her bottom. He was caught off guard, and Axel quickly looked away, spilling the coffee on his shirt and wrist in the process. He walked back into the kitchen and washed his hands in the sink. He grabbed a dish towel to wipe up the floor. He started smiling as he pictured her running by the balcony. *Commando.*

He placed the towel in the sink and slipped out of his shirt. He then went into his room and put on a T-shirt.

"I wore one of your shirts last night. I hope you don't mind!" she yelled from upstairs.

"No, not at all!" Axel yelled back.

"Axel, can you get the outfit from my car for me, please?"

"Sure."

"My keys are on the bar."

Axel found the keys and walked outside. He found the

outfit, took it from the car hook, and walked back inside the garage.

"Axel!" called the unmistakable voice of his neighbor.

"Hi, Jill, how are you this morning?" Axel asked as he walked back out of the garage and waved at Jill, who was loading her kids into the van.

"I see you just got back. Was it a long night?" Jill asked while she climbed into the van with a smile on her face.

"Yeah," Axel answered.

"Nice outfit!" Jill yelled as she pulled out of the driveway.

Axel shook his head and walked back inside the house. He made his way up the stairs to the bathroom and announced himself from the door.

"Thank you. Can you hand it to me?"

"Yes," Axel said and handed it to her from the other side of the door.

He then walked to his bed and noticed it was made. He thought about everything going on and what he was seeing.

She had a change of clothes and her makeup bag for the morning. Was she planning on staying the night last night? No, she's gotta have that stuff with her in case she gets called out. He thought.

Axel turned the television on and caught the latest news from the crime scene he had just left. The news desk reporter announced to viewers they would have the complete story within an hour. Axel was flipping through the channels when Amanda walked into the bedroom from the bathroom. She stood in front of the window, smiled, and tilted her head. He looked at the beautiful woman as the light from the window created a warm glow around her.

Wow, he thought.

"I'll give this shirt back to you now. I'm sorry I didn't ask to wear it, but I didn't have anything else to sleep in."

"No, that's okay. I wanted you to make yourself at home."

"Well, I did. I mean, I slept in your bed. I sat on the other three beds like Goldilocks trying to find the right one and then I ate the pizza after you left. I also watched your television and used your shower," Amanda admitted as she looked down at him while swaying side to side.

He stood from the bed, pulled her to him, and kissed her. "I hope you come back and use more of my stuff."

"I think I would like that, but right now, I gotta go," she said.

"Okay. I'll walk you out."

After he walked Amanda to her car and the two kissed good-bye, he went to his bedroom and finished undressing. Climbing into bed, he looked to the other side where he had tossed the T-shirt she had been wearing. He reached over, picked it up, and smelled her perfume. He allowed her scent to carry him into a deep sleep.

Jeramiah woke up on the couch, and he could still feel the pain in his leg. He slid his feet to the edge of the cushion and placed them on the floor slowly. He made every attempt not to bump into anything. When he looked down, he saw a huge purple bruise on his thigh.

Shit. How am I going to explain this? he thought.

Without moving his leg, he reached for his phone with his uninjured arm. After dialing the number, he shook his head in disgust.

"Hey, boss, it's me. I'm going to need to take a sick day today. I played in a softball game last night and hurt myself. I got plenty of sick time to use… No. I don't have anything important going on in the office… Yes, I can afford to miss the day… Thanks. I appreciate it, and I'll see you later."

Jeramiah placed the phone back onto the receiver and carefully lay back against the couch. He slowly rubbed his leg with his hands. He then reached for the remote and turned the television on.

"I'm here now at the gruesome scene of a double homicide. People close to the investigation say it may be the work of the monster we've come to know as the Pikes Peak Killer. The evidence collected thus far is being compared to evidence from previous cases, and the police hope to have a suspect soon. The names of the victims are being withheld until notification can be made to the next of kin."

Jeramiah watched and listened as she referred to him as a monster.

"Monster!" He whispered.

He rubbed his leg harder as he imagined how he was now being viewed by others. He grew angry and imagined what it would be like to spend time alone with Amanda Crosse. Then he thought about the investigating detective.

"Some of you may be wondering how a nice family with a nice home, like the one I'm in front of right now, could be targeted by a monster who may be living here in the Pikes Peak Region. Hopefully, the police will have those answers before PPK strikes again. I'm Amanda Crosse with Channel Twelve, and we'll have the complete story of what happened here to this family tonight at six."

Yeah. I will have her heart! Jeramiah thought. *What are you thinking about, boy? Don't look at me that way, son. I'll slap the piss out of you, you ungrateful bastard! Who fixed you up last night? I'll tell you who... It was me. I undressed you when you came limping in here. I put the ointment on your leg and shoulder. Your lousy mother didn't have the stomach to deal with it. I knew when you left last night that you were going to get into trouble. It was raining, and I said you should stay home and that it was too dangerous. Did you listen to me? No!"*

"Yes, Father, you told me, and no, I didn't listen to you, and I'm sorry. Can you please forgive me?" Jeremiah begged as he closed his eyes to prepare for the headache building inside his skull.

He hoped his father would have mercy on him and not beat him when he was already in so much pain.

"Are you staying home from work today?"

"Yes, Father, I am."

"You have one lousy work ethic. If I was like that when you were growing up, we'd have all been homeless and starved to death."

"I know, Father. Please. Can I just lie here and relax right now?"

"I don't care what you do!"

"Thank you… and I love you, Daddy!"

The news camera shut off, and Amanda shook her head in disbelief. She had only caught a glimpse of the inside of the home when they were setting up for the shot. Amanda saw into the garage and then farther into the house, and she wasn't prepared to see all the blood. She wanted to call Axel and talk to him, not about the crime but about how she felt.

Chapter 17
Security Guards

The alarm sounded, and Axel reached over to turn it off. He had set it to wake him up at two, giving him enough time to reach the office and contact Beck to learn what he had discovered at the scene in Black Forest.

Axel sat on the edge of his bed, rubbed his eyes, and reached for the TV remote control. As he stood and stretched, he listened to the national news.

"In Washington DC, Senator William Morris was killed late last night in a fire at his home. Senator Morris was alone at the time of the fire. His wife was visiting family in New Hampshire. The fire is being ruled an accident at this time. Investigators from the fire department believe the blaze started from a lit cigarette. The senator was known to be a smoker, and friends close to the family described him as a chain-smoker who would often fall asleep with a cigarette still burning. His family asks that his supporters remember him for the good he did in helping Colorado on major issues that affected them and their state."

Axel remembered the senator as he watched the news display pictures of him on the screen. Morris had worked hard as a representative for Colorado. He led the way for many issues that affected the state, including the death penalty.

After a shower, Axel dressed and left his house at close to three o'clock. He climbed into his car and backed out of his driveway. Pulling out onto Highway 24, he looked at the sky as the sun shined from above. The road looked hot, and it had already dried from the previous night.

The radio was on, and the local news reporter was covering the news and events going on in and around the Colorado Springs area. Axel was thinking about calling Amanda when he got to the office, but his attention was brought back to the news as details of the double homicide were described.

"The police say the homicide is possibly the work of PPK, the serial killer who continues to prey on the citizens of our community. I ask you listeners: What are the police doing to protect us from this maniac? Really! This has been going on too long now. Our police department is stumped as to the identity of this killer."

Axel listened to the radio announcer badger the department for a little while longer and then changed the station. He was upset with the commentary, but deep down, he knew the announcer was right.

Once he reached the police department, he discovered the parking garage was full. He had to park on the street near the building, though he felt it was a bad idea with what had happened to his car the other night.

"Good afternoon, Axel," Lt. Wilson said, greeting him when he exited the elevator.

"Hello, LT."

"I've something to tell you, and I wanted you to hear it from me," Wilson said as he pulled Axel around the corner into his office.

"The FBI has sent a man to assist with the investigation."

Just the sound of the letters F-B-I made Axel's stomach

turn. He looked away from Wilson, ran his fingers through his hair, and tried to take a deep breath so he could compose himself before speaking.

His face showed his disgust, and suddenly every victim's name, their mutilated bodies in the morgue, and their families crossed his mind. Axel pictured the bloody bodies at the scenes. He felt the victims had been discarded like trash. Axel had to speak to each victim's family while they cried and asked him "why" each and every time. Unexpectedly, he let it all come out at once in an unfiltered tone.

"That's bullshit! I've been on this case for months now. Every agency has turned their cases over to us and then this department throws them on my desk. MY DESK! When the media needs someone to blame at the end of this, it's going to fall on ME! Then last night, we get some evidence that can help further our investigation, and they want to send someone from the FBI to assist? That's bullshit! You know it, and I know it!"

Wilson turned and calmly shut the door to his office.

"No, Axel, it's not, and I do know! I told them we could handle it!" Lt. Wilson yelled back. He then collected himself, knowing that yelling at each other wouldn't solve anything. "Look. The FBI sent a profiler, and he has some information that could be useful. Do me a favor and listen to what he has to say. When he's done, tell him thank you and do what you want. I need you to go along with this for now. People higher up are watching the investigation very closely."

Wilson opened the door after Axel nodded in agreement, and both men walked toward Axel's desk. Gary was standing next to a man wearing a polo shirt and dress slacks. He was tall with dark hair, and he looked young. The FBI agent carried a briefcase in his left hand and had a notebook under his arm. Gary, as usual, stood by and smiled at Axel as he and the lieutenant approached them.

"Detective Frost, this is Agent Jaxson Locke. He's here

with some information about PPK and the investigation," Lt. Wilson said as he introduced the two men to each other.

"Hello, Detective. I'm glad to meet you," Locke said as he shook Axel's hand and dropped his notebook to the floor.

"Hello," Axel replied and bent down to help the agent pick up the papers that fell out of the notebook.

"This is great! You guys are already working together, and here I thought it'd be awkward," Gary quipped as he stood over them with a smirk on his face.

After moving into a conference room, Agent Locke explained what he had on the killer thus far from the information he had collected.

"Detective Frost—"

"Call me Axel, and he's Gary."

"Okay then. Please call me Jaxson."

"Agreed," Gary said.

Jaxson sat and opened his briefcase and then his notebook. He organized his files on the table before speaking, while Axel and Gary waited patiently.

"Now. I know you received a profile from Quantico, but I don't think it's completely accurate."

"Then why did you send it?" Gary asked.

"I didn't. A profiler in the BAU sent it," Jaxson answered cautiously.

"Then why did they send it, if it wasn't accurate?" Axel asked.

"Because they think it is."

"I don't understand," Gary mumbled in frustration.

"Okay. Let me explain. The profile you received is partially accurate, but I believe there is more to the killings in relation to the offender."

"Like what?" Axel asked.

"The profile you received resembles the one put together for the serial killer Robert Hansen. He killed women in Alaska in the seventies and eighties. He'd fly them to remote islands and hunt them down with a rifle. There are many similarities between your offender and Hansen. Your offender is an organized serial killer, and he is a white male. Likely, he is between thirty and thirty-five and was and still is physically awkward. He was made fun of as a kid. His discipline as a child was inconsistent; most likely, he was abused by his father... Still with me?"

Both men nodded.

"Good. He's a loner most of the time, he keeps track of the investigation, and he doesn't like being made fun of or being the butt of a joke. He's a hunter, he's socially competent, and he likely was an only child. He has a functioning automobile. He has above-average intelligence. He's sexually competent..."

Axel and Gary listened to Jaxson explain a lot of what they already knew about the serial killer. The profile they received from the FBI earlier in the investigation mirrored much of what Jaxson was covering.

"And—"

"Come on. I think I heard this all before," Gary said sarcastically.

"I've got to agree with Gary," Axel said as he began to stand.

"Well, did you know he doesn't kill anyone under the age of eighteen, he uses a knife with an interchangeable blade or that he made the 'X' mark on the knife?" Jaxson asked and waited quietly.

That information was not in the previous profile. Axel and Gary looked at each other. The two were now intrigued but baffled at the same time.

"Okay, you have our attention. What else do you know?" Axel asked as he sat back down.

"I think he knows the victims or has had contact with them at some point in time before abducting them. I believe every victim is a reminder of the girls he desired as a teenager. I believe that when he was in middle and high school, he was awkward physically in some way. Girls made fun of him or talked about him in their circle of friends. I also think he drives a black, gray, or silver off-road type of vehicle."

"What about the last killing? Do you know anything about it?" Gary asked.

"Only what your lieutenant told me before you arrived. I haven't reviewed anything yet. I know a young male was killed. I know he probably wasn't supposed to be there, and I know the killer left some evidence for you. That is about it."

"Anything else?" Axel asked.

"Yes, but I don't think you'll want to hear it," Jaxson answered.

"What are we not going to want to hear?" Gary asked.

"Well, he probably still lives at home with a parent or parents and…" Jaxson hesitated.

"And what?" Gary asked impatiently.

"I also think he's working in law enforcement."

"What in the hell are you talking about, agent?" Gary asked angrily.

"I think he's working in the security field or in law enforcement."

"You think he's one of us? How in the world could you come up with that idea? I'm finished sitting here, listening to this stuff," Gary protested and stood.

"Gary, wait," Axel said as he looked down at the table.

"You've already thought about that, haven't you, Detective Frost?" Jaxson asked.

"Every time this guy kills someone, he leaves nothing for us to track him down. Up until last night, he's not left one single piece of evidence behind, except the body, at all his crime scenes. The only thing we have is his DNA but no match in the national database. After the third murder, I thought it could be a cop, but I knew if I said something, people would react just like Gary reacted to you just now," Axel explained.

"Gary, I know it's hard to imagine a cop is doing this," Jaxson said. "It's happened before in other cities. Look, he may not be a cop—maybe a security guard at the mall, a car lot, or even at the airport—but either way, he knows police procedure and evidence. The only thing we have right now is that he knows he left something behind at the scene last night and it's going to make him desperate."

Jennifer returned from vacation on an evening flight from Las Vegas. She was soon overwhelmed with grief, and she almost took another day off, after arriving home and learning of her friend Tammy's death. She decided to go to work at the last minute and walked into the security office late in the afternoon. She sat at her desk and looked through the files on the shoplifters that were captured by her security personnel while she was out of town.

"How was your trip?"

Jennifer turned from her desk and saw Jay standing behind her. He was dressed casually with a newly grown goatee. He smiled at her and walked in.

"Did you hear about Tammy?" Jay asked sympathetically.

Jay had worked with Jennifer for over two years in the security office at the store. He was a welcomed addition to the security team, as he stood six foot four and weighed two hundred and eighty pounds. There was more than one occasion when his size had helped her detain a violent shoplifter. Jennifer had hired Jay as a part-time employee because he was still currently employed by the Colorado Springs School District's security department. She paid him a dollar more an hour than the rest of the staff, and she didn't require him to wear a uniform.

Jennifer thought Jay would have resigned by now because he had tried to get hired by various police departments in the area on numerous occasions, but unfortunately for him, he still hadn't made it to any law enforcement agency as of yet.

Turning away and reaching for a tissue, she did not answer. She thought she would be able to talk about Tammy without tearing up, but she was mistaken. Jay reached over and put his hand on her shoulder.

"I'm okay. How is the hiring process going with the police department?" she asked, trying to change the subject from the loss of her friend to something else.

"I think I did okay, but I still haven't heard anything. I think it will be about two or three more weeks before they let anyone know."

"I'm sure you did fine, Jay."

"Well, the third time's a charm. Right?" Jay said with a shrug of his shoulders.

"Your résumé will speak for itself. You're a great security officer at both your jobs," Jennifer said encouragingly.

"Thanks, Jennifer. Hey, before I forget, a customer came by and wanted to review the video of the outside cameras for an accident that happened in the parking lot over the weekend. I told him you would be back today and could call him back after you looked at the video. I would've done it, but you have the password and only access to the files."

"Yeah, I'm sorry I left in such a rush for Vegas that I forgot to write it down for you."

"The customer said he'd come by tomorrow and see if there was anything on the video that would help him with his insurance company. Apparently, they're giving him the runaround about his insurance claim."

"Okay. By the way, have you caught any thieves so far this week?" Jennifer inquired.

"I caught two yesterday. I had to chase one of them down Academy Boulevard," Jay answered. "I also filled out an injury report for myself and placed it on your desk."

"How did you hurt yourself, and why did you leave the property? It's against policy to chase shoplifters outside the store." Jennifer reminded Jay as she looked him up and down.

"I tripped over a curb, chasing that kid down the street. I didn't fall, but I hyperextended my knee. I just won't be chasing anyone else this week or anyone else out of the store ever again."

"Good! What did he steal?"

"I'd rather not say," Jay replied as he turned to walk away.

"Jay, as your boss, I need to know," Jennifer called, leaning against the back of her chair with a smirk.

Jay stopped, turned back toward Jennifer, and stood with his hands on his hips while looking down.

"He swiped a pair of earrings that were on a rack in the jewelry department," Jay mumbled.

"What was the price of the earrings?"

"I think they were five ninety-nine on sale," Jay answered.

"Five hundred and ninety-nine dollars! I'll have to speak to the jewelry manager about placing items that expensive outside the glass," Jennifer said as she reached for the phone.

"Umm, Jennifer, don't call him. The earrings were five dollars and ninety-nine cents," Jay embarrassedly confessed.

"Jay. You chased someone down the street for five dollars and ninety-nine cents?"

"It was a slow day, but hey, I got him."

"Jay, you kill me sometimes," Jennifer said as she shook her head back and forth.

"I'm going to go walk the floor and look for more thieves," Jay advised before turning and walking away.

"Hey! Lunch is on me today!" Jennifer yelled.

Jay didn't say anything. He placed one hand in the air with

a thumbs-up. Jennifer turned toward her desk and worked to catch up on the items and issues facing the security department that she had missed while she was on vacation. She knew she wanted to stay busy with work rather than think about her friend Tammy. She then wrote a note to herself as a reminder to review the video tomorrow morning for Officer Bates.

Chapter 18
Scorned

Axel invited Jaxson to follow along with him and Gary as they reviewed the evidence recovered from the scene in Black Forest. The three men walked into the lobby, entered the elevator, and took a quiet ride down to the basement, where the evidence room and crime lab were located. Gary wasn't convinced that PPK could be one of their own.

"Is this the awkward silence people talk about?" Gary asked.

"Yes. I do believe it is, Gary," Jaxson answered.

"So. Jaxson, how long have you been with the FBI?" Gary asked.

"Just over three years."

"Have you spent all that time in the BAU dealing with serial killers and profiling?" Axel inquired as the doors opened.

"No, actually."

Axel and Gary looked at each other as Jaxson walked past them into the hall.

"Amanda, how is that detective friend of yours doing?"

"Axel is fine. Thank you for asking," Amanda answered Frank, her cameraman.

"Have you gotten him to confide in you about the case?"

"I'm not seeing him for that reason, Frank. Besides, I wouldn't do something like that for a story," Amanda responded sternly.

"I'm sorry, Amanda. I didn't think you would. I was just teasing you a little," Frank said in response to Amanda's defensive remark and her now upright posture.

He knew he had crossed the line. He'd seen many news reporters use their looks to get a story or a lead in the past. He also knew if he didn't apologize, he would hear about it later from his boss. Frank knew of others who had lost their jobs over inappropriate remarks in the workplace.

Why couldn't I have gotten assigned to a male reporter? Frank thought to himself as he looked over the equipment, trying to appear busy.

Amanda saw the look on Frank's face as he began to check his equipment, and she knew he probably didn't mean what he had said in the manner she had taken it.

"Frank, I know some women do that sort of thing, but I wouldn't. Now, if you ever accuse me of that kind of unethical behavior again, I'll…"

"I know, you'll report me to the boss, right?" Frank said, interrupting her.

"No, Frank. I'll tell all the girls back at the station that you wear superhero underwear," Amanda said with a smile.

"How do you know that? I mean, what are you talking about?" Frank asked, trying to pretend like he didn't know what she was referring to.

"Frank, you show more of your backside when you bend over to work on that equipment than you are aware of," Amanda said and laughed, which in turn encouraged Frank to laugh as well.

Frank thought maybe he was with the right reporter. He continued to work on the equipment and laughed as Amanda walked past him, slightly knocking his hat forward over his eyes from behind.

Amanda walked back to the van and sat in the passenger seat. She looked around the area and admired the quiet serenity that the Black Forest community offered its residents. She thought about how nice it had to be to live in a community like this.

How quiet it must be at night, she thought.

Then she remembered where she slept last night and how quiet it was there as well. Sleeping at Axel's house was a great feeling. The smell of his cologne on the sheets had been intoxicating. She thought about the status of their relationship.

If that's what I can call it, she thought. *Maybe he thinks I'm moving too fast.*

She reached into her purse and pulled out her cell phone.

Jeramiah slept for a few hours. After he awoke, he lay there for a few minutes before deciding to get up and try to move around. He felt the soreness in his leg and pulled the sheet back to examine the injury. It was a deep purple and red. He reached for the bottle of Vicodin on the coffee table and unscrewed the cap. He picked up a glass of water from the floor and quickly washed down some pills. He then slept for a little longer before rolling out of bed and into the tub, where the warm water helped to loosen the tightness in his leg and shoulder.

After getting dressed, he took his father's car and drove to the Black Forest neighborhood. Parked on the side of the road, he watched as reporters and their network vans set up their equipment and conducted interviews with other residents in the area. He didn't see many police cars around and wondered if he could walk in the woods without being noticed.

Surely they had searched the woods for the knife or any other traces of evidence. The only reported deaths were the two people inside the house. The people from the car must not have been hit by his gunfire. He was sure they had told the police the direction he ran, but the need to recover his knife was consuming his thoughts.

As he began to open the door, he stopped and sank back down in the seat. He attempted to cover his face. Two crime techs walked out of the woods carrying cameras and plastic bags, most likely containing his knife, or at least that was what he thought.

After the officers passed, Jeremiah made no attempt to exit the car or to enter the woods. The decision to leave without getting caught was the smarter choice. Jeremiah turned the ignition on and looked up and through the trees. He froze when he saw her sitting in the white news van a few hundred yards away.

"Hello. No, I'm not doing anything right now. I'm glad you called… Yes, I think I could meet you tonight after work," Axel said as he spoke into the phone while walking away from his two companions.

"Is that Commando?" Gary asked as his partner smiled and waved him off.

"Commando?" Jaxson asked as he looked to Gary for a response.

"Oh… You want to know about Commando?" Gary asked while speaking loud enough for Axel to hear.

Axel held up a single finger, instructing Gary where he could go and what he thought of his comment.

"Yes, I can meet you at Mario's, and yes, I know where it is. Seven o'clock will be great," Axel said as he nodded his head in agreement while speaking into the phone.

Gary continued to poke at Axel while he tried to finish his conversation. Axel walked in circles, trying to avoid his old friend. Jaxson stood back, leaning against the wall with his arms crossed and watching the two friends with a grin on his face.

"I'm looking forward to it. I'll see you tonight. Good-bye," Axel said into the phone.

"Was that your girlfriend?" Gary asked.

"My girlfriend... How original, Gary. Did you come up with that all by yourself?" Axel asked.

"Why, yes, I did! But you can use it anytime you feel the need," Gary said smugly.

"Weren't we going somewhere, guys?" Jaxson asked.

"Yes, I do believe we were, Agent Locke. Thanks for reminding us. Now, Detective Frost, if you're finished with your personal call, I think we should get back to work," Gary suggested in a light-hearted tone.

The three walked inside and stood in the waiting area until they were buzzed in by Beck. Beck had been working all morning since he'd left the crime scene. He smiled when the trio entered.

"I hope you've got good news for us, my friend," Gary remarked as he sat in a chair behind Beck's desk.

"Hey, get your sorry ass out of my chair!" Beck barked as he limped toward Gary, who stood to allow Beck to sit down.

"You haven't changed one bit, you old bastard!" Gary said. He smiled at Axel, who was pulling a couple of chairs over to the desk.

"Yeah, you wouldn't know what to do if I did change, and yes, Axel, I got more photos of the impression marks from the latest victim this morning. Dr. Ryan's office sent them over. This afternoon, I was able to make a cast of the knife found at

the scene. I then compared it to the mark on Tammy Johnson."
Beck stopped to rub the stubble on his chin with his hand.

"So what did you find?" Gary asked excitedly.

"You know, you interrupt me more than anyone I know, Gary."

"As I was saying before I was interrupted, I compared the impressions, and we've got a match. The knife we found at the scene is the same one used on Tammy, and by tomorrow, I believe we will have a match on all of our other victims, who have the impression, where the knife was pressed hard into their bodies."

"Now that we've got a match, is there any way to tie the knife back to a certain brand or manufacturer?" Axel asked.

"No, Axel. I had my guys run a check through different companies that are in our network. The knife is pretty generic, and I think the skull and bones on the side near the base of the blade were put there by someone after it was purchased, most likely PPK," Beck said as he stood and walked to the wall to flip off the lights. Axel and Gary looked over at Jaxson, who didn't say anything about being right concerning the X mark being affixed to the knife by PPK.

Beck moved next to a laptop computer and used it to display a magnified image of the knife onto a screen next to his desk.

"If you look at the skull and bones here at the base, you can see it was placed there very sloppily, like with probably a five-and-dime soldering kit."

Beck used a laser pointer to direct his audience's attention to the knife on the screen.

"Why do you think the skull and bones were put there?"

"I really don't know, Gary," Beck answered.

Jaxson chimed in. "I think it's being used by the suspect as an alter ego, fantasy, or some other part of his psychological signature."

"Locke, what in the hell are you talking about?" Gary asked.

"PPK uses the impression of the skull and bones on the knife because it represents the illusion of being bad, evil, or even rebellious."

The other men looked around in a way that let each other know that all three men were confused by what Locke was saying.

"Jaxson, pirates used the skull and crossbones on their flags and ships," Axel said as he leaned forward toward the FBI agent, hoping to get more of an explanation from him.

"Right, and pirates were bad guys who went against the norms of society. They broke the laws or the rules. They used the skull and bones to represent their lifestyle. It also took on the meaning of evilness, and the image of the flag on a sailing ship would put fear into their victims. It's also still used today to identify certain poisons on various household items. Some people use it as a sign to others that they live a pirate lifestyle, or they somehow identify that way. Almost childlike."

Axel, Gary, and Beck didn't say anything. They sat quietly and listened.

"PPK believes that when he has his knife, he becomes someone else. Ideally, he becomes his alter ego in his fantasy world. He sees himself as a pirate or simply a person who doesn't have to follow the rules of society. PPK is the total opposite of who he portrays in his everyday life in front of others."

"You're going back to the cop thing again." Gary stood, walked to the wall, and turned on the lights.

"Listen. A cop represents good and a pirate represents bad, if you will. I still believe PPK is someone in the law enforcement profession," Jaxson admitted once more. "You guys have been at this investigation for months. Have you ever really asked why you don't have more evidence than you have? Whoever the suspect is, he's familiar with forensics, and he knows how not to get caught or leave behind any evidence," Jaxson offered and sat down.

"We have some DNA," Beck stated.

"Yes but no match, because he's not in the database," Jaxson replied.

"I think you're right, Jaxson. Gary, let's get out of here and see if we can get anything else going on this. Jaxson, would you like to help us find a killer?" Axel asked.

Jaxson nodded his head and smiled. The three then stood and started to leave.

"Hey, wait. I just got this in an email," Beck said as he walked to Gary, carrying a sheet of paper.

"The gun search you had me do on the Sharon Douglas murder just came back. It looks like a lot of people own a .38 in Colorado Springs."

Axel walked over and looked at the email.

"But the most recent purchase of a thirty-eight in Colorado Springs was by a woman."

"So?" Gary remarked.

"A woman named Elaine Lambert."

Axel and Gary looked at one another and started for the door.

"Gary! Call dispatch. Have them send a marked cruiser out to Richard and Elaine Lambert's home and then get us a radio. I'll get the car," Axel ordered.

"What's going on?" Jaxson shouted as his two new partners ran out the door.

"Something big. I suggest you try to keep up," Beck said.

"May I go with you today, Rich?"

"Elaine, why are you calling me Rich?"

"Honey, you never complained before when I called you Rich. Remember in college, when we were dating, you called me Elle. I miss those days," Elaine remarked. She walked toward Richard as he sat on the edge of their bed, putting on his shoes.

When she reached him, she stood over him, placed her hand on his head, and rubbed the back of it.

"Damn it! Elaine, would you stop! I'm trying to get ready," Richard shouted as he pushed her hand away.

Elaine stood there as her husband walked into the bathroom. She wondered where he could be going. Wherever it was, she would not be with him, nor would she ever know who it was he was meeting with, but she knew who it wouldn't be this time, and that was Sharon Douglas.

Elaine sat on their bed and reached into her sweater. She thought the metal in her hand felt heavy and cold. Tears gathered in the corners of her eyes. She allowed her thoughts to drift to the past, remembering the happy times they had shared.

Memories of staying out late under the stars on a blanket and dreaming about their future together brought tears down her cheeks. She was no stranger to tears, as there were many lonely nights she'd lain awake in bed feeling abandoned, worthless, and wondering where her husband was and who he was with.

"You know crying isn't going to help, Elaine. I'm still leaving, but I'll be back later. I have important matters to take care of before five o'clock," Richard explained from the bathroom while he looked at himself in the mirror.

"What will help us, Richard?"

"What's all of this drama about, Elaine?"

Elaine turned and faced her husband, who had walked back into the bedroom. Her hand was still clutching the solution to their relationship problems. The room spun around her. She sobbed more and placed her hand over her mouth. She looked down at the floor and pulled the .38 from her sweater pocket.

"Elaine, what the…"

"Shut up, Richard! Do you know what I've done for you?" Elaine shouted as she pointed the gun at her husband.

Richard stood motionless for a moment and wondered what he could do or say to get her to calm down. "Elaine, put the gun down and let's talk about this," Richard said as he walked toward her slowly.

She was angry, and all the years of distrust had built to this one moment. Suddenly, they poured out of her at once, in one violent, blood-curdling scream. Elaine's body tensed, and the gun went off unexpectedly. The recoil surprised her. She looked down at the pistol, and the barrel was still smoking in her hand.

"Elaine! What have you done?" Richard asked as he stood in front of her, holding his left shoulder.

Blood poured from the wound, and he started to get lightheaded. He slowly sat on the floor and looked at the women he had hurt many times in the past. Now, for the first time since their wedding, he felt shame for himself, pity for her, and sadness for all he had done to her. Now, it came down to this one moment.

Elaine stood, raised the gun one last time, and pointed it at Richard, who crawled along the floor toward the phone.

Chapter 19
Confessions

Axel and Jaxson reached the car and quickly pulled it around to the back door of the building. Gary soon appeared at the door, wearing his bulletproof vest over his shirt and tie and carrying a radio.

As he reached the car, he opened the front door, not knowing that Jaxson was sitting there. Any other time, he would have argued and had him get out and take the back seat, but for now, he was in a hurry, and there was no time to argue.

"We're going to eleven seventeen Fairview Avenue. Put the red light on the dashboard and turn on the siren with that switch under the radio," Gary ordered from the back.

Jaxson did as he was instructed without question as Axel sped out of the police station toward 1117 Fairview.

"Elaine! Please! Stop it! I know you're just not thinking right now. I'm sorry for all the things I've done to you!" Richard pleaded with his wife to stop what she was doing. For the first time, he saw the strength she possessed that she was now bringing down upon him.

As she stood there, continuing to sob and holding the gun on her husband, there came a knock on the front door. At first, she didn't hear it. She just moved closer to Richard, who had stopped moving toward the phone. He lay on the floor next to the bed, bleeding.

"Police department! Please come to the door," a male voice from outside yelled as someone knocked louder.

"Elaine, let them in… Put the gun down and let them in."

Elaine walked to the window and saw a police car parked a few hundred feet down the street, just as another car pulled in behind it. She watched as three men got out and ran toward the house. Richard continued to lie there as his blood pooled underneath him. Elaine moved from the window to his side. She knelt beside him and rubbed his head. The gun was still in her hand with her finger on the trigger. "So much pain, Richard. I want it all to go away, and I want the source of my pain to go away as well."

"Elaine, please. Please stop. I love you," Richard pleaded.

Elaine bent over and kissed his lips. Her tears fell upon his face. He closed his eyes, and for the first time in many years, he cried. Elaine saw the tears as they ran back to behind his head, and she wiped them away with the sleeve of her sweater.

"I've always loved you, my Richard. Those women thought I'd share you with them. All those women. There were so many, Richard. So many. They never loved you, but I did even after the first. I tried to get you to love me back, but I couldn't. I even tried to stop it all. It was so difficult killing her the other day."

The trio made it to the house quickly, beating the cover officers who were still en route. On the way over, Gary explained to Axel and Jaxson that he had called dispatch and informed them of where they were going. That was when he was told by the dispatcher that she had just sent two officers to the same address for a "possible shots fired" call for service.

"Have you heard anything since you got here?" Axel asked Officer Martinez, who was the first to respond to the residence after a 9-1-1 call came in.

"No. When you pulled up, I saw movement in the window there on the top floor," Officer Martinez answered as he pointed at the window with one hand and held his duty weapon in the other.

Axel looked at Gary and the other two men. He received a nod from his longtime partner. Axel tightened the bulletproof vest he had taken from the back seat when they had arrived. He then leaned forward and tried the doorknob, and he discovered it was unlocked. In a low whisper, he said, "Martinez, tell dispatch that we're making entry into the residence, and you go around back with Agent Locke here. Gary and I'll go in the front door and clear the house. Don't come in unless you hear from us on the radio to do so. I don't want any accidental cross-shooting!" Axel ordered.

Jaxson and Martinez moved to the back of the house. Gary watched from the front step as Jaxson jogged behind Martinez.

"Are you ready?" Gary asked.

"I'm right behind you."

The two detectives entered the front door. They stepped quietly onto the hardwood floor, being careful not to make any noise. Axel stood behind a corner wall next to a painting of Pikes Peak. Gary moved behind him, and they paused. The sounds of someone moaning in pain came from somewhere upstairs. Gary moved from behind Axel and motioned for him to cover him from below while he slowly climbed the stairs.

The stairs were carpeted, which helped mask the noise, helping him make it upstairs without being detected. When he reached the top, he heard someone talking from what he believed to be the master bedroom. He motioned for Axel to follow him up the stairs.

"Richard, look at me please," Elaine said.

Richard, who was beginning to pass out, slowly opened his eyes and looked at his wife, a killer. She was now standing over him with the gun still in her hand.

"You know Sharon and her husband both had lovers other than each other. I tried to stop the affair between you two, and that's how I found out. I went to her home and told her husband. He first acted concerned, but then he told me I should handle my own problems at home and to leave the two of them alone."

"Elaine," Richard said, trying to speak.

"Let me finish. At first, I thought it was just his way of dealing with the news of his cheating wife. So when you continued to sneak around with her, I drove back to their home and saw him pull into the driveway with a woman, who wasn't Sharon. Sure, I thought maybe she was a family friend or relative, but then I saw them embrace each other at the side door of the house. She kissed him and placed her hands down the front of his pants. They both laughed and fell through the door, still embracing each other. It made me sick, Richard. I came home and sat in the living room, waiting for you to come home from work. Then I realized that if he was out with another woman, then his wife was with another man. MY MAN!" Elaine yelled and wiped more tears away. "I bought this gun and intended to kill myself, Richard. Do you know that? I carried it in my pocket around the house. You might've noticed if you ever stopped to hug me or touch me the way you used to do when you loved me."

Axel made his way toward his partner. Gary had taken cover behind the corner of the wall at the top of the stairs.

"The day the 'salesman' came over, I knew who he really was. I could hear everything the two of you were saying from our bedroom window. I knew then that the things you were doing would affect everything in our lives, and in my father's as well," Elaine explained.

Axel stopped behind Gary and waited for his signal.

"I think if my father knew about what you were doing, he wouldn't have been happy. So I didn't tell him, even though I wanted to. I needed someone to talk to. I remember the other day at the park when I walked up to her car and smiled at her like I always have done. At first, I'd planned on asking her to keep quiet about the two of you so we wouldn't be ridiculed in the newspaper. And no, I didn't want to protect you; it was my father I was thinking about. I've decided I'm done protecting you."

Gary motioned for Axel to follow as he moved toward the bedroom door.

"As Sharon put the window down, I remembered the days she and I worked together. All of those fundraisers during the holidays, we worked side by side. You know she smiled at me. It was like she was laughing at me. It was like she was saying how a fool like me could be so stupid not to know that she was sleeping with my husband. I can't even recall how it happened. I just remember standing there with the gun in my hand and looking at her body slumped forward. I didn't even hear the gun go off."

Gary peeked around the corner and saw a woman standing over Richard Lambert, holding a gun.

"I placed the gun in my purse and walked away, and no one stopped me. I continued to look behind me as I walked down the sidewalk, but no one was chasing after me. It was as if I was supposed to kill her, and now, Richard, I believe I'm supposed to kill you."

Elaine raised the gun at her husband's chest and began to pull the trigger with tears falling to the floor. She closed her eyes, and a shot rang out through the house.

Gary quickly entered the bedroom with his pistol focused on his target. For a moment, Elaine stood there with a hole in her chest. Blood flowed down her abdomen; she looked up at Gary and Axel, who were running into the room toward her.

Everything was moving in slow motion. She heard no sounds and felt no pain. She smiled and pulled the trigger, hitting her husband in the chest. Gary fired once more and hit her in the chest again. With the detective's second shot, she fell to the floor, holding the gun. Her eyes were still open when Gary stood above her with his gun still pointed at her. Axel moved to the side of her and took the gun from her hand.

Using the radio, Axel called for an ambulance and a supervisor. Gary leaned down and felt for a pulse in Elaine's neck. There was none. He placed his pistol into his holster and used his other hand to close her eyes shut.

"Gary! This guy is still alive. Grab me a towel from the bathroom."

Gary didn't say a word. He walked into the bathroom where he retrieved a towel hanging from the wall. Axel was squatting next to Richard Lambert. He took the bath towel from Gary and placed it over the wounds as best as he could.

Jaxson and Officer Martinez entered the room with pistols at the ready. Gary walked past them, down the stairs, and out the front door, where he sat on the porch.

The sounds of sirens howled in the distance and grew louder as they neared the house. Jaxson attempted to help Axel stop the bleeding of the now-unconscious Richard Lambert.

"I'll set up a perimeter around the house and begin a roster of the people entering the scene, Detective Frost," Officer Martinez said as he walked back into the hallway.

"I don't think this guy is going to make it, Axel," Jaxson said as he applied pressure to the chest wound.

"Jaxson, all we can do is what we're doing now. Just keep applying pressure," Axel said in response.

Chapter 20
Grief

It wasn't long before EMTs arrived and took over the care of Richard Lambert. Richard was placed on a gurney and rushed out of the room, while paramedics performed CPR on his limp body. Jaxson and Axel walked outside and were sitting in the back of the evidence van that had just arrived when Lt. Wilson walked over.

"Are you guys okay?" Wilson asked after observing the dried blood on the two of them.

"We're okay. It's not our blood," Axel answered.

"Where's your partner?"

"In the car over there," Axel said tiredly.

"The sergeant who arrived first went ahead and took his gun and gave it to Beck to place into evidence," Axel explained.

"How's he doing?"

"I think he'll be all right, eventually. You know how he is. When the sergeant walked up, he didn't have to say anything to Gary. Gary just reached into his holster and handed him his gun. He then walked over and sat in the car."

"Get him to the station. Internal affairs will want to speak to the two of you after they're done here."

Axel and Jaxson had started toward the car when Lt. Wilson yelled for Axel to come back.

"Axel, you were in there. Was it a good shooting?"

"Yeah. There was nothing Gary could've done to avoid shooting her."

"That's what I thought. I went ahead and called our union anyway. They'll have an attorney at the station for the interview with you guys."

"Thank you," Axel replied and then turned and started to walk away.

"Gary will have three days off while the investigation of the shooting is completed. I'll call DJ Thompson and have him report upstairs tomorrow to help you out. He can do the things Gary normally does until Gary returns."

"That'll be great," Axel said.

Lt. Wilson joined Beck inside the house. Axel, Gary, and Jaxson returned to the station to sit through a few hours of questions regarding the shooting.

Jaxson was the first to speak with internal affairs, and after his interview was finished, he left the station without speaking to anyone else and headed to his hotel room. He still didn't know what to do regarding the FBI. After all, he wasn't even supposed to have been there.

The union attorney spoke to Axel and Gary before Internal Affairs. She first sat through the IA interview with Axel. After Axel was done, he went to his desk and told Gary they were ready for him.

"How did it go?"

"I told them just how it happened. You did what needed to be done. Elaine was going to kill her husband, and you had to stop her. If I had entered the room first, I would've taken the shot as well."

"Did I, Axel? I mean, did I do what needed to be done? Did I really save someone?" Gary asked as he stood to walk toward the interview room.

Axel sat at his desk. He had already decided not to leave until Gary was finished with his interview. As he sat there, he thought about Amanda, when suddenly he remembered they had a date this evening. Axel looked at his watch and saw it was getting late. He then reached for the phone to let Amanda know he would still make it tonight, but it may be a little later. When his hand reached the cell phone in his pocket, it rang.

"Detective Frost here."

"Detective Frost, this is Officer Taft. I'm at Memorial Hospital and was told to call when the victim was out of surgery," Taft explained.

"Yes, what do you have?"

"Mr. Lambert is in stable but serious condition. I asked the doctor what he thought, and he said he believes he'll recover."

"Thanks for the call."

"No problem."

Axel hung up the phone and ran down the hall, just as Gary was reaching for the doorknob to enter the interview room.

"Gary! We just got word from the hospital, and you did— save someone I mean."

"Thanks, pal, but was he really worth saving?"

Axel walked back down the hall and took out his cell phone once more to call Amanda.

Axel stayed at the police station until Gary was finished with his interview. He wanted to make sure Gary was okay before leaving to meet Amanda at Mario's. Axel called Carol and told her what had happened and that she should call him if she needed him for anything. Jaxson Locke had not called or said anything about returning the next day to help with the PPK investigation. Axel thought Agent Locke was withholding something. He felt Locke wanted to say more than what he had to the two detectives earlier, and Axel wanted to know what it was.

Traffic was heavy, and Axel ended up pulling into the parking lot of Mario's a little late. He looked around for Amanda's car but was unable to locate it; he was thankful he had arrived before she had. It would allow him time to wind down and think of a lighter topic for conversation other than the shooting.

Axel backed his car into a spot that afforded him an easy exit after dinner. It also allowed him to observe it from the restaurant. As he walked toward the front of the building, he checked to see that the fresh shirt he had taken from his locker before leaving the station was straight.

He also made sure his seams ran down the middle of his body. It was a habit he had developed during his time in the army. Looking down, he tucked his shirt further into his pants using his thumbs. When he looked up, he saw Amanda walking toward him. She wore a caring smile as she walked away from the parking space that occupied her little car.

Axel smiled back and pulled his thumbs from his waistline to wave at her.

How silly do I look?

He felt embarrassed, and it was made worse when Amanda walked up and pulled his shirt out of his pants and twisted it to the right.

"Now that's a little better. You need to relax."

"Thank you, Amanda. My mom's out of town this week, and no one was around to help me get dressed," Axel said jokingly.

The two laughed, and she moved in toward his lips with hers and kissed him softly. "Are you sure this is a good time to have dinner? I heard what happened today."

"I thought I might've seen you over there when the news crews arrived, but I didn't."

"I was in Black Forest, completing interviews with the local residents."

"Did they have anything good to say?"

"The usual. You know. Stuff about how the family was very nice and they're shocked something like that could happen in their neighborhood."

"They're probably saying the same thing in the Woodlake Estates neighborhood," Axel said as he took Amanda by the hand and started toward the entrance.

Smoke swirled in the air above Jeramiah. He placed the skull in its customary position above the crossbones at the base of his new knife. The rays from the setting sun that were coming in from the window behind him allowed the blade to shine as he moved it back and forth in the air.

With his right hand, he held the handle and slowly ran the blade across the left thumb of his other hand. A small amount of blood ran down the side and into his palm. He lifted the knife and stared at his image in the blade, now wet with fresh blood.

Closing his eyes, he stood and ran the knife through the air as if he were a Samurai with a sword, preparing for battle. The pain in his leg was now gone. The numerous pills he had ingested dulled both the pain and his mind.

Jeramiah was still in his own reality when he heard the television in the background and stopped to turn his attention to it.

"Sources say that Elaine Lambert was about to kill her husband in what police believe would have been a murder-suicide. The murder was stopped midway through by Detective Gary Portland, who led officers into the Lambert home, where he shot and killed the suspect, Elaine Lambert. Police are also saying that Elaine Lambert is the main suspect in the murder of Sharon Douglas, which took place a few short days ago near Acacia Park in Colorado Springs."

Jeramiah listened intently to the details as he moved closer to the television.

"Was it a love affair between Mr. Lambert and Mrs. Douglas that drove Elaine Lambert to kill? Mr. Douglas has denied the accusation, but our sources say otherwise. I'm Tina Jones with Channel Twelve Action News."

Jeramiah smiled as he remembered witnessing the murder in the park. Closing his eyes, he recalled how he had started to approach the car Sharon Douglas had been sitting in when Elaine Lambert walked up and shot Sharon in the head.

Jeramiah had learned that the two detectives had planned to meet with a possible witness, and he knew he needed to make the necessary arrangements to kill her before she could talk. From his view on the sidewalk on the passenger side of the car, he watched the blood spatter onto the window and then Sharon Douglas slump forward onto the steering wheel.

He then watched Elaine Lambert walk away from the scene, which made Jeramiah laugh. Never had he been able to kill someone in that fashion and walk away. *In the middle of the day in a crowd of witnesses,* he thought.

John heard of his only child's death by phone. He was alone and the lights were off, except the small lamp in the corner of the room. The lamp illuminated the home office on the main level of his vast mansion. The items that were generally found on top of his desk were now scattered across the room. The disarray of his office would have been worse if John wasn't confined to a wheelchair. After hearing the news of his daughter, Elaine, John had lost control and went into a fit of rage. He ordered his staff to leave him alone for the time being, and every person working for him knew that when Johnathon Willard Davis ordered them to do something, they had better do it.

As the reporter covered the story on television, John closed his eyes and allowed himself the opportunity to remember his precious daughter Elaine as he saw her. For John, Elaine was not the distraught killer housewife. No, for John, Elaine was his one and only precious gift.

He saw her not as a woman but as a child in the backyard, bringing him his tea in a tiny plastic teacup that he had to grasp with his thumb and index finger. Raising her on his own, he was, on many occasions, her only playmate. There were no other children for Elaine to play with, and Elaine's mother had died giving birth to her.

"Mr. Davis."

John opened his bloodshot, watery eyes and turned toward the door to his office, where his assistant, Roger, had entered and said his name.

"Yes? What is it?" John asked.

"I'm sorry to interrupt you, sir, but the hospital called, and your son-in-law is resting. He can have visitors in the morning."

"Roger, bring me my phone, please."

"Yes, sir."

"Visitors? Richard will have visitors soon," John Davis mumbled to himself and closed his eyes once more to return to his memories of his precious Elaine.

Gary pulled into his driveway, placed the car in park, and shut off the engine. He waited in the driver's seat, thinking about the shooting. It wasn't his first shooting in the many years he had spent working as a police officer. He had been placed in that same position to take a life before, when he was a very young patrol cop. In that situation, he had felt bad, just as he did now, but that time he knew the shooting had been necessary.

This time, he wondered if killing someone like Elaine Lambert to protect a man like Richard Lambert had been worth it. Gary believed deep in his heart that she would not have shot him or Axel. In his eyes and mind, Elaine was a threat to only one person, and that person was a pathetic human being who could care little for anyone except for himself. The two detectives weren't the cause of Elaine's unhappiness. From the hallway, Gary had heard everything she said.

Gary sat there unaware that his wife, Carol, had come out to the driveway, where she stood beside his car. She had to knock on the window to get her husband's attention.

"Are you going to sit in the car all night, sweetheart?" she asked softly.

Gary smiled, opened the door, and got out to stand next to his wife. Nothing was said between the two. She just returned his smile, letting him know she already knew. She knew the man she was married to, and she also knew he did what he'd had to do. She simply stood on her tiptoes, kissed his cheek, took him by the hand, and led him into the house.

Chapter 21
9:35

The restaurant wasn't very busy, so the hostess was able to seat Axel and Amanda quickly. They ordered drinks and their food right away.

"How are you doing with this whole thing?" Amanda asked as Axel drank from his glass.

"With the shooting today or with the whole PPK investigation?"

"I guess both. I mean, I'm sure it all runs together for you. What I mean to say is that here, all this time, you're investigating the murders committed by PPK and then suddenly you're at a house where your partner shoots and kills someone."

"I was in the room when it happened," Axel said and drank from his glass once more.

"You mean you and Gary entered the house alone?"

"No, I mean yes. What I mean is we had cover there, but Gary and I entered the front of the house while this uniformed officer, and this FBI agent entered the back."

"The FBI is involved now?" Amanda asked quickly.

Axel had spoken before thinking and wished he could have taken it back. Unfortunately, it was on the table in front of his news reporter friend. Information like the FBI being involved in an investigation was a top story for any reporter.

"Amanda, I know we've talked about things concerning the investigation of PPK, but things we say to one another in private are still private, correct?"

Amanda reached across the table and took his hand into hers. "Axel, anything you say to me in private will never see the inside of a newsreel. If no camera is present, it's just you and me. I respect our privacy, as I hope you respect it too."

"I do. Thank you. Well then, the FBI sent a guy over, and he's supposed to just look on as an observer or something, I think. He's been more than that now. He came up with another profile, or theory if you will, for PPK."

"Wow, what did he say? Who does he think it is?" Amanda asked.

"Remember, we're really off the record now," Axel said, reminding her.

"Agreed. Now, let me have it."

"He thinks like I do. He believes PPK is someone in law enforcement or the security profession. That's something I didn't share with anyone before this agent arrived."

"Why not?"

Before Axel could answer, their waitress reached between them and placed their food down. Both paused the conversation and slightly moved back to wait for the waitress to leave.

"If I had implied that PPK was a cop or had anything to do with law enforcement, everyone would've immediately turned it around, saying I was accusing a cop on the department. I would've gotten the cold blue shoulder."

"You said in law enforcement or security. That doesn't have to mean a cop," Amanda suggested and took a bite of her lasagna.

"That's where this Agent Locke and I differ. He thinks it could be anyone in law enforcement or in security. I think it's someone in our department, but I haven't told him or anyone else that theory until just now."

"What?" Amanda asked as she leaned forward across the table.

"Amanda, when the first killings occurred, I made detailed plans to catch this guy. I arranged to have unmarked cars parked near the entrances of North Cheyenne Cañon and Rampart Range every weekend, trying to catch this killer before another murder happened."

"Axel, you couldn't have predicted when he would kill someone and then hope one of those unmarked units would've caught him in the act."

"You don't understand. That's not the point. Only cops knew these undercover cars would be there on those particular nights."

"So? I guess I'm still missing what you're trying to explain to me," Amanda admitted.

"Okay. The killings continued on those nights we had stakeouts in place. PPK just used a different spot to take his victims to. Before the stakeout nights, PPK used North Cheyenne Cañon and Rampart Range exclusively, to either have his way with his victims and then kill them or to dump their bodies after he killed them someplace else. This was true until the very first stakeout I organized. Then, on those particular nights, he used the other locations. But when we weren't watching North Cheyenne Cañon and Rampart Range, he went back and used them again," Axel explained before taking a bite of the spaghetti noodles that he had spun onto his fork.

"Do you think it was a cop on the stakeout?" Amanda asked.

"No. There are so many entrances to those areas that extra cops were used, and the department paid overtime. When cops hear about overtime, word gets around fast, and everyone knows what it's for. Besides, PPK continued to kill on those nights, but he did it at other locations, so it couldn't have been one of those cops."

Axel stopped talking for a moment to drink from his glass. Amanda sat quietly, using her fork to move the remaining parts of her lasagna around her plate.

"I think PPK heard about it from other cops working the overtime," Axel confessed.

"You haven't told anyone about this yet?"

"Just you."

"Why not Gary?"

"Gary is my friend and partner. He would've told me it was crazy to believe a cop was doing these things to young girls. Besides, Gary tells everything. I love the guy to death, but he can't keep his mouth shut to save his life. And when Agent Locke said it was someone in law enforcement, Gary got pissed."

"Sir, can I get you another drink?" the waitress asked.

"No, I think I'm okay, but thank you," Axel answered.

The two finished their meal as their conversation turned toward the brighter side of everyday life. She asked him about his interests, and he, in turn, asked about her future goals. They were, in a sense, feeling each other out more than they'd had the opportunity to do in the past when they were alone together.

The two said good-bye in the parking lot with a warm, passionate good-night kiss. Axel waited for her to pull out of the parking lot before walking to his car to head home.

On the trip back to his house, Axel's thoughts drifted back and forth from Gary to Amanda to PPK. As he drove past Peterson Air Force Base, he thought about turning around and going to Gary's house but decided it was too late for a visit. He wanted and needed to know that his friend was okay.

The lights of the city faded in the background, and the fields next to the road grew dark as he drove west, away from

Colorado Springs. He turned the radio up and listened to a familiar love song.

Once again, he thought about Amanda and wondered if she was someone he could fall in love with—or if she could fall in love with him for that matter. Subconsciously, he daydreamed about being with her and having her in his life on a more committed level. He imagined them going to the lake during the summer and riding on his jet ski together, while Gary slaved over the grill, making hamburgers. Bathing suit… Axel smiled when he imagined Amanda lying in the sun next to the water, wearing a tiny bikini.

After the song was over, he still thought about the two of them being together until the radio started to report the news about the day's events. The topic of Elaine Lambert was the main story, of course, followed by PPK. Axel listened for a short time, but he quickly grew tired of it all and changed the car stereo over to his cell phone, so he could hear the music of his choice for the remainder of the trip home.

FRIDAY, JULY 6TH

Jennifer arrived early to the office and worked on the video for Officer Bates concerning the accident in the parking lot over the weekend. As she sat there drinking from her coffee cup, she moved through the recording at a high rate of speed, trying to get to the correct time of day. As the video went from day to night, she saw images of people moving in and out of the store. She thought it was funny at how the cars sped through the parking lot like ants hurrying about the ground.

As the time passed the nine o'clock hour, she noticed the parking lot was nearly empty except for the occasional employee who would walk out from the mall and into the employee parking lot, where all mall employees were required to park per policy.

At exactly 9:35 p.m., Jennifer watched an individual approach someone in the parking lot, and then without warning, he or she appeared to hit the other. Jennifer quickly and clumsily reached for the stop button to freeze the images, spilling her coffee over. She grabbed a napkin and wiped up the mess. She then rewound the video, zoomed in, and replayed the incident in slow motion.

Her eyes watered when she watched a dark figure approach her friend Tammy Johnson in the parking lot. She knew it was Tammy from the car she stood next to. The recording was dark, and the image was hard to make out, but clearly, the unknown person who'd attacked her towered over her small frame.

Jennifer picked up the phone to call the front desk to the police department and asked to speak with the detective in charge of the Tammy Johnson murder. She was put on hold for a moment and then she was connected to another phone that rang and went to voicemail.

"This is Detective Frost of the Colorado Springs Police Department. I'm not in right now or am away from my desk, but if you leave a message and a phone number, I'll get back to you as soon as possible. Thank you."

"This is Jennifer Walters at Landing's Department Store in the mall, and I'm calling you because I've got a video of the individual who killed Tammy Johnson in the security office here at the store. I'll be here until I hear from you. Please call me back soon!"

Jennifer was upset she had to leave a message and was unable to speak to Detective Frost directly. She bit her lip and looked at the video playing on her screen. She decided to work on the video recording in an attempt to make the images clearer so she could see who Tammy's attacker was in the parking lot.

The video equipment at her disposal was the best in the city, and it rivaled that of the police department. It was the one thing she had asked for in her budget request last year, and it had been installed one week before Tammy's murder. Jennifer was confident she could crop the images, bring them closer into view, and add light where there didn't appear to be any. She stood and refilled her coffee cup. She wiped her eyes and then sat behind her computer to work on the images.

DJ was sitting behind Detective Frost's desk, waiting for him to arrive. Lt. Wilson had called and requested that DJ come in and assist with the investigation while Gary was out. DJ was examining an odd doll when the frantic message from Jennifer Walters came in. He excitedly ran his fingers through his hair as he listened to it. He then quickly stood and walked toward the door.

"What did you do to your leg?" Lt. Wilson asked as DJ walked out from the cubicle with a slight limp.

"I was breaking horses the other day and fell off," DJ answered.

"I didn't know you broke horses."

"Oh, yeah. I've been doing it for years."

"Well, I'm glad you came in today, because we need help. I think we're just waiting for another call from dispatch telling us another girl has been killed. With everything that's going on, I think Axel is overwhelmed. And now, since Gary isn't here and won't be for at least four more weeks, I'm assigning any case that comes in to you," Wilson explained.

"Four weeks? I thought officer-involved shootings took about three days to investigate to clear the officer."

"They do, but Gary called this morning requesting additional time off, and I decided to give it to him."

"Okay, boss. Let me know what I can do, and thanks for giving me a chance to work in homicide for a few weeks."

"No problem, and thanks for doing it," Wilson said and walked back into his office.

DJ continued back toward the hallway, where he got into the elevator and took it to the first floor. He thought it would be best for him to contact Jennifer Walters about the video rather than bother Axel with it.

Stepping off the elevator, DJ ran into Beck who was going down to the basement.

"Good morning," Beck greeted as he passed DJ.

"Morning," DJ mumbled as he brushed by Beck.

Beck entered the elevator and pressed the down button, then scratched the back of his head. Beck thought DJ had been slightly rude to him. Maybe something was bothering him. Either way, the CSI investigator blew it off and continued downstairs.

As Axel pulled into the parking lot, he passed DJ driving out of the parking garage. Axel waved, but DJ went by without waving back and left in a hurry. Axel found a spot for his car on the fourth floor. When he got out, he opened the back door and took out his suit coat he had hanging in the back seat. Instead of putting it on, he threw it over his arm and walked into the building. Once at his desk, he picked up the phone. Dialing the numbers from memory, he was soon connected to his friend's home.

"Hello?"

"Carol? This is Axel."

"Hey, Axel."

"Hello. How's my partner?"

"He's okay. He's been in the garage most of the morning, putting things into the motorhome. He's planning on taking me to Florida tonight."

"Really?"

"Yes. He just got off the phone with Lt. Wilson and cleared it with him. The DA's office is still looking into the shooting, but based on the interviews with internal affairs, the district attorney believes Gary will be cleared of any wrongdoing because he had no other choice but to shoot the woman."

"I told Gary that too."

"We watched the news last night, and all they kept saying was what a wonderful person she was and how much she had done for the community."

"I know, but they always do that. With what happened yesterday, he would've been damned if he did and damned if he didn't by the media."

"You're right, and I think he knows that. Do you want to speak to him?"

"No, let him pack and get the two of you out on the open road. I'll call tomorrow morning and find out where you guys are."

"Halfway to Florida hopefully!" Carol said.

"I hope so."

"I hope to meet your new friend soon."

"My new friend?" Axel asked suspiciously.

"Yes. Your new friend, Commando. I hear she's a baseball fan too," Carol said and snickered into the phone.

"Okay. I thought you were my friend and left the jokes to your other half."

"I normally do, but sometimes I have to step in when he's not up to it."

"I get it. Take care of him."

"I will, good-bye, Axel."

"Good-bye, Carol."

Axel was still thinking about Gary when Jaxson walked into the office. Axel immediately noticed the agent looked different. His shirt wasn't straight, and his suit coat collar was flipped up on one side.

"Jaxson, are you okay?" Axel asked as he watched Agent Locke walk by and slump into a chair.

"No. I need to tell you something."

"What is it?" Axel asked.

"I'm not assigned to the PPK case. I'm here on my own, using vacation time to help you out," Jaxson admitted.

"What do you mean you're not assigned to the case?" Axel asked as he leaned forward in the chair, looking dismayed.

"I've been trying to get into the BAU within the bureau, but I haven't been accepted yet. I think a lot of what the BAU is doing is outdated. They're still using data that was collected when they first started the BAU."

"So?"

"So, I've created some of my own theories, techniques, and psychological profiles."

"How's that?"

"Take the profile you received from the BAU before I arrived."

"Yes…"

"Did any of it help you identify the killer?" Jaxson asked.

"Not really."

"Right. But what I gave you about the knife and how he made the cross and bones was correct."

"Yes, it was."

"What if I told you I've determined his psychological signature?"

"The taking of the hearts. Is that what you're referring to?" Axel asked.

"Exactly. His taking the hearts of his victims has some psychological meaning to it."

"What psychological meaning is represented by taking the hearts?"

"I think PPK was a type of outcast in his teenage years. I believe he never found love, or, for lack of better words, I don't believe he ever won the heart of a girl or a woman as an adult," Jaxson suggested.

"A person in love doesn't win someone's actual heart," Axel corrected.

Jaxson shook his head from side to side. "No. It's the symbolic meaning of winning someone's heart, and it's the reason he takes them. Taking the heart is PPK's psychological signature. He possesses their heart both figuratively and literally."

Axel thought on it for a minute. "Let's say I agree with you. What else do you think you know about PPK?

"He probably has more than one vehicle. Two, maybe even three most likely. As I said before, they're gray, black, or silver. One is an off-road type of vehicle, and all the vehicles are probably American made. I think he lives in or near the woods around the mountains. After looking at a map of the area, I think it's somewhere close to the city of Colorado Springs, most likely west toward the mountains."

"Well, that, I think I can use," Axel replied.

Chapter 22

Landings Department Store

DJ pulled into the mall parking lot near Landings Department Store. He parked near the security entrance in an area hidden from the public eye. He knew about the security door from working extra duty at the mall. After looking around, he walked to the door where no handle could be located on the outside.

The only way in was with the use of a unique key that DJ pulled from his key ring. After shutting the door behind him, he waited for a moment in the hall. He heard the voice of Jennifer Walters, the security manager.

"Hey, mister. Where have you been?" Jennifer yelled from her office.

"Everywhere!" DJ answered as he walked with a visible limp toward the open office door. He entered the office and moved behind Jennifer. "What have you been up to?"

"I've been working on this video. I think it will show who killed Tammy. It's a video with a view of the parking lot. I was asked to look for an accident in the parking lot over the weekend, when I came across this guy attacking Tammy," Jennifer explained excitedly.

"Yeah, I know. I'm working with Detective Frost on the investigation. I heard your message on his voicemail."

"Great! I was wondering why he didn't call me back."

"Well, he's been pretty busy with the case. Have you got anything yet?" DJ asked.

"No. I'm waiting for this last image to come up on the screen. I had to lighten some areas and darken others to get a good picture. All I know is he's a big man. He might be bigger than you," Jennifer suggested as she looked up at DJ who was towering over her from behind.

"Well, that would be pretty big," DJ said as he moved closer toward her.

"Look, DJ, the image is coming up. Oh my God…" were the only words Jennifer could muster together as she watched the image take on the form and identity of the Pikes Peak Killer.

"That's too bad, Jennifer," DJ, David Jeramiah Thompson, said as he leaned back with his right hand and swung his closed fist at the back of Jennifer's head.

Jennifer didn't have time to react. She was still looking at the screen that displayed the face of PPK. The powerful blow sent her onto the counter. She gripped at the corners tightly, which kept her from falling to the floor.

"What the hell is going on?" Jay yelled as he entered the small office.

Jeramiah turned to see Jay coming at him. Jeramiah immediately moved toward Jay while pulling his knife from his waistband.

Jay stepped to the side and tried to prepare for an assault as Jeramiah raised the knife into the air. With both hands, Jay caught the arm wielding the blade.

Jeramiah would not be outdone. He used his free hand and pushed Jay's arms and hands away from his own, freeing up his knife hand. Jeramiah smiled as he looked into his victim's eyes as he sank the knife deep into his chest. Jeramiah pushed the knife through Jay's chest, into his heart, and finally through his back to the wall behind him.

Jennifer slowly regained her balance. She turned toward the fight taking place next to her. She heard Jay gasping for air as he desperately tried to pull a knife out of his chest.

"DJ, stop it!" she begged.

Jeramiah, without moving his right hand from the knife still inside of Jay, picked up the telephone next to him on the desk with his left hand and swung it to his side where Jennifer stood. It struck her left temple, quickly knocking her unconscious. Jeramiah looked down at Jennifer and slowly pulled the knife from Jay's chest. He watched as the man's body fell to the floor next to Jennifer.

Axel was at his desk speaking to Jaxson when he saw the red light flashing on his desk phone.

"Let me check this message really quickly," Axel said.

Jaxson waited for Axel to get off the phone. He watched Axel's facial expression change as he listened to his message.

Suddenly, Axel slammed the phone down, leaped from his chair, and started for the elevator.

"Where are you going?" Jaxson yelled.

"We got a new lead. Let's go!" Axel explained as he bypassed the elevator, choosing the stairs instead, while Jaxson ran behind him, trying to catch up.

The two men hurried to the parking garage, quickly got inside Axel's car, and sped out of the gate.

"Can't you use the red light and siren?" Jaxson asked.

"It's only used in emergency situations. Right now, we don't have an emergency. Just a gut feeling that we need to get there fast."

Traffic was heavy on the road, and it was just as busy at the mall. Many shoppers were pulling into and out of the mall parking lot. Jaxson was becoming impatient as he sat in the passenger seat, looking out the window watching everyone else move through the light they were sitting at.

"Go around or something!" Jaxson said impatiently.

"Jaxson, we'll get through in a minute. If I change lanes now, I'll have to get back over when we get through the light. Please relax. You're making me nervous," Axel said.

Jaxson looked at him. "I need to relax?"

Jeramiah grabbed Jennifer by the hair and pulled her to the side so that the door to the security office would close. Jay was on the floor beside his boss, but his body was lifeless. Blood covered the tile floor around them.

Jeramiah looked through the video. When he found what he was looking for, he removed the thumb drive, placed it into his pocket, and removed his picture from the screen.

Jeramiah then bent over and pulled Jennifer's head up by her hair. He lightly slapped her face.

"Wake up, Jennifer. It's DJ. I got a question for you. Come on now. I know you're still in there somewhere," Jeramiah said as he shook her.

Finally, out of frustration, he let go of her and allowed her head to fall to the floor with a loud *thump*. Jeramiah looked up at the security monitors and watched for a moment as someone he recognized exited a car in the parking lot.

"Damn it! Well, Jennifer, I guess we're going on a date," Jeramiah said as he stood and walked to the door. After opening it slowly, he walked into the hall and found a large empty box sitting on a wheeled cart.

"I'm Detective Frost, and this is Agent Locke. We're here to see Jennifer Walters in the security office," Axel explained to the young girl who was straightening a display rack filled with discounted clothes.

"Their office is downstairs near the west wall. Take the escalator and walk to the right," she replied and pointed them in the right direction.

"Thanks," Axel said and the two men quickly walked away.

Axel and Jaxson stood still on the steps of the escalator as it carried them downstairs toward men's apparel.

"You think we will get anything useful?" Jaxson asked.

"Yeah, I do. Or I hope we do," Axel replied.

Jennifer started to wake, and she moaned as Jeramiah was placing her in the back seat of his SUV. Her head throbbed with pain, and her clothes felt wet and sticky to the touch. She knew she was awake, but she could not see anything around her. She thought she was under a blanket or coat, and she began to pull at it.

Reaching into the cargo area of the vehicle, Jeramiah pulled out a small leather sap. He looked around the parking lot for witnesses, and when he was sure no one was looking, he hit Jennifer in the head with the lead-filled weapon. Her body went limp onto the seat.

Jeramiah threw the weapon back where he had taken it from before pushing her into the floorboard and shutting the door. He walked around the back of his SUV, climbed behind the wheel, and pulled out of the parking lot.

"Here we are, Jaxson," Axel said as they finally found their way to the hidden security office.

Jaxson knocked on the door and waited for an answer. Axel looked around the hallway and down at his feet, where he saw a familiar red liquid oozing from under the door.

"Move, Jaxson!" Axel whispered urgently, pointing at his shoes.

Axel grabbed the handle with his left hand and with his right, he pulled his gun from his holster. Jaxson immediately followed Axel's lead and drew his own gun from his side. The two prepared themselves while Axel opened the door slowly. Covering the door, Jaxson watched as the experienced detective entered the room.

After ensuring the office was clear, Axel bent down and checked for a pulse in Jay's neck. His body was still and getting cold. He knew before he reached down that the man was dead.

"Is he alive?" Jaxson asked from the doorway, where he was still covering them from any possible surprises.

"No," Axel answered and stepped back over his previous footsteps to exit the room. He pulled his cell phone out and called dispatch as he holstered his weapon.

"This is Detective Frost. I need Lieutenant Wilson and CSI Ken Beck to respond with his team to the mall. I have a homicide and need a perimeter set up with marked units."

Jaxson walked out of the hallway toward the security entrance of the building, following some blood-stained footprints. He opened the door and found a cart next to the sidewalk that led to the parking lot. A box lay open on its side. He turned and looked at Axel who had just gotten off the phone.

"We just missed him," Jaxson said.

"Jennifer! Are you alive back there? I need you to answer some questions for me," Jeramiah said as he reached back behind him and lifted the blanket that he had placed over her.

With his hand under the blanket, he ran it along her breast and down to her crotch. After a few moments, he felt for her face. He placed his hand over her mouth and felt for the movement of air.

"I knew you were a tough one," Jeramiah mentioned as he turned the radio up and moved his head to the beat of the music. He merged onto I-25 and made his way toward the woods of Rampart Range. He thought the area in and around the national forest would provide him the privacy he wanted with Jennifer.

It's dark, Jennifer thought to herself after she had awoken.

She was afraid to move, and she forced herself to ignore the pain in her head. She decided to wait for the right moment to attempt to get away. The timing had to be right because she knew she was in no condition to fight a good fight.

"Jennifer, are you awake back there?" Jeramiah asked.

Deciding it was best not to answer, she remained silent. She heard the music and felt the seat in front of her. She kept still and thought about her situation. She knew she was in the back seat of some car. She knew her attacker, DJ Thompson, the police officer she had worked with numerous times in the past, was her kidnapper and the Pikes Peak Killer. He had always been so friendly to her and helpful.

Why's he doing this? she thought to herself. *Maybe I'm dreaming!*

She hoped she would soon wake up and find herself in her home, in her bed, safe and sound.

Jeramiah was in a hurry as he drove through Ute Pass, which would eventually bring him to the small town of Woodland Park. From there, it was a short drive and he would be in the national forest, where he could be alone with Jennifer.

Jeramiah hoped he had not hurt her too badly. After all, she needed to tell him if there were any more copies of the security images or video that he would need to retrieve.

Jeramiah raced his black SUV through the mountain curves, passing slower traffic. He wasn't ready for the police car that pulled up behind him with his lights flashing. Jeramiah looked for a secluded road to turn onto as the police cruiser inched closer. Jeramiah tilted his rearview mirror downward and viewed his passenger under the blanket.

She's still unconscious, he thought.

He reached for his gun on his hip and removed it from the holster and placed it in his lap.

"What've we got, Axel?" Beck asked as he walked up, carrying his bag.

"One dead body in here. There are footprints around the body in the blood. I think there could be other evidence," Axel indicated.

"This is really messy, Axel. Something happened here other than killing this guy," Beck explained as he surveyed the room and the bloody footprints that led down the hallway and out to the parking lot.

"Yeah, I think we or someone else surprised him," Jaxson said.

"You think he was looking for something?" Beck asked.

"I think we have one of the three people who were in this room when this all went down," Axel answered.

"I agree. Look over there, in the far corner. There's a partial footprint. It's smaller than the others, and it doesn't match this guy's print. I think three people were in here, and I think the third person, a woman, was carried out," Jaxson explained.

"I agree, Jaxson," Beck said, nodding in agreement.

"PPK may have another victim with him. Beck, I need you and your team to get in this room and see if there is anything on those cameras or the hard drive," Axel ordered.

"I'll get on it right away." Beck gave orders to his team and took photos of the scene.

"Axel, what do you think we got?" Lt. Wilson asked as he walked up to Axel and Jaxson.

"Our guy was here today," Axel stated.

"Why was he here?" Wilson asked.

"He came by to get something. We're waiting for Beck to finish up and let us know if there is something on the computer security recorder. I don't believe we're going to find anything. He came here for something, and I think he may have left with it."

"Why?" Wilson asked.

"Jaxson and I came here after I got a message on my voicemail from Jennifer Walters. She said she had a video recording of the killer in the parking lot with Tammy Johnson. When we got here, this is what we found." Axel pointed at the body on the floor.

"What else?"

"I think the smaller footprint belongs to Jennifer Walters, and I think he took her with him. The scene indicates there were more than two people inside the security office. I bet he came here to get that video," Jaxson explained.

"Guys, I'm sorry, but I can't picture this guy coming by now and trying to get the video. I mean, why didn't he come by earlier after the murder of Tammy Johnson? Why did he wait a couple of days?" Wilson asked.

"I spoke to the store manager while we waited for Beck. Jennifer has been on vacation for a couple of days, and she has the password and access to the security footage. If the killer knew it, then he waited until she came back to work to try to get the video recordings," Axel replied.

Jeramiah turned off the main road onto a private driveway leading to what looked like a vacant home. He made sure he pulled up far enough so that he and the police cruiser were out of sight of the passing cars. The police cruiser stopped close behind him with its red-and-blue lights still flashing in Jeramiah's rearview mirror. He gripped the pistol tightly in his right hand and waited for the officer to approach. As Jeramiah waited, he thought he heard his passenger stirring in the back seat, but there wasn't enough time to attend to her before the officer was at his window. Jeramiah watched his side-view mirror as the unsuspecting Manitou Springs Police Officer approached the vehicle.

"Good afternoon," Officer Daniels said before he saw a flash of light. He fell backward onto the ground. The bullet struck him in his right eye and exited the top of his skull to the left.

Jeramiah, without looking down at Officer Daniels, placed the gun back in his lap, turned the wheels to the left, and pulled back onto the main road. His heart was racing. He looked to the front and to the rear for other police cars that he knew had to be on the way.

He pressed harder on the accelerator, creating distance between him and the driveway where Officer Daniels lay dead. He ran his hand through his hair and soon realized he was passing other vehicles at a high rate of speed. He looked to the right and signaled for a lane change. When he finally calmed and slowed his vehicle to the speed limit, he reached behind the seat and again felt for his sleeping passenger. Once Jeramiah was satisfied that she was still unconscious, he turned his attention back to the road.

Jennifer had felt the car stop. She'd heard a man's voice and then she heard the loud gunshot. She was frightened, and she didn't dare move, even when Jeramiah reached back and felt for her.

As Jeramiah approached the town of Woodland Park, he saw the flashing red-and-blue lights of a Colorado State Patrol cruiser pass him, going in the opposite direction down the Pass. When he reached the Rampart Range turnoff, Jeramiah signaled right and turned off the main highway once again.

Chapter 23
"Are You Awake Yet?"

"**H**ello, stranger."

Axel turned and saw Amanda approaching. Her crew was behind her near the van, unpacking their equipment. She wore a beige top with a matching skirt that went to about two inches her knees. Amanda smiled as she moved in closer to the detective.

"Have I been reduced to being a stranger?" Axel asked jokingly.

"Well, I haven't seen you in a few hours."

Axel and Amanda looked at one another in the parking lot. He smelled her perfume when the wind shifted. He wanted to take her into his arms but knew he could not. He knew they needed to be professional in front of other people.

Amanda was also enjoying the moment as she admired how her new friend looked in his suit. She was still looking him up and down when she noticed blood on his shoes. She walked closer and extended her hand. She also knew how they should act in front of others. The two shook hands and smiled at each other.

"Is that blood on your shoes?" she asked quietly.

"Yes, it is."

"Are you okay?" she asked, still shaking his hand.

Axel did nothing to pull his hand away from Amanda's. "Yes. I'm fine, babe," Axel answered before thinking.

"Okay then. The reporter has to make an appearance now," Amanda replied. She heard him say babe, and it made her feel good. "Detective Frost, is there anything you can share with the citizens of Colorado Springs about what occurred here today?" she asked professionally.

Axel stood straighter and smiled. He knew she had a job to do, and he did too.

"I'll be prepared to give a statement to the media in about five minutes. If you can have your equipment set up by the front entrance of the mall with the other news channels, I'll come over and answer the questions I can."

"Thank you," the reporter replied, and her cameraman walked toward the mall entrance to set up his equipment.

"Now, are you and I still on for dinner tonight?" Amanda asked without missing a beat.

"Yes. If I get done with all of this in time," Axel answered.

"I'll call you later, if that's all right."

"That'll be great," Axel answered.

Amanda smiled and extended her hand once more, then placed it inside of his. When she began to walk away, Axel held her hand firmly and stopped her. She paused and looked back at him.

"I just wanted to say that you're a sight for sore eyes."

Amanda smiled and blushed. "Thank you."

The two separated and went back to their own people. It was as if two captains from different teams had just met on neutral ground and discussed the rules. Each had a mutual understanding and respect for the other's position.

"Beck was just telling me about what he found in the office," Jaxson said as Axel walked up.

"You guys were right. There were three people inside the room when the man was killed. I think someone was picked up off the floor and dragged outside. The box over here has blood inside of it. I had my computer forensics technician take a quick look at the computer and video recording equipment. Someone deleted some video files and then shut all the cameras down."

"So there is no video evidence of anything?" Axel asked.

"No. Not unless he took it with him on a thumb drive. And that's a possibility. There was a cover to a thumb drive on the desk next to the screen but no drive."

"Damn! Jennifer had something on this guy," Axel said in frustration.

"The killer was sloppy on this one. I found a bloody fingerprint on the phone. I think your guy was surprised by the security officer we found dead," Beck explained.

"Do we know who the dead man is?" Jaxson asked.

"Yes. The store manager came in and identified him as one of the security officers here. He also said that Jennifer, the security supervisor, was also in the building today," Beck said.

"I think we've got to assume that the other two people in the room were PPK and Jennifer," Jaxson said.

"I agree," Axel replied.

"Do you think she's dead?" Beck asked.

"No," Axel said quickly.

"If she were dead, he would've left her here. He took her with him, and he had a reason. We need to find this guy now," Jaxson said.

"Axel, the media is ready for you," Lt. Wilson said as he walked up.

"All right."

"Before you go over there, let me ask you: Where do you think this guy is going right now?" Wilson asked.

"I think he's heading for the mountains with her. In

the past, he has always taken his victims west, out of town. I think we should contact the state patrol, the Teller County Sheriff's Office, and the Manitou and Woodland Park Police Departments."

"What do we advise them to be looking for, Axel?" Wilson asked.

Axel turned to the FBI agent. "Tell him, Jaxson. Tell him everything," Axel ordered and then walked toward the waiting cameras.

Jaxson took a deep breath. "Let them know to look for an off-road vehicle, black, gray, or silver. They're looking for a white male, approximately thirty to thirty-five. Tell them to be careful and that he may be armed with a firearm."

"You think he's still carrying that gun to go along with his knife?" Wilson asked.

"Most law enforcement professionals carry one," Jaxson quickly offered up.

"A cop? A fucking cop! Is that what you're telling me?" Wilson said excitedly.

"We think so."

Axel made his way toward the reporters who had gathered at the front entrance to the mall. His eyes were fixated on one specific reporter who stood out from the others. She was beautiful, and she was prepared for her interview with her microphone in hand.

The detective walked in front of the various news stations that were eager to question him about the murder.

The interview with the media was quick and painless, Axel thought as he made his way back to Lt. Wilson.

"We just got a call that a Manitou Springs officer was shot

in a private driveway just off Ute Pass on Highway Twenty-Four. He radioed in that he was stopping a black SUV that had been speeding in the westbound lanes. When they called him back over the radio, he didn't answer. They sent another officer out, and that's when they found him shot in the head in the driveway," Wilson explained.

"Did we get a plate number?" Axel asked excitedly.

"We got the cruiser dash camera and—"

"What about a suspect?"

"No. The plate was listed to an SUV, but the plate was also listed as stolen a few months ago."

"How many people were in the vehicle?" Axel asked.

"They can only see the back of the driver in the video, but if this is our guy, he could have had her tied up and lying down," Jaxson suggested.

"We're going up the pass. Can you call the tactical unit, the K-9 units, and get them started there too?" Axel asked.

"Okay, Axel. Keep me informed on what you got going on," Lt. Wilson ordered.

"I will," Axel answered and raced out of the parking lot in his car with Jaxson in the passenger seat.

Jeramiah continued driving deeper into the woods, until the road changed from asphalt to dirt. A feeling of relief swept over him when he finally passed the last house before entering the national forest. The dirt road was maintained, but still, the summer's evening rains had created washboard bumps along the way.

He maintained his course until he reached the Y in the road, where he veered onto Route 312, which took him deeper into the forest. The area was popular during hunting season, when deer and elk ran through the dark timber, dodging hunters in their bright-orange vests and hats. During the summer months, there usually weren't hunters in the forest.

Except for me, he thought.

The washout on the dirt road became more severe the deeper they went into the black timber. The SUV rocked back and forth.

The pain in her head was still there, but Jennifer collected herself and finally got the courage to slowly use her right hand to pull the blanket back slightly. She saw the front driver's seat and knew her back was against the rear seat and that she was lying on her left side on the floorboard. She moved her toes and fingers on both sides, testing her body for unknown injuries. She then shifted the blanket over even more so she could see under the driver's seat in front of her.

"Are you awake yet?" Jeramiah asked.

Jennifer didn't answer. If he believed her to be dead or unconscious, then she may have an element of surprise when she needed it. Very carefully, she moved her left hand forward, under the driver's seat, she felt for anything she could use as a weapon.

"Jennifer, you and I are going to have some fun. I must admit though, you are a little older than my regular dates," Jeramiah said and laughed loudly.

As her hand searched the floor under the seat, she felt something hard. She grasped the object that she believed to be metal and pulled it toward her. Using the little amount of light available, she recognized the base of an old jack that was approximately four to five inches wide and seven to eight inches in length. She placed her hand in the small rectangular hole in the center and grasped it tightly.

Jeramiah pulled off the route and parked the SUV. He looked around cautiously before opening the driver's door. After turning the engine off, Jeramiah got out and stretched.

Once he was satisfied that no one else was around, he opened the back door on the passenger side of the SUV. He stared down at Jennifer, who was still lying motionless.

"Jennifer, it's time to get up and answer some questions!"

Jeramiah grabbed Jennifer's feet and pulled her out the door, allowing her body to drop to the ground. The blanket remained over her upper body, which prevented her from seeing her attacker.

"Jennifer, I need you to talk to me, and then we'll have some fun," Jeramiah said as he bent down and removed the cover from his victim.

The bright light from the sun blinded her for a moment, but she was still able to see her target. She swung the jack base hard and fast, and she struck Jeramiah in the head.

He staggered and moved backward while holding his head. Jennifer stood, and she, too, staggered a bit as she hurried toward her kidnapper. When she was in range, she swung her arm around and struck him a second time in the chin.

Jeramiah fell to the ground, and Jennifer screamed with conviction and went after him again. Jeramiah looked up and saw her coming at him. He reached for his gun, pulled it from its holster, and fired it. The shot echoed through the wilderness as it hit Jennifer in the left shoulder.

When the bullet passed through her, Jennifer bent over in pain and screamed. Jeramiah scrambled to his feet. Shaking his head, he looked over at Jennifer, and for a third time, he felt the impact of the metal base to his head after Jennifer threw it from about two feet away.

Jeramiah leaned to his right and shook his head. He then stood and turned around to face her again but found her running madly into the thick dark forest.

Jennifer cried as she ran away, holding her wounded shoulder. She didn't know where she was or what she was running toward. Her head began to throb once more, and she lost her balance when she tried to descend a steep hill littered with pine needles. After falling to the ground, Jennifer rolled on her side to the bottom.

Jeramiah ran after her and tried to stop the bleeding on his face at the same time. He was angry, and now he wanted her dead. His heart raced as he followed her into the woods. Looking down at the bottom of the hill, he watched as she tried to stand. Slowly, he raised his gun and aimed at her. He smiled as he began to pull the trigger.

"Stop!"

When Jeramiah turned around, he saw two men running toward him, carrying rifles. He refocused his aim at them and pulled the trigger. The two unknown individuals sought cover behind different conifer trees. Once more, Jeramiah turned the gun toward his first target, who was on her hands and knees, trying to crawl away.

The cracking of the wind over Jeramiah's head caused him to duck as he fired blindly at his target. He dropped to the ground, attempting to dodge another bullet fired by one of the two men. He looked at the bottom of the hill once more and saw Jennifer lying on her stomach. Jeramiah believed he hit his target, so he stood back up and fired at the gunmen who were moving up the hill toward him.

Running back to his SUV, Jeramiah continued to fire blindly behind him, hoping to slow his pursuers. When he reached it, he jumped inside and started to back up, when a bullet came through his rear window, sending small pieces of glass onto his shoulders and back.

Jeramiah ducked and pressed the accelerator but failed to see where he was going. He rammed into the tree behind him. When he looked again, he saw one of the gunmen aiming his rifle in his direction once more. Jeramiah dropped into the passenger seat just as another bullet whipped over his head, as it came through his windshield.

He sat up quickly and fired his pistol once more at the determined rifleman who was seeking cover. Jeramiah put the vehicle in drive and sped off, leaving a trail of dust and his combatants behind him.

He drove for about ten minutes, but he could not concentrate on the road. The pain in his leg and shoulder had returned, and his head throbbed as blood trickled into his eyes, preventing him from seeing the road clearly. When he drove back onto the pavement, the slight residue of dirt on the asphalt created a slippery transition, and Jeramiah fought for control of the wheel as his rear tires spun out over the road. The loss of traction sent the SUV into a ditch. It came to a sudden stop against a tree, where he tried unsuccessfully to get it out and back on the road.

Good job! Jeramiah thought sarcastically to himself as he stepped out of the car.

He climbed his way up the embankment as quickly as he could. When he reached the road, he started toward the small town of Woodland Park.

"Look, Jaxson. That's where the officer was shot," Axel said and pointed toward the passenger side of the car, where police cruisers lined the highway near a private driveway.

"Man! There are a lot of cars here," Jaxson commented as their vehicle continued past the scene at a slow pace.

"Jaxson, if this guy is a cop, then he knows he's got to get rid of the car. Every cop on duty right now is looking for it."

"What would you do if you were him?" Jaxson asked.

"I wouldn't take a chance by stealing another car with a victim still in my possession. I'd wait until after I got rid of her and then I'd start looking for a new ride."

"Okay. Then we still may have a chance if he takes her to the mountains, right?" Jaxson asked.

"Yes. I think PPK is heading for Rampart Range through the town of Woodland Park."

"What makes you think he's going to Rampart Range and not to one of his other body drop locations?"

"Because he shot a cop here, and that would mean he's already passed any turnoff or side road that would take him to one of the other locations. He's got to be going to Rampart Range," Axel said as the two continued toward the national forest.

"Jaxson, how did you know his vehicle was an SUV and black?" Axel asked.

"Because this guy is dark. I mean, he feels a need to be intimidating, and the only way he knows to do that is to make people fear him. He views himself as a dark figure. The color black, psychologically speaking, represents evil, power, and death. He probably doesn't even know he chooses black for those reasons. He probably just tells other people when they ask that he just likes the color black. The off-road vehicle is the type of vehicle he needs to travel into the mountains with his victims."

"Interesting. It all makes sense," Axel replied.

Chapter 24
Tom and Laura

Jeramiah had been walking for about ten minutes when he heard sirens coming up the road. He ran toward a ravine and concealed himself from the occupants inside the ambulance as they sped by. He waited motionless on his stomach before standing and surveying the area for any police cars that were sure to follow. Once he stood, he saw another car off to the side of the road near a hiking trail.

"There's my new car," Jeramiah said quietly as he started toward the car with his pistol drawn.

"Tom, did you bring me up here to take advantage of me?" Laura asked and giggled as Tom unsnapped her bra from behind.

The two had parked near the road and walked a short distance up the trail where they could be alone during their lunch break.

"No! I brought you here so you could take advantage of me," Tom answered.

"Do you think we should? I mean, an ambulance did just go by," Laura said as she allowed her bra to fall to the blanket.

"I think we should," Tom replied.

"Okay," Laura agreed and pulled his face toward hers.

The two were deep in each other's arms when they heard a car window break from near the bottom of the trail.

Jeramiah had used the butt of his pistol and shattered the driver's side window of the small compact he had come across. He reached in and unlocked the door. He then opened it, sat in the driver's seat, and looked for a key.

"What the hell are you doing?"

Jeramiah turned to his left and saw Tom standing next to him.

"I need your keys!" Jeramiah yelled.

"Kiss my ass!" Tom said as he moved closer to the would-be car thief.

Jeramiah pulled his gun from his lap and aimed it at the man. Tom backed away with his hands in the air as Jeramiah got out of the car. The killer smiled and pulled the trigger. There was no loud explosion from the barrel nor a slight recoil. The only sound that could be heard was a metallic click of the hammer slamming forward on an empty pistol.

Tom waited, expecting the worst, but when he heard the click, he was relieved. "Now what, asshole?" Tom asked as he ran toward Jeramiah. Tom wasn't as large as his opponent, but he was never known to back down from a fight, no matter the odds.

Jeramiah stepped forward, and with the pistol, he struck Tom in the temple. Tom fell to the ground but was still conscious. He was screaming in pain as Jeramiah rummaged through his pants pockets for the keys.

"Where are the keys?" he asked as he pulled his knife out and placed it to the throat of the already-injured man.

"Please don't!" Laura pleaded from a short distance away.

"I have the keys. It's my car. I'll give them to you, but you have to let him go first."

Jeramiah looked at the girl standing a short distance away.

He thought about killing both of them, but he knew there was no time for that. He had to get away before the woods were filled with cops and forest rangers.

"Throw them over here," Jeramiah ordered.

"Let him go first!" Laura called.

Jeramiah was still hovering above Tom with his knife in one hand and Tom's head in the other. He thought for a moment as the sound of sirens grew louder in the distance. Jeramiah released Tom and stepped back. Tom quickly stood, ran toward Laura, and stood next to her.

"Now give me the keys before I come over there and kill the two of you," Jeramiah ordered.

Laura threw the keys over. Jeramiah picked them up and quickly got inside the car.

The phone on Axel's hip rang as they entered the town of Woodland Park. He reached down and answered it.

"Hello."

"Detective Frost, this is Dora with dispatch. I was told to call you and let you know that a girl is on her way to the hospital from Rampart Range."

"What's her name, Dora?"

"We don't know yet. She's been shot and beaten up pretty bad. A couple of men who were target shooting in the woods found her. Your boss wanted me to call you and let you know. He said he'd tried a couple of times to call you, but your phone wasn't working or something."

"We were in the mountain pass, and my phone doesn't get service there," Axel explained.

"I'll let him know."

Axel dialed the Woodland Park Police Department and was

able to get the information he needed. After he got off the phone, he explained everything to his anxious passenger. He turned right off the highway and entered the area of Rampart Range.

"Hard to believe that one place can have so much beauty," Jaxson noted about the surrounding landscape.

"You've never been to Colorado before?"

"No. I don't take a lot of time off," Jaxson answered.

"Maybe when this is all over, and we catch PPK, I'll take you sightseeing," Axel said to Jaxson who was staring out the window.

"Depending on how the FBI feels about my actions, in this case, I may have plenty of time to go sightseeing," Jaxson replied.

The road transitioned from pavement to dirt, and the men soon found themselves with the Woodland Park Police. They pulled off the road, where Axel and Jaxson got out and walked to the crowd of uniforms gathered near an ambulance.

"I'm Detective Frost, and this is Agent Locke," Axel said as he introduced the two of them to the crowd of uniforms.

"Hello. I'm Detective George with Woodland Park PD. I got word that you were on your way."

"I thought our victim was on her way to the hospital," Axel stated, as he realized the ambulance was still on scene.

"She is. They took her to the hospital in town, and a helicopter is taking her to Memorial Hospital in Colorado Springs. They figured it'd be quicker with her injuries and the traffic beginning to build up. This ambulance is for our other victims."

"Our other victims?" Jaxson repeated.

"Yes, it appears your man got in a shootout with these two guys over here when he was trying to kill the girl. He grazed one of them and then stole this couple's car," George explained as he pointed at the couple sitting in the back of the ambulance, being treated by the paramedics.

"He stole their car?" Axel asked.

"Yeah. He hit the guy with a pistol," George answered.

"Did anyone provide a description of the suspect?" Axel asked.

"The guys who exchanged gunfire with him said he looked big. They never got close enough to get a good look at him. Your victim from the city was unconscious when the paramedics arrived. The guy in the ambulance got a real good look at him though."

"Good. I want him to come to the station with me," Axel said.

"All right, Detective. I'll see that it happens."

"By the way, George, we still need to locate his SUV."

"I got some guys on that now."

Axel entered the back of the ambulance and sat with the couple, who were holding hands.

"Hi, folks. I'm Detective Frost with the Colorado Springs Police Department, and I need to speak with you for a moment," Axel said in a calm, reassuring voice.

"That man was going to kill Tom," Laura said quickly.

"I know. I heard Tom got a pretty good look at him."

"I did," Tom said slowly. "I was going to kick his ass, but he pulled that gun out and hit me with it. Laura here threw him the keys when he pulled the knife out and put it to my throat. She saved my life!" Tom replied after collecting his thoughts.

"I don't doubt it. Why did he use the knife and not the gun?"

"Damn thing was empty. The jerk pulled the trigger, but it just clicked. That's when he hit me with it. It caught me off guard."

"Did you plan on fighting him?"

"Hell, yes! That car is all we got. We're married and work at the same restaurant, and Laura is going to school at night while I work a second job. The guy was big, but we needed that car."

"How big, Tom?"

"Maybe six five or six seven."

"I have a police sketch artist at the police station. Can you describe him?"

"Yes."

"Detective Frost! We found his vehicle," George yelled.

"Great! Guys, I've got to go now, but I'd like you to come to the station after you go to the hospital. Agent Locke here will go with you."

"I will?" Jaxson asked as Axel exited the ambulance.

"I want you to stay with them at the hospital until they're finished. Then I want you to bring them to the station. While you're at the hospital, find out about Jennifer Walters. I'm going down to the SUV with these guys. Then I'm going back to the station to talk to Beck. I hope he's got something by now," Axel said as he walked away from Jaxson.

"How am I supposed to get to the hospital?" Jaxson yelled.

"In the ambulance with them!" Axel yelled back.

Jeramiah drove until he reached the local grocery store, where he pulled into the parking lot. He used a towel and a bottle of water he found in the back seat to wash his face off. He exited the car and limped around, searching for a new getaway car.

After a few minutes, he watched as a woman parked her car, got out, and walked into the store. Jeramiah went inside and cautiously followed her down the aisles. After a few minutes, she provided an opportunity for him to steal her purse from her grocery cart when she bent down to retrieve a case of soda from a bottom shelf. He quickly placed the purse under his shirt and exited the store.

When he reached the car, he took the purse out from under his shirt and retrieved the keys. He pressed the key fob, deactivating the car alarm and unlocking it. Once inside, he adjusted the seat, turned the ignition on, and left the parking lot.

"How long do you think it will take before she notices her car is missing, Jeramiah?"

"I don't know, Father."

"I don't think I need to tell you how bad you messed this up. If I told you once, I've told you a thousand times: girls are nothing but trouble for you."

"I know! Why do you continue to speak to me as if I'm still a child?"

"Because you act like one, boy. Don't you ever question me again! Do you understand me?"

"Yes!"

"Yes, what?"

"Yes, Father, I understand."

"Lieutenant Wilson, this is Axel. I'm on my way back to the station."

"I've been waiting for your call. Beck is finished at the scene, and he's working in the lab on the fingerprints he recovered."

"Okay. I have Agent Locke going to the hospital to see Jennifer Walters and then he's going to bring the witnesses to the station to describe the suspect to a forensic artist."

"I'll have one called in and make sure they're here when the witnesses arrive."

"Can you contact Beck and get him to send a crew up here to Woodland Park? The suspect's vehicle was found, and it's filled with blood and prints."

"Sure. Did anyone check the VIN number?"

"It was checked, and it came back as stolen. It was reported about six months ago to our office," Axel explained as he drove down through the curves of Ute Pass, hurrying back to Colorado Springs.

"Axel, you're breaking up. I can't hear anything you're saying."

Axel was still speaking when he heard the familiar beep from the phone, indicating he had lost his cell service.

"Damn!" Axel said as he raced along the curves. He was driving fast, and his tires were squealing. The most critical piece of evidence sat in the passenger seat, and as he rounded a bend, it slid between the door and the cushion. When he reached a straight run on the highway, he recovered it. It was a thumb drive that had been found in the abandoned SUV.

He gripped it tightly and continued down the road. After a few minutes, he saw the ambulance carrying Agent Locke and the two witnesses speeding up behind him. He moved into the right lane and watched the ambulance pass by.

Jaxson and the witnesses rushed to the hospital. Tom, the eyewitness, had fallen unconscious. In the emergency room, the attending physician and nurses took Tom and Laura into a trauma room to evaluate him. Jaxson walked around the ER until he found a nurse to help him.

"I'm Agent Locke with the FBI, and I'm here to see the young girl who was brought in from the mountains," Jaxson explained to the nurse on duty as he displayed his credentials.

"That's Jennifer Walters, and she's in recovery."

"Recovery already?"

"Yes. The bullet wound to her shoulder was treated without surgery for now. Her head injury didn't require surgery either. Just some stitches and observation for a couple of days, due to her concussion. The doctors suspect she'll be with us for some time, and she will need surgery to repair her shoulder in the future when she's stronger."

"Do you think I can see her?"

"Probably, but don't excite her in any way."

"I won't."

"Good. Follow me."

Jaxson followed the nurse as she led him down the hall and onto an elevator, which they took to the sixth floor. When the doors opened, Jaxson walked off and waited for the nurse.

"You're on your own from here. I've got to get back to the ER. Jennifer Walters is in room sixty-five ten," she said as she pointed down the hall to his right.

"Thanks."

Jaxson turned and walked toward the room. Once inside, he was greeted by an irate man who immediately confronted the agent.

"Who are you?" the man demanded.

"I'm Agent Locke with the FBI, and I'm here to see Jennifer Walters," Jaxson explained quickly as he once again displayed his gold badge.

"Have you caught the man who did this?"

"We're working on it. It's why I came here. I need to speak to Jennifer," Jaxson said.

The irate man took a deep breath and walked to a chair to sit down.

"May I ask who you are?"

"I'm her father. Her mother went downstairs to get our other daughter."

"Has she woken up yet or said anything?"

"No. She just got here in the room. The doctors worked on her shoulder to stop the bleeding but put off any surgery until later. They didn't want to do much more because they felt she's too weak."

"That's what I heard. Do you mind if I sit with you in case she wakes up?" Jaxson asked.

"Yeah, you can stay. Have a seat over there, Agent Locke," Jennifer's father said as he pointed at a chair on the other side of the room.

Axel arrived at the station and rushed downstairs, looking for Beck. He found him in the lab, sitting in front of his computer, running the fingerprints he had recovered from the security office at Landings Department Store.

"I ran some of the prints, and so far, I've got the deceased's fingerprints identified, along with those of Jennifer Walters," Beck said as he spun around in the chair to face Axel.

"I also sent a team up to Woodland Park to recover evidence from the suspect's vehicle. Lieutenant Wilson came down for a little while but had to leave when the chief called."

"Well, I got something here if you're interested," Axel said as he held up the thumb drive."

"We can start watching the videos while this last print runs through the database. It may take some time to come back with anything," Beck said as took the thumb drive from Axel's hand.

The two walked to another computer, where Beck inserted the thumb drive. They sat behind the screen for Beck to access the files, and Axel's cell phone rang.

"Hello, Detective Frost speaking," Axel said without looking at the caller ID.

"Hi, handsome! Are you busy?" Amanda asked.

"A little. We got a lead. I don't know if I can make it tonight," Axel explained.

"I kind of thought so. I heard about what was going

on, and we've had crews out all day running down your counterparts, looking for the big story."

"Amanda, we're getting close to PPK. I know we'll get him soon."

"Call me later and be careful. I've grown a little fond of you, Detective Frost."

"I will. I feel the same about you. Good-bye for now."

"Good-bye, handsome."

Axel placed the phone back in his pocket just as it rang again.

"Just can't get enough of me, can you?" Axel said before looking at the caller ID once again.

"Axel, this is Jaxson."

"Oh, sorry, Jaxson, I thought you were someone else."

"That's all right. Jennifer Walters is coming around. Do you want me to question her, or do you want to come down and do it?

"I'll be there in about ten minutes, but you can get started."

"We're here in room sixty-five ten on the sixth floor. Our witness from the woods is still in the emergency room. I'll see you shortly," Jaxson said and hung up.

"I'm going to the hospital to try to interview our victim. That was Jaxson, and it seems she's coming around. Do you need me to do anything before I leave?" Axel asked.

"No. I got it. I wonder what's taking that fingerprint so long," Beck questioned as he got up from his chair and walked to the computer.

"You've got to be kidding me!"

"What's wrong?"

"I forgot to hit enter on the computer, and for the past few minutes, this print has been sitting here not doing anything. I guess I got distracted when you came in with the thumb drive."

"Hey, you know, it happens. Don't worry, just give me a call when or if you find something."

"I will," Beck answered in frustration.

Axel turned and walked out of the lab. He was tired and upset about the error but decided it would not be a good idea to share his dissatisfaction with Beck. Besides, Beck was as tired and overworked as he was. The mistake was a minor one that anyone could have made.

Jeramiah finally made it home. His leg and shoulder ached, and his head continued to bleed. He parked the stolen car away from his home and walked the last two miles. Once he was out of his clothes, he ran a hot bath, downed more pain killers, and sat in the warm water.

He closed his eyes and replayed the events of the day in his mind. He was angry with himself over the mistakes he had made. Every few minutes, he rubbed his leg and tried to work the stiffness out of his shoulder. He hadn't been prepared to fight with such a determined opponent, nor had he been ready for the shooters in the woods. It was frustrating.

The cop was probably dead, and Jennifer was too. The only people who got a good look at me was the couple in the woods. Could they identify me? Jeramiah asked himself. *What about the shooters? No, they were too far away.* Satisfied that he had gotten away clean, he soaked.

Chapter 25
"You Really Messed Up This Time."

"Hello, Jennifer, I'm Agent Locke with the FBI. How are you feeling?"

"Tired," Jennifer answered in a soft, sleepy voice.

"Jennifer, can you hear me?

"I'm so tired."

"I know, but I need you to talk with a detective from the police department when he gets here."

Beck had run through many file folders on the thumb drive and had not found anything. Then, he clicked on one file folder titled TJ. The folder contained one image. Beck clicked on it and waited for the image to appear. Then he heard the computer chime that the last fingerprint recovered from the security office was ready. When he stood to walk to the other computer, the image of a man's face filled the screen in front of him.

Axel got off the elevator, walked down the hall, and was about to walk into Jennifer's room when his cell phone vibrated.

When he walked into Jennifer's room, he heard Jaxson ask Jennifer who had attacked her. He then answered his phone.

"Hello, Detective Frost here."

"Jennifer, who attacked you, sweetheart?" Jaxson asked again as he leaned closer to her face.

"Axel, this is Beck! PPK is—"

"Officer DJ Thompson did," Jennifer mumbled.

"Axel, did you hear what I said? PPK is Officer David Jeramiah Thompson!" Beck said once more over the phone.

"I heard both of you," Axel answered.

"Call Wilson and tell him. I'll start heading to DJ's house. Beck, did you hear me?"

"Yes. I'm going upstairs now."

"I'll need the tactical unit. Tell Wilson, and he'll get them started."

"I can't believe you guys were right!" Beck said.

"I wish we weren't," Axel replied. He turned on his heel and walked back to his car with Jaxson close behind him. When they were on the road, he took his cell phone out once more and called dispatch.

"Dora, this is Axel. I need the address to DJ Thompson's home, and I need it quickly."

"The address is twenty-three twelve Valley Drive in Green Mountain Falls. Is it true, Axel?"

"Dora, I don't know how you guys know already, but please stop the conversations and gossip for now. I can't have anyone calling him or letting him know what's going on."

"I know, because I paged the tactical unit a few minutes ago at the request of Lieutenant Wilson. No one else knows," Dora explained.

"Good. I got to go. Please keep me informed of everyone's arrival in the area."

Axel placed the phone on his side as he drove his unmarked

car back up Ute Pass toward the small mountain community of Green Mountain Falls.

Jaxson was sitting beside him, not saying anything. He wanted to speak but thought it would be best to allow Axel to start the conversation if there was anything he needed to say.

"We were right, you know." Axel finally said.

"I know, Axel."

The two said nothing more as they continued to make their way up the pass. When they arrived at the turn to Green Mountain Falls, Axel pulled the car off the road and waited for backup to arrive.

He pulled the radio from the car charger and called for Lt. Wilson. The two decided to meet at Axel's current location. There, they would make plans for entering the house. Beck called Axel's phone and told him they were getting a warrant signed by a judge and that they would be at their location in about an hour.

Axel and Jaxson took a few minutes to put their bulletproof vests on. Axel then used his phone and called Gary.

"Hey, old man."

"So, it's DJ Thompson," Gary said.

"I figured you already knew. I don't think anyone can keep things like this quiet."

"Well, when things like this happen, everyone knows. I bet he knows you're about to come a-knocking too."

"Probably. I called because I didn't want you left out of the loop. After all, we worked on this together."

"I wish I could be there," Gary confessed sadly.

"I wish you could too."

"I know. I'll be up all night until I hear from you."

"All right. I'll speak with you later," Axel said before ending the call. He then dialed another number. "Hey, it's Axel."

"Hello, handsome," Amanda cheerfully replied.

"I'm sorry we can't get together tonight, but something

big is about to go down. I'd like to make it up to you though."

"I understand. It's been a busy day for everyone. They've got me going to the police station to interview the chief for the ten o'clock news."

"Well, I'll call you in the morning then and... —"

"No, you call me when you get home," Amanda corrected.

"If you insist, babe."

"I do." Something in Axel's voice made Amanda feel uneasy and concerned. She wanted to know what he had going on at that moment but knew he couldn't say if she asked. "I don't know what you're up to, but I want you to be careful."

"I will. Good-bye."

"Bye-bye."

Jaxson walked over to Axel as he tightened his vest and checked his pistol. "Something Beck said earlier has me concerned," Jaxson admitted.

Axel gave the agent a worried expression. "What?" He asked.

Locke slid the pistol in his holster. "PPK has left DNA with most of his victims. Why? I mean, he knows better than that."

"Maybe he didn't think about it," Axel offered.

"No, not this guy."

"What are you thinking, Jaxson?"

Jaxson crossed his arms over his chest. "He's not going to prison. He's decided to die before he lets that happen. It's why he's not worried about the DNA."

Axel nodded. "That's good to know before we go in."

Jeramiah woke to the sound of water running onto the floor that had overflowed from the tub. He climbed out and unplugged the drain, then carefully dried himself off. His leg was stiffer than it was before, and the pain pills were wearing off.

He limped into the bedroom and sat on the edge of his bed. He carefully wrapped himself in a blanket and closed his eyes as he lay back onto the bed. Once again, he ran through the events that had taken place earlier. He remembered hearing Jennifer's message, going to the mall, and killing the security officer. He remembered loading Jennifer into his car and placing the thumb drive in the center console of his SUV.

"The thumb drive!" Jeramiah shouted as he sprung from the bed, allowing the blanket to fall to the floor.

"You really messed up this time, didn't you, boy?" his father said loudly.

Axel, Jaxson, and Lt. Wilson met with Lt. Jenkins and Sgt. Denton from the tactical unit at the staging site to develop a plan. The consensus of the group was for the tactical unit to make an unannounced entry. If they knocked on the door, it would alert the trained police officer that they were coming in. A killer who was experienced in police tactics presented a dangerous scenario for any tactical team.

"We have everyone ready. We are limited on backup if this goes sideways. A large wildland fire is burning out of control near Manitou Lake. The Woodland Park Police, the Manitou Police, and both county sheriff offices are having to respond to that. We have our tactical team ready and three marked units at the end of the driveway blocking it," Lt. Wilson explained as the officers prepared to execute their plan.

"Let's do this!" Lt. Jenkins said.

As the tactical team made their way to the target's house, Beck arrived with the search warrant in hand. Lt. Jenkins was directing his people over the radio as Axel and Jaxson prepared for entry at the front door behind Tactical Team One.

"The snipers haven't seen any movement from inside," Lt. Jenkins said to the entry team over the radio.

"Remember, Detective Frost and Agent Locke are going to wait at the door after Team One goes inside, and they'll act as an extraction team if needed. The home is large, and it belongs to our suspect's parents. If they're contacted, they're to be brought out of the house and placed into separate cruisers until we can speak with them. The sheriff's department wants to be updated as to what's going on since this scene falls within the county's jurisdiction. Lt. Wilson will keep them updated as we move on this," Sgt. Denton explained in detail.

"We would like this guy alive, but it's going to be up to him. Remember, everyone goes home tonight," Lt. Jenkins added.

Jeramiah was getting dressed when he saw a tactical van pull up to the front of the house. He grabbed his knife and gun with extra magazines and ran down the hallway.

"Go! Go! Cover the back, Team Two!" Lt. Jenkins ordered over the radio as the van came to a stop. The tactical officers dressed in black filed out the side of the van and ran up to the front door. Axel and Jaxson trailed close behind the trained entry team. The first officer used a metal ram to knock the door down quickly.

"Police department! Search warrant!" the tactical team yelled as they entered the house with weapons at the ready.

Axel and Jaxson stayed at the door and waited until they were called inside. Jaxson was breathing hard. His heart was pounding underneath his vest. His hands were sweating, and even more sweat dripped down his forehead into his eyes. He looked over at Axel, who was down on one knee at the other side of the door.

The team went through the house as they had planned and precisely the way they were trained to do. No room was missed, and no closet unopened. After about twenty minutes, Sgt. Denton walked out the door between Axel and Jaxson and radioed to Lt. Jenkins that the house was clear.

After the team checked the surrounding structures, Axel and Jaxson met with Wilson in the living room of the home. The house was immaculately clean, and there didn't appear to be any sign of people living in the home. The house seemed to be more of a museum than a residence.

CHAPTER 26
NORTH CHEYENNE CAÑON

A xel and Jaxson had expected there to be a gun battle between the entry team and PPK. The men were surprised to find the house empty. They moved around the living room, then paused and looked at each other suspiciously.

"Where are his parents?" Jaxson asked as he looked at Axel.

"I don't know. The house is still listed to them, and their mail is here on the table," Axel replied.

"I'm going back to the station to update the chief," Wilson announced as he walked out the front door. It was evident he was disappointed. He, like the others, really wanted to apprehend PPK.

Axel watched as his boss walked toward the door. "We'll finish up here," the detective said.

"All right," Wilson replied without turning around as he walked to his car.

Axel turned around to face Jaxson and Beck, who remained at the house to gather evidence, and said, "He's upset."

"Yeah, but he'll get over it," Beck suggested.

"I guess we should get started," Jaxson suggested as he walked down the hallway.

"I'll cover the bedrooms upstairs," Axel said as he walked up the stairs from the front entry.

"I'll cover the living room and kitchen if you can check the other rooms down here Jaxson," Beck said.

"Got it," Jaxson replied.

Jaxson started down the hallway from the foyer, and Beck walked into the kitchen. The house was decorated in a mountain décor with pictures of wildlife and mountains. Jaxson continued walking down the hall and stopped a few times to look at the decorations.

The hallway was filled with large pictures, and Jaxson moved from one to the other, slowly studying them. It was the forensic psychologist within him that forced him to try to understand his suspect's behavior, his life, his choices, and his thinking. Moving by the pictures along one wall, Jaxson stopped to analyze one specific painting.

The painting ran from the floor to the ceiling. It was framed in a dense dark wood that appeared to have been carved by hand. The picture was of a grizzly standing on top of a mountain, overlooking a herd of elk. The grizzly was large, muscular, domineering, and a bit demonic.

"This is him," Jaxson said quietly.

Jeramiah watched from the peephole from the other side, in his panic room. The painting concealed the entrance to the secret room. The small holes he had cut in the tapestry allowed Jeramiah to observe the FBI agent on the other side. Slowly and quietly, Jeramiah placed his gun down the front of his pants and gripped his knife tightly.

Jaxson turned away from the painting to look at one of Pikes Peak on the opposite wall. He was examining it when he started thinking about the grizzly and how it was watching the herd of elk.

The grizzly was watching his prey as they grazed, Jaxson thought to himself.

He slowly turned back around to look at the grizzly once more. He looked up and then down at the entire painting and determined the picture was approximately the same dimensions as a door. Jaxson leaned in closer to the canvas and saw two small holes. He quickly backed up, drew his pistol, and held it at chest level just as PPK burst through the painting. Jaxson fired, shooting from the close-quarter position.

At first, Jaxson didn't notice the knife, nor did he feel the blade enter his torso between his ribs. He tried to speak but couldn't while looking into the eyes of a killer. PPK pushed Jaxson against the other wall and slowly pulled his knife out. Jaxson dropped to his knees.

"Tell Axel I'm still watching," PPK said.

Jaxson slumped backward against the wall as PPK moved past him, toward the front door. He leaned forward and fired at PPK. A round struck the wall next to his head. PPK, angry now, turned and faced Jaxson once more and lifted his gun to finish the agent off, when suddenly Axel appeared at the top of the stairs with his gun in hand and began firing at the killer before he had a chance to shoot at Jaxson.

PPK quickly pointed his pistol at Axel and fired multiple rounds at the detective. Axel ducked. He then stood and fired once more from behind cover, but it was too late. PPK had run from the house.

Axel ran down the stairs and heard Beck screaming from the hallway.

"Axel! Jaxson is down!"

Axel entered the foyer and looked out the front door and then down the hallway, where Beck was kneeling over Jaxson.

"Go! I'll take care of Jaxson!"

Axel ran across the yard and into the driveway. The driveway led to a garage that sat alone, away from the house. He moved to the side of the open garage and cautiously looked inside with his gun drawn. He turned the flashlight on at the bottom of the barrel of his pistol. It allowed him to see where he was aiming. The garage was dark, so Axel moved slowly. A black pickup truck occupied a portion of the garage.

As Axel passed the front of the truck, the lights came on and illuminated him. He then heard the truck crank as the motor came to life. Axel turned and faced the truck with his gun pointed at the driver's side. There, sitting in the driver's seat, staring at him, was PPK. Gunfire erupted from the driver's side window, which forced the detective to roll to his left and fire blindly at the truck as it charged forward at him. The flash of red was all Axel saw from the taillights as it passed him.

Members of the tactical team ran from the main road and fired at the truck as it passed them as well. Axel watched as it disappeared down the driveway.

"Damn, damn!" Axel shouted and kicked the garage door.

"Axel!" Beck yelled from inside the house.

Axel ran back into the house and hurried to Jaxson. He knelt on the other side of him and looked at Beck, who was applying pressure to the wound on Jaxson's side. Axel grabbed the agent's hand and held it tightly. The three men sat quietly and waited for the tactical emergency medical support team to come inside. Axel listened to the radio. Officers were explaining how PPK had successfully crashed through the barricade. He then heard the police cruisers were damaged, and they weren't able to pursue the suspect. Axel shook his head and looked at Jaxson.

"Hold on."

When the ambulance arrived, Axel climbed inside and sat next to Jaxson, while Beck stood at the back door.

"You'll be all right," Beck said and looked at Axel.

"I'll take care of him," Axel assured as the doors shut. He

was looking down at Jaxson when he heard the sirens wail from the rooftop of the ambulance as they started down the mountain.

"Can you contact my boss?" Jaxson asked from the gurney.

"I'll call them."

"Why am I sleepy?"

"Because they gave you something to relax you. Now, just lie back and think about all those pretty nurses who are going to be waiting on you hand and foot for the next few days."

Jaxson closed his eyes, and Axel looked up at the paramedic.

"The medication is working. He's looking good on his vitals right now," the paramedic said.

"Thank you."

At the hospital, Axel made the necessary phone calls and waited until Jaxson was out of surgery. He was tired, and before long, he dozed off, only to be awakened by agents from the FBI. Agent Moore identified himself as the special agent in charge and quickly informed the detective there were many questions he needed to answer.

Axel followed Agent Moore to the cafeteria, where they each got a cup of coffee and sat at an empty table, away from anyone who could hear them. Axel explained how he had asked Agent Locke for his assistance in the investigation. Agent Moore looked as though he knew Axel was lying, but he didn't ask any follow-up questions about the matter. Axel figured the FBI would be content with the explanation if they could say Agent Locke was asked to help.

After surgery was over, Axel was the first visitor who entered Jaxson's recovery room. He spoke in a low voice to Jaxson, who appeared to be half asleep.

"Are you awake?"

"Yes," Jaxson whispered.

"How are you feeling?"

"Really good," Jaxson answered slowly.

"Well, that's how you're supposed to feel."

"What time is it?"

"It's late or early, depending on how you look at it. You should get some sleep. I'll come by later and see how you're doing. If anyone from the bureau comes in, make sure you tell them that I asked for your assistance with the investigation."

"But you didn't. I just—"

"I know what you did, and I should've asked for some help sooner. Maybe others would still be alive if I had."

"You did everything you could."

"Thanks." Axel started to walk out the door just as a nurse walked in, carrying a syringe. She smiled and made her way to the IV drip and added the contents of the needle to the line going into Jaxson's arm.

"This will help him sleep," the nurse explained and left the room.

"Watch your back, Axel."

"What?"

"He told me to tell you he's still watching," Jaxson said as he slid deeper into unconsciousness.

"What else did he say, Jaxson?" Axel asked as he moved closer to the bed from the door.

"I tried to find Lisa," Jaxson whispered, right before he passed out.

Axel tried to get Jaxson to continue talking, but the medication quickly took him somewhere else. Axel patted his friend's leg and walked into the hallway. Before leaving the hospital, he spoke to the FBI agents waiting for their turn to see Jaxson. Axel then spoke to Jaxson's doctor. He learned that the blade had been pushed away from Jaxson's vital organs, thanks to the bulletproof vest he had worn. The wound was more of a hindrance to the muscles and one artery. Axel left knowing the FBI agent should recover quickly.

A ride back to the station was easily found in the emergency room, as cruisers came and went every few minutes in a busy city like Colorado Springs. Once he was back at the station, he called Beck, who had left him a message through dispatch. The message was short and to the point. Axel learned the house had provided plenty of evidence. He also learned that two coffins had been found in PPK's hidden room that Beck believed contained the remains of the killer's parents. The CSI team also found PPK's trophies, which he kept in glass jars in the same place as his deceased parents.

At his desk, Axel worked on his report concerning the events of the day. When he was finished, he sat back in his chair and wondered where DJ would have gone. He then thought of the warning for himself that was given to Jaxson by PPK.

What did he mean by he's still watching? Why me? he asked himself.

"I'm still watching," Axel whispered. He closed his eyes and slowly started to fall asleep. He thought of Amanda. He thought of the nights they'd had dinner together and remembered each one separately. The first night at the restaurant had been perfect, up until he went out to his car and saw the damage.

Axel jumped to his feet and remembered what had been written on his door. DJ must have been following him that night.

But why? he asked himself.

He paced back and forth in front of his cubicle.

Why was PPK following me that night? There must be some reason, but what is it?

Then it hit him, and he stopped pacing. It wasn't him who was being followed that night. It had been Amanda!

He pulled his phone out and dialed Amanda's number. It rang once before he heard her voice on the other end.

"Hello," Amanda said as her voice began to crack.

"Amanda," Axel said. "Amanda, are you there? Amanda! Amanda! Answer me!" Axel shouted into the phone.

"Amanda is indisposed right now and can't speak. She's tied up. I can take a message, and maybe she'll call you back, but I doubt it," PPK said into the phone.

Axel said nothing. He just listened.

"Oh, come now, Axel. Surely you knew this would happen. After all, you don't think people can go on television and call someone a monster and get away with it, do you? I thought it'd be a good idea to let her get to know me after calling me a monster."

"DJ, you don't have to do this! Where are you?"

"I can't tell you where I'm at now, but I'll tell you where I'm going to be."

"Where?" Axel asked calmly.

"North Cheyenne Cañon in tunnel one. Why don't you try to make it there?" Jeramiah asked.

"You can count on it," Axel answered.

"Axel, I don't believe I have to say this, but I will. Come alone," Jeramiah ordered.

"I will. Now let me speak to Amanda again."

"No. But we'll see you at five in the morning."

The phone went dead.

That's a lot of time. He could do anything to her in that amount of time, Axel thought.

Axel sat at his desk, trying to figure out what he should do. After a few minutes, he rushed out of the building and got into his car. He had an idea.

"Amanda, don't cry… There'll be plenty of time for that later."

Amanda couldn't stop crying. Her hands were tied behind her back, and her feet were bound at the ankles. She wondered if she would make it out alive. She thought of her parents and her sister. She tried to remember the last time she had spoken to any of them.

"You and I are going to have fun before we're finished tonight. Do you think he'll show up? I think he will," PPK said sarcastically as he ran his hand over his captive's bare leg. PPK had Amanda in the back seat of her car.

"I need to rest before we meet with Detective Frost," PPK said before placing her car in drive and leaving the parking lot of the police operation center. He left Amanda's cell phone taped to the driver's side door of Axel's car, where he was sure to find it.

SUNDAY, JULY 8ᵀᴴ

The drive up to Gold Camp Road was slow. It was agitating Axel, as he wanted to get there as quickly as possible. The thoughts of what could be happening to Amanda enraged him. The images of the other victims flashed in his eyes, and it made him drive dangerously faster. As he sped up, the car slid out more than once, almost sending him over the edge and down to the bottom of the North Cheyenne Cañon.

The final curve before the tunnel was only a few hundred feet away, and Axel reached down and shut his lights off. He brought the car to a stop, took his pistol out, and flipped on the light on the bottom of the barrel. Holding the gun in one hand, he looked at his cell phone in the other. PPK had sent him a photo of Amanda. She was tied up in the floorboard of her car. She was crying, and she was scared. The rope around her ankles was the same as what had been found on the other PPK victims. The text that accompanied the photo had two words and a question mark. 'Final Victim?'

Axel threw his cell phone to the side and pressed the trunk release. He got out, shut the door, and walked toward the tunnel. He adjusted his vest while consciously surveying his surroundings for PPK.

When he got to the entrance to the tunnel, he saw a light at the other end, and he stopped momentarily. He took a deep breath and walked down the center of the dirt-packed road. Axel knew he was walking into a trap. Halfway through the tunnel, it began to turn, and the light became brighter. As he got closer, he saw a car sitting in the tunnel with the headlights on. In front of the car was Amanda, still bound at her wrists and ankles.

Axel's heart beat faster, and he ran toward her. He was about to reach Amanda when he saw a flash of light. The impact of the bullet sent him backward. The sound of the pistol firing echoed through the tunnel.

"No! No!" Amanda shouted.

"Shut up! Shut up!" PPK yelled louder as he walked from his hiding place at the side of the car. He moved toward Amanda and looked down at her, still holding the gun as smoke drifted upward from the barrel.

"You killed him, you bastard!"

"Maybe, maybe not, but we'll soon find out," PPK said as he started toward Axel, who was still on the ground, not moving.

PPK cautiously walked toward the motionless Detective Frost with his gun at his side. The lights of the car illuminated him as he stood over what he believed to be his latest victim. PPK smiled and positioned himself to send the final shot into the head of the man who had been following his every move.

Then suddenly, the car's light beams were interrupted by someone walking in front of them, directly behind PPK.

PPK turned and saw the figure of a man standing in the light. The man stood in front of Amanda, blocking her from her kidnapper. He turned and looked at Axel, still on the ground.

"I said alone, didn't I?" PPK shouted.

"Hey, monster," the man said. His voice echoed down the tunnel.

The word *monster* angered him. "What did you call me? I'm no monster! No one has the right to judge me. I've been judged my entire life by people like her. She doesn't know me, and neither do you!" PPK shouted in anger and raised his gun hand at the figure in the distance.

Axel took advantage of the distraction and raised his own gun at PPK. PPK saw the movement from the corner of his eye and turned to face Axel, just as a flash of light from Axel's gun brightened the tunnel. The round hit PPK in the chest, and he winced in pain. DJ fired his gun once more and caught Axel in the leg.

PPK fell next to Axel. The dark figure at the other end of the tunnel ran toward the two of them on the ground. Axel had followed PPK's large body with the barrel of his pistol as it fell next to him.

"Don't do it!" Axel yelled as PPK lifted his gun slowly toward the detective.

"No!" The dark figure and Axel shouted at the same time and then fired their guns at PPK. The killer jerked many times before they stopped filling him full of lead.

Jaxson knelt beside his friend. "Are you okay?" He asked as he placed his hand under Axel's back to help him up.

"Yeah. I am now," Axel answered.

"Good," Jaxson stated as he slapped Axel on the back. "How's Amanda?"

"Physically, she looked okay when I passed by her. I think she's probably scared," Jaxson replied.

The two walked back to Amanda, and Jaxson untied her from her bindings. Axel dropped beside her on the ground. Amanda reached for him, and he pulled her into his arms.

"I'll call everyone. You take care of her," Jaxson said and slowly walked back down the tunnel toward Axel's car, holding his free hand against the cut on his side that had begun to bleed.

Jaxson had been off his medication for about three hours. That was when Axel had shown up in his hospital room with a plan to save Amanda. He still had some lingering effects from the medication. His side hurt, and he winced in pain as he walked and breathed in and out slowly. He didn't know if Axel's plan would work, but he knew he had to come through for him, no matter the cost to himself or his career.

Amanda held Axel close to her. She was still scared. "Is it over?" she asked.

"It is," Axel answered as he looked down the tunnel at the body that lay on the ground.

EPILOGUE
THE BAHAMAS

Jaxson found that the instructions to the house were easy to follow, and after a short drive from Colorado Springs, he and Brandi were pulling up to the home of Axel Frost. Jaxson was in no hurry to get back to work, and Axel had invited him and his plus one to his house for a party. Besides, Jaxson had a month off from work and needed to find something to do. A thirty-day "vacation" hadn't been his idea. It was the FBI's idea, in response to his behavior during the PPK investigation. Jaxson, at first, was upset over the thirty-day suspension. But on the day he was officially released from the hospital, he received a visit from the special agent in charge of the BAU. They wanted him in the unit, but he still had to be disciplined for his unusual behavior.

There were other cars in the driveway of Axel's home, and Jaxson saw a man, a woman, and two young girls walking into the garage. He and Brandi got out of the car and made their way into the house through the garage, behind the others they saw going inside.

"Hey, everybody," Axel said after opening the door.

He smiled and invited everyone inside. When Jaxson

entered, the two men looked at each other, smiled, and hugged. No words needed to be said. Jaxson then introduced Brandi to his friend. Brandi said hello and made her way inside, carrying a dessert dish. She walked to the kitchen counter to put it down and was greeted by Jill. Axel and Jaxson stood there for a moment, talking.

"How are you feeling?" Axel asked.

"I should be asking you the same thing," Jaxson answered.

Axel shrugged his shoulders. "I'm good. A little stiff, but good. The bullet went straight through. I should be up and around and back to work in about a month," Axel explained.

"What about you?" Axel asked as they moved their conversation into the kitchen.

Jaxson chuckled. "About the same, but my month off isn't by choice."

"Yeah. I heard, but I also heard that you've been asked to join the BAU."

Jaxson smiled. "I was," he answered happily.

"Good for you. By the way, who's Lisa?" Axel asked.

The FBI agent gave his friend a surprised expression. "Lisa? What about Lisa?"

"You mentioned her name before you passed out in the hospital."

"Lisa is—was my sister. She—"

Amanda walked up and stood next to Axel. She placed her arm behind his back and then kissed his cheek. "Is this the famous FBI profiler, Jaxson Locke, that I've heard so much about?"

"I wouldn't say famous, but yes. I'm Jaxson."

"Well, you may not be famous now, but people who are good profilers usually become famous. Some even work on television after their careers in the FBI."

"I guess we'll have to wait and see then," Jaxson replied.

The guests moved about the home, eating and drinking

while a baseball game played on the television in the background. The party lasted into the night. Jaxson and Brandi were the last ones to leave. Axel walked the two of them out to their car to say good-bye.

"What are your plans after the weekend?" Axel asked Jaxson after he opened the door for Brandi to get into the passenger seat.

"I'm actually going to the Bahamas on Monday with Brandi for a week."

"Really?"

"Yes, really. But I'll be back to check out what Colorado has to offer the week after."

"Good. The bedroom upstairs needs someone to stay in it for a few weeks."

"Sounds good, Axel," Jaxson said before climbing into his car and driving away toward a new adventure.

Amanda waited for Axel at the door, and when he walked inside, she hugged him tightly. The two kissed passionately for a few moments in the kitchen until she slowly backed away. Axel just watched her as she sauntered toward the bedroom. When she reached the bedroom door, she turned toward him, pulled her dress straps off her shoulders, and allowed her summer dress to fall to the floor. Axel stood there frozen, with his eyes wide open.

"I believe the term you're looking for is commando!"

THE SECRETS
OF
TAYLOR CREEK

AGENT JAXSON LOCKE FBI MYSTERY THRILLER SERIES BOOK 2

THE SECRETS OF TAYLOR CREEK
PROLOGUE

SUNDAY, APRIL 18, 1965

It was a cool April evening in 1965. The loud music and laughter from the invited guests, the who's who and well-to-do of North Carolina, could be heard in the distance. Delia Snipes looked back once at the old plantation home that bordered Taylor Creek. She was tired, intoxicated, and ready for bed. Her red high-heeled shoes made her feet ache, and the flower print, form-fitting dress she wore was way too tight. Delia felt more comfortable in a pair of jeans and a loose shirt, but the man who had requested her presence this evening required her to dress how he wanted.

Ben Arrington made all the girls who were of mixed race dress how he desired. The lights from the house were but a small glimmer from the long, dark driveway that led to the main road. The shadowed figures of the drunk politicians, businessmen, and party "treats"—like Delia Snipes—danced past the windows to the beat of the Rolling Stones.

The house belonged to the Arrington family of Beaufort, North Carolina. To visitors of the area, the home was described as an antebellum plantation home. It was white with tall pillars that supported the roof, which extended over a large ground-level balcony. To folks living in the area, especially black folks, it was known as the Old Klan House on Taylor Creek.

Delia had made an early exit from the Gentlemen's Social through the servant entrance in the back. She was satisfied with the hundred dollars she had earned servicing the wealthy white men attending the social. Delia never gave much thought to the things she did for the men nor to their special requests at parties. Besides, she was not paid to ask questions. She believed it was a necessary means to an end. After tonight, she had enough money to move herself, her sister, and her mother to Virginia Beach, where she hoped they could all find work and a different life. Maybe they would head farther away, to Pennsylvania, where her aunt could help her get a job in a factory. Either way, she and her family would be leaving Beaufort just as quickly as she had left the social tonight.

Delia allowed her intoxicated mind to drift toward thoughts of Virginia and Pennsylvania as she staggered down the driveway in the direction of the main road. The driveway was long and dark. It was best described as more of a tunnel of Spanish moss that hung overhead from the rows of trees lining both sides of the gravel driveway. The farther Delia walked from the house, the darker it was. She always felt uneasy about the area and was more comfortable on the main road. From there, she hoped to catch a ride with the workers heading to the docks.

The feeling of someone watching her caused her to stop. She stood motionless and listened for a moment. She squinted her eyes as she peered between the trees into the dark brush on both sides of the drive.

There ain't nothin' or nobody out here but you and God! Stop imagining things. You just drunk! Delia told herself. Slowly, she walked forward once more while singing Shirley Ellis's new hit song, "The Name Game."

When Delia got to the middle of the chorus, she heard something. She turned quickly, "Who dat!" Delia shouted. She looked for who or what had ruffled the bushes behind the trees off to her left.

"I know somebody there! Is that you, Charlie White? I'm done for the night, and I ain't giving you no special attention. I'm goin' go home! Besides, you ain't never got money," Delia called.

She was afraid, and she stood quietly as the waves from Taylor Creek lapped against the shoreline. Still frightened, Delia turned and walked once more.

Delia only sang a few more words to the song before being struck in the head from behind. She didn't remember falling to the ground, but she soon realized she was lying on the ground, looking through a small opening in the Spanish moss at the moon. Warm streams of blood trickled down her cheek and into her eyes, and the moon faded away as darkness overtook the light.

CHAPTER 1
BEAUFORT, NORTH CAROLINA

Agent Jaxson Locke entered the town of Beaufort, North Carolina, shortly before five o'clock in the afternoon and quickly found the sheriff's office. He parked in the visitors' parking lot and made his way inside. He wasn't sure if he would find anyone in the office so late in the day on a Friday. Once inside, Agent Locke was greeted by a tall, thin man in his twenties with a strong Southern accent.

"May I help you?" he asked.

"I'm Agent Locke with the FBI, and I'm here to see Sheriff Maggie Turner. I believe she's expecting me."

"I'll go see if she's ready for you."

Jaxson waited in the lobby where he saw a wall dedicated to the deputies who had been killed in the line of duty. At the top was Sheriff Dwight Carter. Jaxson recognized the name from the one in the file he carried. He was reading the circumstances surrounding Carter's death when the side door next to the lobby opened.

"Sheriff Turner will see you now," the young man announced from the door.

Jaxson followed the man down a short hallway to the office at the end. When he entered the office, Sheriff Turner was sitting at her desk. Upon seeing Agent Locke, she stood, walked around from behind her desk, and approached him while extending her hand.

"I'm Sheriff Turner," she stated professionally as she shook the agent's hand.

"I'm Agent Locke with the FBI," he replied while displaying his credentials.

"Please have a seat." She gestured toward the chair on the other side of her desk.

"I'm here to recover a car—"

"Yes, I know. The very popular and very collectible 1965 Shelby Mustang GT350 that belonged to Agent Nathan Emerson, which we now have in our impound lot," she said, interrupting him.

"Right. I was hoping to look at it this evening."

"That won't be possible. My guys have already gone home for the evening, but you're more than welcome to look at it tomorrow. I have already scheduled one of the fellas to be there for you in the morning."

Jaxson's eyes widened. "Well, okay then. I guess I'll find a place to stay the night and—"

"I booked you a room at the Beaufort Bed and Breakfast. It's at two thirty-one Ann Street. The sheriff's office is picking up the tab for your stay this evening," Sheriff Turner explained.

The FBI agent nodded his head. "All right. Do you know where I can find—"

"The widow Mrs. Josephine Arrington and Mr. William Turner Junior?" she asked, interrupting once more.

"Yes," he answered with a confused look on his face.

"Josephine goes by Stormie, and William Turner Junior, my father, would rather be called Will," she stated and then stood. "They're both over at Mrs. Stormie's home on Taylor

Creek. You can follow me over there. Do you have any questions so far?" she asked as they walked out to the parking lot.

"Do you know where I can find Agent Nathan Emerson?" Jaxson asked comically.

The sheriff turned and gave him a disapproving glare. "No, but maybe you'll find him before you leave," she remarked as she got in her car. "Now, just follow me."

Jaxson did as he was instructed, and after a short drive, he pulled into a long driveway that led to a beautiful home on the water. When he got closer, he saw two people sitting on the porch. Jaxson parked beside Sheriff Turner, then got out of the car and followed her up the steps and onto the porch.

"Hi, Mrs. Stormie, Daddy," Sheriff Turner said politely to the two of them. "This is Agent Locke with the FBI, and he wanted to come and speak to the two of you."

Agent Locke reached out his hand and greeted the two of them. Mr. Turner was an elderly black man in his sixties who was well dressed and spoke with a deep voice. Mrs. Stormie was older, and based on the information in the file, Agent Locke knew she was eighty-three years old.

"Please have a seat," Stormie said and gestured for Jaxson to sit in the chair across from them.

"I'm here to—"

"To recover Agent Emerson's car that the department of transportation road crew found on Wednesday, over where they're putting in the new highway," Will responded, interrupting Agent Locke.

Like father, like daughter. At least she comes by it naturally, Jaxson thought to himself.

"Yes, sir, I am," Jaxson replied.

"What can we help you with, Agent Locke?" Stormie asked.

"Is there anything you can tell me that's not in this file?" Jaxson asked, holding up a thick folder he had brought with him.

"No, I don't think there is," Stormie answered solemnly and then looked at Will.

"I agree. I don't think we left anything out when we spoke to the other agents who were here questioning everyone in nineteen sixty-five."

"I just thought maybe you could tell me why Agent Emerson left his car here, in the woods, instead of taking it with him," Jaxson asked, looking back and forth between the two of them and waiting for an answer or some type of observable behavior.

"I have no idea. He did leave in a hurry," Stormie answered and then slowly turned away toward the water.

"He came here to look into the deaths of those young girls, and the next thing we know, everything was turned upside down. Nathan got out of town as quickly as he could," Will said when he noticed Stormie looking away.

Odd. Will Turner just referred to Agent Emerson by his first name, Locke thought to himself.

"Well, unless you have any further questions, I don't think they have anything to add, Agent Locke, but after you look at the car tomorrow and you find that you have other questions, then just reach out. We'll see if we can help," Sheriff Turner said as she stood, hinting to Agent Locke it was time for them to leave.

"No. I can't think of anything right now," Jaxson said as he stood.

He thanked them for their time and followed Sheriff Turner back to their cars. She gave him directions to the Beaufort Bed and Breakfast and to the county impound lot where he could find the car. Jaxson found the directions easy to follow, and before long, he pulled into the parking lot of the converted Victorian-style home and checked in with the owner.

After unpacking and cleaning up, he read over the file once more. Jaxson asked his supervisor before leaving Charlotte as to why he was being sent to recover a car belonging to an FBI agent who disappeared in 1965. Jaxson's caseload usually involved unsolvable cases, cases where there were no leads, and cases that involved serial killers. Jaxson, unlike others, had a sense about him that most investigators did not. He had the natural ability to notice things that were out of place or that other people simply overlooked.

Jaxson was told that Agent Emerson was wanted for the murder of two, maybe three people. He had come to Beaufort on his own accord and conducted an unauthorized investigation into the deaths of three young girls of color in 1965. The current media attention surrounding the case has been centered on the discovery of his personal car, an original 1965 Shelby Mustang GT350. Car collectors had reached out to the FBI, wanting to know what was to become of the car once the FBI was finished with it. The town was full of media personnel waiting to get a photo of the rare vehicle.

Jaxson ordered pizza from a local pizzeria and sat at the small table in his room, reading over the file concerning Agent Emerson. He learned Agent Emerson had gone to the University of Oklahoma and played in the Orange Bowl in 1958. After graduation, he went to law school at Duke.

Interesting. Agent Emerson grew up in North Carolina, went to the University of Oklahoma, played in the Orange Bowl against Duke University, and came back to Duke to go to law school, Jaxson thought to himself.

He also learned Agent Emerson was involved in some highly publicized civil rights cases in the sixties. Jaxson sat back in his chair. The things Emerson was accused of and the things he was a part of in his short career weren't adding up. Jaxson then focused on reading the reports from the investigating FBI agents, the sheriff, and the coroner. Once more, things didn't add up. They were also very brief. They contained little information about the people Emerson had supposedly killed, the disappearance of Agent Emerson, and the deaths of the girls. One thing that the FBI agents' and the sheriff's reports had in common was the guilt of one person: Agent Nathan Emerson, who suddenly disappeared into thin air, leaving an expensive car in the woods.

Jaxson finally moved on to the few available photos that had not been destroyed or misplaced in the past fifty-plus years. He reviewed autopsy photos, crime scene photos, and photos of victims in the hospital. There were photos of young Stormie and Benjamin Arrington in the hospital, recovering from their extensive injuries. At about twelve-thirty, Jaxson finally decided to go to bed. After lying there for about thirty minutes thinking about the case, he fell asleep

SATURDAY, JUNE 1

Jaxson woke up at about seven and quickly got in the shower. It was there where he was still trying to wake up when a thought occurred to him. He turned off the water and hustled toward the table with the files on it. He shuffled through the photos and finally found the right one. There it was, a detail in the image right in front for everyone to see, but it seemed no one ever had... until now.

Jaxson made it down to the impound lot and met with the man Sheriff Turner said would be there. His name was Tim, and he was overly helpful yet slightly hard to understand when he spoke. Jaxson had found him in the office sitting over a large portion of biscuits and gravy. Outside along the fence, were news vans and media people waiting to get a glimpse and a photo of the car. Tim led Jaxson through a door into the garage bay, where Jaxson got his first look at the 1965 Shelby GT350.

"I towed the car inside the shop out of view of the cameras until you got a chance to look it over," Tim explained.

"Thank you. Did you have a look inside it?" Jaxson asked.

"Nope, I just lifted the hood and made sure all the critters were out of it before I brought it inside."

"No critters?" Jaxson asked.

"Nope. The car was buttoned up pretty good. All the windows were up, the keys were in the ignition, and the doors were unlocked. I'm pretty sure the guys who found it went through it and took some photos. I found smudge marks in the dust inside from where people had climbed around before I got there."

"Well, thanks. I guess I'll take it from here," Jaxson said as the man walked out of the building.

Jaxson took photos of the outside of the car and then moved to the inside to take more. After an hour, he sat in the front seat to document and log the items he found in the glove box. He finally moved to the back seat, and under the passenger seat, he came across a journal written by William "Preacher" Turner.

Jaxson took the journal from the car and walked to an old chair sitting in the corner to read it. After about an hour, he realized he had discovered an amazing story, but he still had questions. Jaxson collected his things and made his way to his car. He placed the journal in the passenger seat and headed toward the two people he believed could answer those questions.

Once again, he drove down the driveway leading to the home on the water. On the porch, Stormie and Will sat, appearing as if they were waiting for his return. Jaxson walked onto the porch holding the journal.

"My father couldn't let the truth die. He told me before he died that he'd written everything down. I just didn't know where he'd left it," Will admitted.

"Can I have the truth that goes with the journal?" Jaxson asked.

"I think you already know the truth," Stormie answered.

"I think I do. I found it this morning in this photo." Jaxson handed her a copy of one of the evidence photos. In his very brief investigation, Agent Jaxson Locke believed he had found the truth in the photo. The journal confirmed it, but still, there were unanswered questions.

Stormie looked at the red circle that Agent Locke had made. She smiled and then looked back up at Agent Locke. "Start reading, and Will and I can fill in the blanks."

Jaxson sat in a chair across the table from them. He opened the journal, took a deep breath, and read aloud from the beginning.

ABOUT THE AUTHOR

Michael grew up in Pensacola, Florida, where he spent the summer months as a youth at the beach, tubing down the river or splashing around in a pool near his grandmother's home. After graduating from high school, he joined the US Army and served in the Military Police Corps. After nearly seven and a half years, Michael left the military. He took a position at the Colorado Springs Police Department, where he served the community for ten years. An injury on duty forced him into early retirement from policing. Currently, Michael is the Department Chair of the Criminal Justice Department at a local community college. Michael earned a Bachelor of Science in Sociology with an emphasis in Criminology from Colorado State University and a Master of Criminal Justice from the University of Colorado.

Michael started his writing career as a ghostwriter for a publisher of textbooks. Eventually, he co-authored a textbook. Michael has always had the desire to write fiction. Through the encouragement of his family and friends, Michael started writing mystery fiction and hasn't stopped. Michael's wife, Stefanie, still catches him daydreaming as he drives down the highway thinking about different stories. The facial expressions that he makes reveal to her that somewhere in his mind, he's reviewing a chapter, scene, or dialogue between characters for a new book.

Made in United States
North Haven, CT
04 January 2024

47051940R00153